Death in Advertising

A Tobi Tobias Mystery

Laura Bradford

LYRICAL UNDERGROUND
Kensington Publishing Corp.
www.kensingtonbooks.com

LYRICAL UNDERGROUND BOOKS are published by

Kensington Publishing Corp.
119 West 40th Street
New York, NY 10018

All Kensington titles, imprints, and distributed lines are available at special quantity discounts for bulk purchases for sales promotion, premiums, fund-raising, educational, or institutional use.

Special book excerpts or customized printings can also be created to fit specific needs. For details, write or phone the office of the Kensington Sales Manager: Kensington Publishing Corp., 119 West 40th Street, New York, NY 10018. Attn. Sales Department. Phone: 1-800-221-2647.

Lyrical Underground and Lyrical Underground logo Reg. US Pat. & TM Off.

First Electronic Edition: February 2017
eISBN-13: 978-1-5161-0206-8
eISBN-10: 1-5161-0206-1

First Print Edition: February 2017
ISBN-13: 978-1-5161-0207-5
ISBN-10: 1-5161-0207-X

Printed in the United States of America

For Erin and Jenny . . .

Never stop believing.

ACKNOWLEDGMENTS

I remember the moment Tobi Tobias popped into my head. I also remember the fun I had bringing her to life on my computer. She has the kind of quirkiness about her I always wished I had. But that's part of the fun of writing—getting to be someone else for a little while.

A huge thank you goes out to my dear friend Lynn Cahoon for giving me the shove I needed to share Tobi with all of you, and to my Kensington editor Esi Sogah, for liking what she saw.

Having people in your life who believe in you and your abilities is truly a blessing; one for which I am most grateful.

1

Desperate times call for desperate measures.

A cliché? Perhaps. But a cliché, after all, is a truism. Which, in layman's terms, means whoever coined the *desperate measures* thing knew what they were talking about.

Frankly, if you ask me, *I* think the girl (or *guy,* in the interest of being politically correct) was a genius. How else could you define someone who'd so accurately described my state of mind without ever having met me? I mean, my life was the epitome of desperate times, my recent behavior the poster child for desperate measures.

I'd tried it all:

Nail biting, check.

Increased chocolate consumption, check.

Hiding from the mailman, check.

A lit match, check.

But none of it had worked.

Wait. Let me rephrase a moment. Technically, the lit match *worked* (along with the smoke detector and ceiling sprinklers) but we won't go there. Besides, it was a temporary fix.

Which brings me to today's final act of desperation. Granted, it hadn't worked when I was five and trying to clean my room, but with age comes wisdom (or stupidity, as my grandfather was fond of saying).

I yanked open the top drawer of my desk and pulled out a white paper napkin left over from yesterday's brown-bag lunch. Laying it carefully atop the mountainous stack of singed envelopes, I squeezed my eyes shut and willed myself to become one with the Amazing Mumford.

"A la peanut butter sandwiches . . ."

I opened my eyes slowly and looked at my paper-strewn desk,

everything exactly where it had been when I dove off the deep end into insanity (with not so much as a poof of smoke for my efforts). "Damn."

Maybe a top hat would help. Or a moustache . . .

"You okay, Tobi?"

I'd been so intent on running through my mental list of magic paraphernalia that I hadn't noticed JoAnna standing in the doorway. But there she was, a strange look plastered on her softly wrinkled face. I knew that look. I'd seen it a lot lately. Mostly in the mirror.

"Oh. Hey. I, um, can expl—"

JoAnna held up her hand, a knowing smile creeping across her face. "No need. I know exactly what you were doing." She strode across the room and stopped in front of my desk, her eyes soaking up the source of my shenanigans in one quick sweep. "Unfortunately, a magic spell isn't going to pay these, sweetie."

I leaned back in my chair and nibbled the inside of my cheek. She had a point. Or—

"Do you happen to have a cape I could borrow?"

She raised an eyebrow at me.

"A wand?"

She shook her head.

"Maybe my cadence was just off."

Judging by her eye roll, I'd say cadence wasn't the issue either.

"Do you have a better suggestion?" I finally asked.

JoAnna folded her arms and lifted her chin. "As a matter of fact, I do."

It was nice to feel the twinge of hope surge through my body at those words. Maybe I hadn't resigned myself to true Eeyore status yet. "Okay, lay it on me."

"Land a campaign."

My left nostril flared, my mouth fell open. It wasn't one of my best looks, but it was all I had at the moment. I mean, *land a campaign*? What did she think I'd been trying to do the past six months (beyond becoming proficient at finding the minus key on my calculator)?

"Good Lord, Tobi, you can't go in with *that* face."

I dropped my head into my hands and searched my memory bank for different magic words that would make *everything* vanish. Including me.

Alakazam, perhaps?

"Okay. I give up. What are you talking about?" I knew my words were muffled, but I just didn't have the energy to pick up my head.

"Ever heard of Zander Closet Company?"

I blew a piece of hair off my forehead in a half-hearted attempt to at least *appear* as if I were making eye contact. "Zander who?"

"See. They need you as much as you need them."

I tried to stifle the groan before it left my lips, but I wasn't entirely successful. "You lost me, JoAnna. Any chance you could try English this time?"

"Fine. Two very attractive men from Zander Closet Company are sitting in the conference room waiting for you. They're kind of hoping you can turn their company around."

That did it. My head snapped upward and that nostril/mouth thing happened again. Only this time my eyebrow was in on the action.

"Here? Now?"

"Here. Now. Waiting. For you."

"How?"

"They just showed up. Said they needed to see the head of Tobias Ad Agency. And, sweetie, that's you."

I pushed back my chair and stood, my legs feeling a bit like Jell-O when you first pull it from the fridge.

"Do my eyes look okay? My hair?"

"Yes. Your eyes are beautiful. Your hair looks sensational. But—" JoAnna met me as I came from behind the desk, her hand brushing against my wrist as she plucked a piece of tricolored hair off my sleeve. "There. *Now* you look perfect. Not a piece of cat fur anywhere."

"Maybe they're animal lovers, and they'll hire me out of a sense of loyalty." At this point I'd take any pity job I could get, just so long as it came with a paycheck.

"Have faith, Tobi. They're going to love you."

I felt a familiar catch in my throat as I looked at JoAnna. I'd been blessed a hundred times over since she'd walked through my door six months ago. She'd come in looking for a secretarial job and quickly became a loyal friend. Her knowledge at getting a business off the ground had allowed me to focus my attention on marketing the agency in the hopes of landing a few big campaigns. She'd done a great job with her tasks. But I'd failed to accomplish mine. Big time.

And now I was faced with the very real possibility that I would have to let JoAnna go. Sure, it would be heartbreaking. But allowing her to stay on without a paycheck was worse.

I grabbed her hand and gave it a quick squeeze. "Cross your fingers, okay?"

"I'll give you my toes too."

I looked up at the ceiling and took a long, slow breath, waiting for a moment to see if Scotty would, you know, beam me up to wherever he takes you. I counted to thirty in my head, just in case he was busy, but nothing happened. Not a big surprise when you considered Scotty's gender. After all, if I've learned anything from my broken engagement to Nick Harmon, it's that you can't count on a man.

Shaking off all sudden yet undeniable thoughts of revenge and torture, I forced myself to focus on the occupants of the room at the end of the hall.

I can do this. I know I can . . .

"Here I go."

"I'll hold your calls."

Oh how I wish I could keep from snorting when I laugh. It's one of those less than stellar habits I can't seem to shake. A vice I didn't even know I had until I started moonlighting at the To Know Them Is To Love Them pet shop and Rudder Malone started mimicking the sound from atop his little metal perch.

I looked back at JoAnna. "Ah, that's right. I forgot. The president of Anheuser Busch was supposed to call today, wasn't he? Something about that million-dollar campaign he handed me on a silver platter last week . . ."

"It could happen someday." JoAnna waggled her fingers at me. "But it won't if you don't get in there, talk to those men, land their campaign, and keep this place open."

"Is that *all* I have to do? *Seriously*? Why didn't you tell me this before?"

Again, with the eye roll. The woman had them down to an art form. "To-bi! Now go!"

When JoAnna syllabized my name like that, it meant she was losing patience. And when she lost that, there was hell to pay. Trust me.

"Okay, okay. I'm going."

I headed toward the conference room at the end of the hallway, but stopped just outside the bathroom door. I'd strategically placed the mirror where it could be used for a quick grooming prior to all client meetings. It wasn't used very often.

I flicked on the light and stared at myself for a moment. My blond hair shimmered in the overhead light and my Carolina Herrera outfit from the resale shop looked surprisingly new. All was good there. But my face was a different story. There wasn't much a brush and well-honed bargain radar could do for the tiny spray of freckles that danced across my cheeks. My parents always said it gave me a sweet look. Which, translated, meant I looked like a kid. And how many business executives wanted to put their company's livelihood in the hands of someone who could pass for a cheerleader minus the pom-poms?

I stuck my tongue out at my reflection and then laughed. Sinking ship or not, I was still Tobi Tobias.

Was I still broke? Yes.

Was I still teetering on the edge of homelessness? Yes.

Would I be defeated? No.

At least not yet, anyway . . .

I flicked off the switch and looked at the closed door that separated me from the chance to turn things around. For JoAnna. And for me.

"It's now or never."

I turned the handle, plastered a smile on my face, and pulled the door open. The rush of hushed voices inside the room grew silent as both representatives of Zander Closet Company rose to their feet.

"Good afternoon, gentlemen, I'm Tobi Tobias."

It wasn't hard to miss the look of surprise on the face of the taller, better-looking man. It was the same look I'd seen all my life.

The second man had a slightly different expression, but not one I wasn't familiar with. *His* had nothing to do with the masculine moniker my parents had saddled me with at birth. It did, however, have every-thing to do with his species' tried-and-true MO—the part that makes them scope women regardless of age or availability (hers or theirs).

Bitter? *Moi?* Not a chance.

Well . . . maybe. Just a little.

But even if I *was* projecting, I was fairly certain my read on Mr. Roving Eyes wasn't too far off the mark.

While my buddy puffed out his chest to the point of near-button-poppage, the better-looking one grasped my outstretched hand.

"Ms. Tobias, thank you for seeing us without an appointment. I'm Andrew Zander and this is my brother, Gary."

Andrew Zander was a handsome man. He was a good six inches taller than me, so I figured him to be about six feet. His hair was the color of sunlit sand, his eyes an emerald green. The faint lines around his eyes deepened as he smiled, and I suddenly had that Jell-O feeling in my legs again.

"Tobi Tobias, huh?" Gary stole my hand from his brother and held it tightly. "I knew a Kitty Kitrina once."

Reluctantly, I pulled my gaze off Andrew to acknowledge his brother. It wasn't a surprise that Mr. Roving Eyes—I mean, Gary—would know a Kitty Kitrina. In fact, I was pretty sure he knew a lot of women with cutesy little names like that. They were probably all employed just over the Mississippi River in what's known in male circles throughout St. Louis as "The East Side." But it wasn't his boyishly tousled brown hair, thick gold chain, or overly charming eye contact that tipped me off. It was simply the result of a newly tuned radar—a radar that had been draped in naïveté until the day my heart was broken.

But I didn't have to give the guy my heart, just a pitch that would knock his socks off.

"Mr. Zander," I replied as I disengaged my hand.

"You can call me Gary."

I'd only been in the room a grand total of about two minutes, but I could already sense that the Zander brothers were about as opposite as they come. And, if I believed in gambling, I might just be willing to bet the farm on the guess that their relationship with each other was strained. Then again, if I'd had a farm, it would've been repossessed by now.

I motioned to the chairs and invited the men to sit. The dirty look Andrew shot Gary was quick but not missed by me. It was obvious that Andrew was the professional, and Gary the whatever.

"What can I do for you this afternoon?" I sat in a chair across from the two men and employed a trick I'd learned from my days at Beckler and Stanley Ad Agency: I leaned forward, my attention squarely on the prospective client.

"We've got a radio spot coming up on Tuesday, and we are without a slogan thanks to that idiot, John Beckler."

I felt my mouth start to gape at the mention of my former boss but managed to recover before anyone was the wiser.

Andrew cleared his throat and waved his right hand in the air in an obvious attempt to gain control of the conversation from his brother. "I'm sorry, Ms. Tobias, let me give you some quick background."

"Tobi, please. And, yes, background is good."

"We own Zander Closet Company. We specialize in closet organization systems. We opened about six months ago and business has been really slow. I couldn't figure it out for the longest time. I mean, we do just as good a job as these other companies and we're using better materials. Yet no one is calling." I couldn't help but notice the way his emerald-green eyes darkened as he spoke. Mood eyes. Like mine. I tried to focus on his words as he continued. "I was at my wits' end one day and so I did a search on closet companies in and around St. Louis. I figured I'd call some of our competitors and see what kind of deals they were offering. When I flipped to the section for closet companies, I got a glimpse at one of our problems."

Ah, yes, the joys of alphabetical order. A true business killer if there was one.

"It takes a while to weed through the companies who vie for the first spot, doesn't it?" I commented.

Andrew's face brightened. "Exactly. I mean, how many *A*'s can you really put in front of a name?"

"So we need to make you stand out. Make people remember Zander Closet Company." I reached for the pad of paper I kept on the table and pulled a pen from the holder. "Now, what's this about a radio spot and John Beckler?"

"We've got what could be our first real break coming up. You've heard about next week's Home Showcase out in Chesterfield, right?"

Yeah, I'd heard about it. I'd been staring at the ads for weeks, drooling over all the business I didn't have. To Andrew, I said, "Are you one of the businesses being featured?"

"We are. It was a huge coup, but we got in. We're supposed to install one of our premier organization systems into a home owned by Preston and Mitzi Hohlbrook."

This time I was a bit slower when it came to recovering my slackened jaw. "Preston Hohlbrook? As in the Car King himself?"

"The one and the same," Gary interrupted. He drummed his hands on the table and shifted in his seat. "You ever seen those commercials he does sitting on top of the camel? Wearing a crown on his head? Comes across as this hip guy? Well, it's a farce. He's as boring as they come."

It's a good thing Andrew muttered something to his brother at this point because they were too preoccupied to hear me snort. Gary Zander really was a piece of work.

"Yes, Tobi, Preston Hohlbrook from Hohlbrook Motors," Andrew said, shooting daggers in his brother's direction.

"That's great visibility for you."

"It certainly could be. But we've got to get Zander Closet Company in people's heads *before* the Showcase. Otherwise they won't be looking for our work. And that's why we're here."

I nodded, my thoughts still on the name Gary had uttered earlier. As much as I wanted—no, *needed*—this job, I had to know if John was involved.

"You mentioned John Beckler before. Is he working on part of your campaign?"

"That lazy sack of—"

"Gary, enough," his brother said.

But for once, I wanted Mr. Roving Eyes to continue. Slimeball or not, Gary Zander obviously had a handle on the personality of my former boss. So good, in fact, that I had to wonder if I'd been a bit rash in my estimation of Andrew's brother.

"Hell, Andrew, he's that and more. We've got 'til Monday afternoon to come up with a slogan that's gonna make us stand out. That's *three* days. He dragged us around by the ear only to come up with zip."

Sounded like the John Beckler I knew, all right. Sit back, do nothing (or do something incredibly stupid), and then leave the task of damage control to his business partner.

"So you *were* working with John, but you're not now?" I could feel my cheeks pushing upward, the adrenaline coursing through my body. This was sounding a lot like a chance to show John who was best once and for all.

"We fired him," Andrew said before his brother could speak again. "We should have known better when we met with him and he kept talking about all his *other* clients instead of focusing on us. And the partner? Mike Stanley? He basically sat there the whole time and didn't say a word. Just kept chewing tobacco through the whole meeting—"

The first few notes of the theme from *Jaws* interrupted the conversation. I wasn't surprised to see it was Gary's phone. How fitting. Women beware.

"Gary here . . . Oh, yes, Mr. Hohlbrook . . . *what?*"

I tried to busy myself with my pad of paper, the name Zander Closet Company already sprawled across it in block letters, but it was hard. It didn't take a rocket scientist to note the tension in Gary's voice or to see the worry in Andrew's eyes as he listened to the one-sided conversation.

"I'll take care of it, Mr. Hohlbrook. He'll be removed immediately."

Gary flipped the phone shut and made little effort to bite back the string of obscenities that poured from his mouth.

"What's the problem, Gary?" Andrew's eyes moved from his brother to me and back again. "No, actually, wait."

I felt sorry for Andrew. The man seemed torn between finding out what happened and wanting to apologize for his brother's foul mouth.

I pushed back my chair and stood. "Why don't I leave you two alone for a few moments so you can discuss whatever you need to talk about, then we'll get started on what you're looking for from me."

Gary's voice brought an immediate end to the flicker of relief in Andrew's face.

"No. You don't have to go." Gary turned to his brother. "It's Blake. He's ogling Hohlbrook's wife out at the site. He's outta there."

Andrew shrugged an apology in my direction. "Blake's our cousin, Tobi. He's a Zander too, only he's more the labor side of our business."

"Not anymore he's not," Gary snarled.

"C'mon, Gary, don't you think we owe him the chance to defend himself? That doesn't sound like Blake and you know it."

"Hell if I know that. He's outta there."

I saw Andrew shake his head in disgust. The pieces were coming together just as I'd suspected. Andrew was the professional. Kind. Hardworking. Fair. Gary was the hot-headed playboy who wanted things done *his* way and on *his* time. Sounded a lot like my old boss.

I admired the way Andrew worked to keep his cool when he spoke to his brother. "Then who's gonna install the rest of the system? The preview is next Thursday."

"Don't you worry. *I'll* do it, that's who," Gary growled through clenched teeth.

Now, I must admit, that wasn't a piece of the Zander family puzzle I would have expected. Gary didn't seem the type to take on menial labor. In fact, I'd have to put him as the type who drew a paycheck for doing nothing but sporting the same last name as the company. Interesting . . .

I could see Andrew visibly struggling with the desire to engage his brother in further battle. But, after a moment of tense silence, he simply shook his head and looked at me.

"Look, I don't want to waste either of our time by dragging out this meeting longer than necessary. We have a pre-Showcase radio spot to fill starting Tuesday, and we are completely unprepared. Our company is riding on this campaign. Do you think you can help us?"

Their company was riding on this campaign?

I thought of the overdue bills on the desk in my office. I thought of all the hours spent cleaning cages at the pet store just so I could hang on to my lease here. I thought of my apartment and the eviction letter that was surely waiting for me from the landlord. I thought of my dream to be a successful business owner doing what I loved most— creating words that left an impression long after they were gone. And I thought of wiping that self-satisfied smirk off John Beckler's face once and for all.

Zander Closet Company and Tobias Ad Agency was a match made in heaven.

"Oh, yes, Mr. Zander. I'm sure I can help. In fact, by the time I'm done, Zander Closet Company will be a household name."

2

I was just finishing a bowl of Cocoa Puffs when I heard my alarm clock. It took me a few seconds to figure out exactly what it was. The ring sounded much quieter, less obnoxious than usual. Probably because I was already dressed and in another room, rather than burrowed under the covers dreaming about cashing in a winning lottery ticket.

I set my bowl on the counter and wiped my mouth with the dishtowel. I hadn't slept a wink all night. In fact, I'd spent most of the moonlit hours sitting cross-legged and staring at the inside of my closet. I had studied the shoe organizer slung over the back of the door (though the empty-to-full ratio was a sad commentary on my current financial situation). Then I considered the sparse row of business attire hanging on the upper clothes bar and my casual everyday duds below. As I'd sat there in the shadows, I noted everything about a closet that could be noted. Bars, hangers, cubbies, wire racks—all boring stuff that I had to turn into a slogan capable of sticking in the consumer's head.

And I couldn't be any happier. This was my *thing*. Maybe even more than chocolate, if that was possible.

Growing up, I was the kid who, when asked to sing in the choir for my third-grade Christmas pageant, sang the commercialized version of each carol. You know—*dashing through the snow to my Barbie dream ho-tel* and *My fro-sty mak-er, I can make one by myself, with a col-or pack and a set of cones . . .*

I ended up being the narrator that year instead.

When my friends were making pitchers of lemonade for one of our summer money-grubbing stands, I was always the poster maker. And *our* signs didn't just say *Get Your Lemonade Here* or *Lemonade*

10 cents like the other kids in the neighborhood. No siree. Ours were the talk of the town. Looking back, I can see why. How many ten-year-olds create a sign that reads *Lemonade: A splash of summer that'll wet your whistle?*

We made fifty bucks the day I hung up that sign, and I was hooked.

While my classmates had picked and changed (and picked and changed) their career paths over the next nine years, I'd stayed focused on the one job I knew I wanted: Advertising.

Shaking my thoughts back into the present, I rinsed my bowl and spoon and set them in the drainer. No sense running the dishwasher for just a few items. It'd help keep the water bill down. I headed into my bedroom for my purse and keys, and flipped off the alarm clock.

Mary Fran wouldn't be at the pet shop for another thirty minutes. But that was okay. The extra up-and-around time was exactly what I needed. The more time I had to stroll around outside, the more time I had to brainstorm.

I thought about what Andrew Zander had said as he was leaving my office yesterday. He wanted a slogan that was fun, unique. Something that would appeal to the young homebuyers, as well as those in the older, downsizing group. A tall order for sure. But I had every faith I could pull it off.

I grabbed a light jacket and stepped outside, the early autumn sun unable to squelch the morning chill.

"Where are you off to this early in the morning?"

Uh-oh.

I twisted the key in the lock, allowed myself the inner groan that always accompanied the sound of my next-door neighbor's voice, and then turned around.

"Hello, Ms. Rapple. How are you?"

The woman raised a bony hand to her cotton-top and tucked a wiry strand of hair back in place, the loose skin beneath her arm swaying with the movement.

I shivered.

"I've been better. My knees are acting up. Winter is on its way." Ms. Rapple pulled her orange housecoat more tightly against her body and pointed to the second-floor window above my door. "Carter didn't get home until nearly two o'clock this morning. That's a little late, don't you think?"

"He's thirty-five-years-old, Ms. Rapple. I'm sure he's fine." I looked down at my watch and mentally ran through a variety of excuses I could give that would enable me to get away from the old biddy—I mean, *Ms. Rapple*. But before I could try one out, she started yakking again.

"I don't care if he's *fifty*. He still needs to be considerate of his neighbors when he's sneaking around at all hours of the night."

Let's pause and take stock here for a moment, shall we? Carter doesn't sneak. He prances. Literally. If he's out late, it's not because he's barhopping or bringing home a new flavor-of-the-day. It's usually because he's working his on-again/off-again job as the makeup and hair guru for the community theater house down the block. Carter is a genius when it comes to color, and he is absolutely invaluable when you're going on a date.

I looked at Ms. Rapple and counted to ten in my head. Sometimes I needed to remind myself that she was an old lady.

Reminder aside, I still felt compelled to defend my faithful friend. "It's funny, but I was awake at that same time, and I didn't hear Carter at all." I shifted foot to foot in an effort to dodge the evil eye that was suddenly trained on me.

"Well, he *sneezed* on the sidewalk. And it woke up Gertrude."

Ah yes, Gertrude. Where *was* the little rat?

I looked around the blooming mums to the right of my front stoop. The orange flowers jiggled in the windless morning, an indicator that everyone's favorite kick-me dog was near. I looked at Ms. Rapple in her orange coat, then back at my orange mums. Sure enough, Gertrude ran from behind the flowers in her orange sweater, carefully crocheted from the same material as Ms. Rapple's housecoat. They matched. How cute.

Wait a minute.

Did she actually pinpoint Carter's late-night rudeness to a *sneeze*?

A quick mental replay of the woman's words served as confirmation.

"I'm sure if you let him know, Carter will try not to sneeze outside when Gertrude is sleeping."

I tossed my keys into my backpack and walked down the six steps to the sidewalk. "Anyway, have a good—"

"Wait right there, young lady. You never answered my question," Ms. Rapple said, her hands planted firmly on her hips. "*Where* are you going this early in the morning?"

It was a good thing I was raised to respect my elders . . .

"To the pet shop."

"Oh?" Ms. Rapple pointed to the second floor of her own building. "Mary Fran hasn't come out yet."

I wondered what would happen if I counted to twenty this time. I tried. It didn't work. I was still approaching edgy.

"I know she hasn't. It's still early. But I've got a few things to do before we open the shop." I started to wave and then stopped. A focus group was a focus group, right? "Ms. Rapple, what comes to mind when I say closet?"

"In or out?"

I stared at her for a moment, waiting for her to explain the odd question. But, for once, Ms. Rapple was silent. And surprisingly, there was no sign of the arctic blast I'd always expected to accompany such a feat.

"In the closet, out of the closet, it doesn't really matter. I'm just curious what you think of when you hear the word *closet*."

The woman swung her head upward in the direction of the apartment above mine. "Carter."

I laughed. Snort and all. I couldn't help it. Ms. Rapple was the antithesis of forward thinking through and through.

"Thanks, Ms. Rapple."

I slung my backpack over my left shoulder and headed down the block. My time to wander had been cut short thanks to my nosey next door neighbor. But hey, I got some slogan material, right?

I turned the corner at McPherson and Euclid and headed south, the early morning sun bringing warmth to my face and a spring to my step. Autumn was my favorite time of year in the Central West End neighborhood located on the outskirts of St. Louis. Something always spoke to me—the crisp air, the changing leaves, and on and on. Today, it was the bright patches of yellow, orange, white, and red that lined many a walkway leading to the two-family homes common in this area of town.

"Hi there, Tobi."

I looked up and smiled. Passing Mr. Houghtin at this same spot each morning was as much a part of my day as brushing my teeth and combing my hair. I bent down and gave his faithful companion, Sandy, a quick scratch behind her ear while I engaged in the usual conversation with her owner.

"Looks like Sandy had a visit to the dog salon yesterday."

Mr. Houghtin raised his fist to his lips and cleared his throat, a byproduct of his two-pack-a-day smoking habit, no doubt. "She sure looks mighty pretty, doesn't she? Mary Fran says Sandy must have been a debutante in another life. Swears she seems upset when her nails don't get painted after being clipped."

"I wish you'd bring Sandy in on the weekend sometime. The dogs I end up grooming aren't quite so docile." I looked down at my hand and mentally inventoried last week's fading scratches—a souvenir of my hellish encounter with a Husky.

Oh, what I wouldn't give to have my weekends free . . .

I wiped Sandy's doggy drool onto my jeans and looked up at Mr. Houghtin, his shadow shielding my eyes from the sun. "Can I pick your brain for a moment?"

"Sure, Tobi."

"Give me the first thing that comes to mind when I say this word."

"Okay, hit me."

"*Closet.*"

"Disaster."

The word was no sooner in my ear when Valerie Mollner from across the street emerged from her door with her mutt, Ragu. Sandy tugged her leash so hard I landed on my backside.

Mr. Houghtin feigned concern, but I knew better. Sandy wasn't the slightest bit interested in Ragu. He was beneath her. But Mr. Houghtin was a different story. He had the hots for Ragu's owner. And Sandy, well she liked the treats Mr. Houghtin passed her for running in Ragu's direction.

I yelled my gratitude at Mr. Houghtin's back and picked myself up off the ground. I had exactly fifteen minutes left to conduct my informal market research.

At the corner of Euclid and Maryland, I crossed. Fletcher's Newsstand was a staple in this neighborhood, much like its owner. Jack Fletcher had worked beside his father from the time he was four, counting back change and stacking papers. The pictures that hung from a clothesline beneath the awning told their story to people like me, who hadn't grown up in this part of town.

Even so, it hadn't taken long to realize, all on my own, that Jack was an admired member of this community. He was, in a lot of ways, like the barber my Grandpa Stu used to go to twice a month when I was a little girl. Only Jack's stories weren't collected over the buzz of a razor or the snip of a scissors. His were accumulated over the ping of silver into the same tin bucket his dad had used so many years before.

"Hi, Jack."

"Hiya, Tobi. You're sure looking pretty today."

I looked down at my baby-blue sweater and stonewashed jeans. Nothing special. But that's one of the things that made Jack Fletcher everyone's friend. He was simply a nice, upbeat kind of guy.

"Thanks. How's business this morning?" I reached for a copy of the *Central West End News* and dug around in my pocket for thirty-five cents.

"It's good. Perfect day to be outside, I say."

"That it is."

"Working at the pet shop again this weekend?"

I nodded. "But, if I play my cards right, I won't be working there much longer."

"Why's that?"

"I just got a new client yesterday. With any luck, things will start looking up very soon."

Jack pushed a strand of hair out of my eyes and smiled. "I hope so, Tobi. You deserve it."

Why did the good guys always have to be gay, married, or older than dirt?

"Thanks." I tucked the paper under my arm and looked around. There was a temporary lull in Jack's customers so I seized the opportunity. "If I say a word, will you tell me the first thing that pops into your mind?"

Jack flashed his infamous cock-eyed smile, the one that illuminated his face like the brightest Christmas tree on Christmas morning. "Shoot."

"*Closet.*"

"Full."

"Full?"

"To capacity."

Oh.

I smiled and waved a thanks in Jack's direction as a customer stepped up to the stand. It was just as well. I had less than five minutes for my three-block walk to the pet shop. Which meant I was less than five minutes away from spending yet another beautiful Saturday inside.

As I walked, I thought back over the words I'd gathered so far.
Full.
Disaster.
Carter.
Ah yes, a winning assortment of slogan possibilities if I'd ever heard one.

Mary Fran was just opening the front window of the shop when I came around the corner. The quiet morning was shattered by barking, meowing, croaking, and creaking. The creaking was Rudder Malone's contribution to the fray, a spot-on imitation of the sound the window makes when you slide it open each morning.

I pushed open the door and listened as the ringing of the overhead bell was quickly echoed by Rudder from atop the perch in his oversized cage.

"Hey there, Rudder."

"Hey—hey there, Rudder."

I laughed. "That's what *I* said."

"That—that's what I said."

Working here, with Rudder, was like being in second grade all over again. I just thanked my lucky stars that he'd never heard someone say *I know you are but what am I?*

Rudder Malone was an African grey parrot. And that alone makes him interesting. His breed of bird imitates voices, words, and assorted sounds. He's such a gifted impersonator, in fact, that I literally hide him in the back room when Ms. Rapple comes in with Gertrude. Hearing her voice once was more than enough.

"I see that sparkle in your eye, Tobi. Who is he?"

Mary Fran Wazoli was as subtle as a sledge hammer. She didn't believe in beating around the bush or holding her tongue. In fact, I think *Direct* was her middle name. But I loved her anyway. She'd taken me under her wing when I moved into my apartment two years ago, introducing me to everyone in the neighborhood. She'd been there when I first met Nick, consulted on my outfits before each date, celebrated with us when we got engaged, dried my tears when I caught him cheating on me.

I closed my eyes against the moment that had changed me more than any other—the sounds and visuals associated with walking in on my fiancé and the voluptuous waitress from our favorite restaurant still as vivid and painful as the what's-a-guy-to-do look he'd given me when he saw me standing there, stunned and heartbroken.

Focus, Tobi.

Focus.

I forced myself to breathe. To redirect my thoughts back to the grinning woman in front of me now.

Mary Fran was truly the best friend I'd ever had. And even though she'd been divorced three times and held little faith in men, she still encouraged me to get out and meet new people. Though sometimes her encouragement could be better classified as a shove.

Or, better yet, a punch.

"There is no *he*." I set my backpack behind the counter and pulled a Tupperware container out of the small fridge to my left. "Wait. Technically, that's not true."

Mary Fran squealed and jogged in place. "I knew it, I knew it."

I pulled the container top open and removed three pieces of kiwi. "It's not a *he* in the normal *he* kind of way, Mary Fran."

"Spill it, Tobi. There's either a he or there isn't."

I set the kiwi down on a small cutting board and began slicing it into tiny pieces, the blade of the knife banging against the board every time I cut through the fruit.

"B—bang. Bang. Bang."

"It's coming, Rudder."

"It's—it's coming, Rudder."

If anyone had ever told me that my route to being a successful advertising executive would require a stint at a pet shop, I would have laughed. Guess the joke was on me, huh?

I picked up my conversation with Mary Fran. "Look, a guy— well, actually, two guys—came into my office yesterday. They want me to come up with a slogan for their company."

"Two guys?" Mary Fran asked, her feet starting to move once again.

I laughed.

"Snort."

I stopped slicing kiwi to cast a disapproving glare at Rudder and then returned my attention back to Mary Fran. "You did hear the *slogan* part, right?"

Mary Fran waved aside my words as she crossed to the first hamster cage and its tenant, Max.

Undaunted, I continued. "Anyway, these guys are in just as bad a shape as I am. But if I can come up with a slogan that'll get them noticed, it might be just enough to turn things around for me *and* the agency."

I watched Mary Fran painstakingly move all of Max's bedding to the bottom of the hamster condo, an effort I never understood since we all knew he was just going to load up his cheeks and take it through the tunnel again in an hour. But I knew her decision to clean the cage at that moment was as much about distracting herself as it was a necessary task. My Saturdays at the pet shop had become a kind of girls' day out—a time to laugh, to gossip, and to fool around. If I got my agency on track, working here would no longer be a necessity for me.

"S–snort. Snort. Snort."

Heaven forbid I stop cutting kiwi to have a conversation. I scooped up the pieces with my hand and carried them over to Rudder's cage. "Breakfast is served."

"Break–breakfast is served. Snort."

I opened the food door, dropped the kiwi pieces inside, and then shut it once again. "Why does he snort even when I'm not?"

"He remembers repetitive sounds." Mary Fran shoved the last handful of bedding onto the lower level of the hamster condo and rested her face against the glass that separated her from Max.

"Repetitive sounds? Gee, thanks."

Mary Fran smartly changed the subject. "There was a really cute guy in here late yesterday afternoon. And he wasn't wearing a wedding ring."

I reached for the broom and began sweeping around Rudder's cage. "Did you ask him out?"

"Now, Tobi, let's not go down that route again. I'm saying he was cute for *you*."

I stopped sweeping long enough to raise my right palm. "Uh, no. We've been down *this* road, remember? Say it with me now: I. Will. Not. Set. Tobi. Up. On. Any. More. Blind. Dates. Ever."

Mary Fran turned from the hamster cage and put her hands on her hips. "C'mon, Tobi! I had no way of knowing he was a bigamist with a foot fetish."

I shuddered. Some memories were just too traumatic to revisit.

"No more blind dates," I said firmly.

"Suit yourself. But you're missing out. This guy was a little grungy, but cute."

"Grungy?"

"Yeah, his clothes were kinda paint-spattered and a little, uh, outdated."

Some things were better left alone. The guy's inability to dress was really not an issue since I had no interest in meeting him. Instead, I pushed the straw and droppings into the dustpan and knocked them into the trash can.

"Why'd he come in?"

"To take Sadie home."

I whirled around and stared at the cage that, just last weekend, had held my favorite cat in the whole store. Sadie was a calico and a world-class cuddler. She and I had bonded, each seeming to sense when the other needed a little extra attention. I would have brought her home long ago if my landlord didn't despise pets so much.

I walked over to the now-empty cage and looked inside. All that was left of Sadie was the little pink ball we used to play fetch.

I felt Mary Fran's hand on my shoulder, but I didn't look up. Maybe I would miss this place more than I realized.

The bell over the door rang. And so did Rudder.

"Hey, Mom. Hey, Tobi."

Sam. Mary Fran's son from her first marriage. A fifteen-year-old dynamo who had no use for sports or getting into trouble like his peers. All he thought about was cameras; I'd been the same way about advertising at his age.

Sure hope things turn out better for him.

"How's things going, Sam?"

"Did Mom tell you?"

I looked at Mary Fran and saw the instant sparkle in her eye. I looked back at Sam. "No. Tell me what?"

"I got it."

"Your picture?"

Sam nodded, his silver-adorned smile stretching across his narrow face. "Yup. Got the letter yesterday. I placed first in the teenage photography division."

I pulled him in for a quick hug, my eyes suddenly moist. I knew that feeling, that validation of your talent. There was nothing in the world like it. "Congratulations."

"Thanks, Tobi." He stepped back and grinned at me. "I'm really pumped. But what about you? Anything new?"

I leaned against the counter. "I have a shot at a campaign. I just need to find a slogan that'll stick in everyone's head the second they hear it."

"Can I help?"

I studied Sam for a full minute before I finally answered, my mind running in a million different directions. If I pulled off this slogan, Andrew Zander said the radio spot would lead to a color brochure and maybe even a commercial. Both would need a photographer.

"What's the first thing that comes to mind when I say *closet*?"

Sam hoisted himself onto the counter, letting his feet dangle over the side. "That's easy. Skeletons."

3

I was about to break Mike Stanley's cardinal rule regarding a pitch session and it wasn't because of naïveté. Stupidity, perhaps. But not naïveté.

Sunday had come and gone in a flash as I'd juggled words and ideas with graphics and color. So absorbed was I, the phone had gone unanswered the few times it rang (sorry, Mom), Gertrude's incessant bark-a-thons from next door had barely registered against the back-drop of my gurgling food-deprived stomach, and I'd even turned down Mary Fran's invite for popcorn and a movie with her and Sam. But it was the way I always worked once an idea started to form.

I looked at the storyboard I'd drawn up and prayed the added work would not be wasted. But most of all, I prayed that Andrew and Gary Zander saw the slogan's fun factor as a way to reach a broad audience— a way to turn their company—and, *cough*, mine—around.

A soft knock on my office door interrupted my thoughts, and I looked up. "Oh hey, JoAnna. C'mon in."

"Andrew Zander is here, sweetie."

My stomach tightened as Mike Stanley's monotone voice rushed through my head. *Always bring three slogans with you. One of them is bound to catch the fly.*

"Tobi?"

Had I not seen the note in my mail Saturday? The one that said I had fourteen days to pay my rent or I would be evicted? Had I not no-ticed that Cocoa Puffs and chocolate bars didn't span all recom-mended food groups? Had I not just spent my entire Saturday being mocked by a bird with an attitude?

I sunk into my chair and buried my face in my hands. "What have I done, JoAnna?"

I heard her footsteps as she crossed the office, felt her hand on my shoulder as she tsked in my ear. "What's wrong, Tobi?"

"How much time do you have?"

"You looked so self-assured when you came in this morning, what happened?" JoAnna asked.

"Reality." I looked up as I felt JoAnna lean against my desk, the worry in her eyes impossible to miss. "I'm sorry, JoAnna. I'm just second-guessing myself."

"Good heavens, Tobi, why?"

I straightened in my chair and met her gaze head-on. "Because I'm putting all my eggs in one basket. Actually, scratch that. I'm putting my singular egg in a singular basket."

"Is it a good one?"

"Huh?"

"Your singular egg. Is it a good one?"

I looked at the slogan I'd slaved over the previous day and read it again as if I was seeing it for the first time. "Yeah. It is. It's a good one."

"Then you don't need a second egg."

I felt that catch in my throat again. The one I got every time I was reminded just how much this woman meant to me. Just how much she brought to my life. I pushed my chair back and stood, giving her a quick hug as I did.

"You're right, JoAnna. It's a great slogan and I know that. It's everything he asked for. Fun, unique, memorable."

"Then go get him."

I hooked the tiny loops of my dark-brown fitted jacket but left the top third open to the gold-and-brown beaded necklace below. I'd opted to go casually nice that morning in an effort to give off the same youthful, breezy feeling Andrew Zander was looking for in a slogan.

"Is Gary in there too?"

"No."

For some reason I found that tidbit of information to be a little unsettling. I was far more comfortable with Andrew (not to mention the fact that he was gorgeous) but I had my looks to fall back on with Gary if the slogan fell apart—desperate times and all, you know?

I pulled my hair from behind my left ear and took a deep breath. Things were going to be okay. They had to be.

"The easel is all set up in the conference room. And so is your water."

I looked at JoAnna and smiled. The woman was a mind reader. She knew exactly what I needed at all times. I simply could not afford to lose her.

"Thanks." I squeezed her hand, then grabbed my pitch materials and headed for the door. "Get the chocolate ready, we're gonna have a party when this is done."

"That's my girl."

I headed down the narrow hallway, past JoAnna's spotless desk, my attention completely fixed on the open doorway to the conference room. Unlike the first time I met with Andrew Zander, I didn't bother to look at myself in the mirror. Sometimes you just feel put together. Thankfully, today was one of those days.

I stopped just outside the room when I realized Andrew Zander was on his phone, his back to me.

"Yeah, Gary, I'm here now. I'm waiting on Tobi. Look, I'm not worried, I think this girl is going to come up with something awesome."

I felt my cheeks warm, my mouth stretch wide with a smile. This guy didn't know me from Adam, yet he believed in me somehow.

"Yeah, I know we've got to get a slogan to WKST by three o'clock. I'll take care of it. You focus on getting that closet system in at Hohlbrook's and leave the rest to me, okay?"

It's funny how certain voices just go with certain people. Andrew's was deep, yet gentle, a perfect match for his muscular build and kind face (not that I'd noticed or anything). As I continued to listen, I noticed his voice becoming increasingly agitated. "Is that Mrs. Hohlbrook in the background? Has she complained to you about Blake?"

I couldn't help but commiserate with Andrew's plight. Owning a business was anything but easy. So many factors came into play when determining if you'd survive or not. And simply having a passion for the work wasn't enough.

I switched the storyboard from one arm to the other, the thick material brushing the trim work around the door. Andrew Zander spun around in his chair, the surprise in his face giving way to a smile as we made eye contact.

"I've got to go, Gary," Andrew said into his phone. "Tobi's here."

He stood, slipped his phone into his pocket, and crossed the distance between us in mere seconds. "Hi, Tobi. You look great."

Score one for my wardrobe selection. "Thanks."

"Did you have a nice weekend?"

"It was busy. But nice."

"You didn't spend your entire weekend working on this, did you?"

My whole weekend? No. The rest was spent sweeping up poop, shaving teeth-baring dogs, bagging up goldfish that never live long anyway, diverting discussions with Mary Fran onto something other than men, and trying desperately to help Rudder find a new sound to mimic. None of which I felt comfortable sharing with present company.

Instead, I took a breath and composed my real answer carefully. "Helping you and your company is something I take seriously. So, yes, it was a big part of my weekend. By choice." I motioned for him to sit down again, but he remained standing. "Would you like some coffee or some soda?"

He shook his head. "No. I'm good. I stopped by the coffee shop on the way here. I needed a shot of caffeine, badly."

"Busy weekend?"

"Busy night. I was woken up every few hours."

"By loud music?" I asked.

"Nah, by my new girl. She'd rather fool around than sleep."

Alrighty then. More information than I really wanted to know.

I changed the subject. "Shall we get started?"

"Absolutely."

I walked around the table and set my boards, face down, in front of my usual chair. I could feel his eyes on me as I pulled the easel closer. "When we spoke on Friday, you said you wanted Zander Closet Company to be remembered. That you wanted a slogan people would fall in love with and immediately associate with your company."

Andrew nodded, his eyes locked on mine (which, truth be told, was making it rather difficult to concentrate on anything other than their uncanny way of making my legs feel all jiggly).

"You also expressed a desire to have your slogan be something that new homebuyers would enjoy without alienating their more seasoned counterparts."

"A tough call, I know," he said. "But I've watched my parents and their friends over the years. They seem almost turned off by companies who opt to go the route of popular music or slang to promote their products. And, right now, I can't afford to push away either group."

I nodded. "Makes perfect business sense. But, like you said, it's a tough job and there's not much common ground to be found between the groups. That's why I opted to take a humorous route instead."

I didn't miss the way Andrew's eyebrows furrowed or the way he shifted in his seat when I said that. And I didn't miss the way my palms dampened in response.

Stay the course, Tobi.

"By playing on an expression that has been around for years, we're throwing a bone to the older demographic. By bringing a humorous connotation to it, we're creating a youthful feel that will speak to first-time homebuyers too."

Grabbing the top board from the table, I placed it on the easel. With any luck, Andrew Zander wouldn't notice the way my hand shook.

"The first thing we need to do is get your name out there. Very often, slogans place the name of the company at the end, if they incorporate it into the slogan at all. Most don't. They simply splash it across the television screen when the commercial is winding down, or in a small corner of a print ad.

"But we need to connect your name with this slogan so that when people hear it, or recall it, they remember your name as quickly as they do the saying."

Andrew nodded, casting his eyes upward for a moment. "You know, I remember a political commercial from when I was in high school. It had this little jingle, sung by children. *Congress-man Peters picks our pock-ets.* It was brilliant. I didn't care about politics, certainly didn't know who was or wasn't running, but I remembered that jingle."

I could feel my excitement mounting as I watched him sell himself on my plan of attack. It was almost a textbook pitch session, and I hadn't even unveiled the slogan.

"And you remember his name fifteen years later, don't you?"

"I sure do." He leaned forward against the table and grinned. "Can you really do that for us?"

"Yes, I can."

I cleared my throat quickly and reached for a glass of water. Someone had once told me that drinking tepid water before speaking made your voice sound better, clearer. And there was no doubt that the way a slogan was read had a big impact on how it was received.

Pulling the cover sheet upward, I looked from the slogan to Andrew as I spoke, my voice surprisingly calm and self-assured. *"Zander Closet Company. When we're done, even your skeletons will have a place."*

Now, I'm not exactly sure what I expected when I unveiled the slogan, but I know it wasn't a blank look and utter silence. Apparently, Andrew Zander hadn't gotten the memo that detailed appropriate responses to a woman's labor of love.

Men.

As I stood there, studying his face, I could feel the enthusiasm rushing from my body, and hear the self-recriminations beginning to overpower the little voice that had been so certain one slogan was enough.

My voice was quiet when I finally spoke, the wind totally sucked out of my body as I racked my brain for something, anything, that might serve as a backup. But there was nothing. I truly believed in the power of my slogan. I still did.

"Mr. Zander, I'm sorry, I—"

My words were cut short as Andrew's hand hit the table. "Tobi, it's perfect!"

I stood there, dumbfounded, as he walked around the table, wrapped his arms around my shoulders, and pulled me in for a hug.

"Then you *do* like it?"

He stepped back and met my eyes, his cheeks sporting a slight pinkish hue. "Like it? Are you kidding me? It's spectacular."

The fear that had gripped my heart just moments earlier released its hold, and I let my smile fly. Not an engaging, professional smile, of course. No siree. My infamous Tobi Tobias face-splitting smile that invariably leads to a laugh. And, you guessed it, a snort.

Today was no exception.

Fortunately, I was saved by the sound of Andrew's phone, a fairly innocuous melody that drowned out my idiosyncrasy quite nicely, thankyouverymuch.

"It's official, Gary. We've got a winner. Let me put you on speaker so you can hear for yourself."

He set the phone on the table and nodded at me, his smile threatening to swallow me whole.

"Good morning, Gary," I said, moving closer to the table.

"Hey darlin'."

"Would you like me to go through the whole pitch as to why I created the slogan I did?"

"Nah. Just give it to me. And by it, I mean the slogan.... For now, anyway."

Andrew's stance tensed, and he shook his head in disgust. When he spoke, his voice carried a mixture of disdain and embarrassment. "I'm sorry, Tobi, my brother thinks he's being funny."

I mouthed an *It's okay* at Andrew and turned my focus back to the phone. "Gary, I've come up with a slogan that will appeal to people across the board, regardless of demographic, as well as one that will bring instant name recollection."

"Okay . . ."

"*Zander Closet Company. When we're done, even your skeletons will have a place.*"

"Come again?"

"*Zander Closet Company. When we're done, even your skeletons will have a place.*"

"Oh my God, that's it!"

I felt my mouth turn upward again, my snort-filled laugh bubbling just below the surface.

Andrew looked at me and grinned. "So you're good with it, Gary?"

"Good with it? It's fan—"

"Catch you later, Gary." Andrew pressed the disconnect button, silenced the ring, and winked. "He needs to install a closet system."

If it weren't for my broken heart and the old adage about not mixing business with pleasure, I could so see myself with this guy. He was funny. Cute. Sincere. But my heart *had* been broken. Badly. To work around that would require trust, and that wasn't something I was willing to do these days. Besides, Andrew Zander was off-limits, thanks to the new roommate who couldn't sleep through the night without his attention . . .

I forced my mind back to the campaign. It was a much safer place to dwell. "I took the liberty of creating a script for your radio spot that incorporates the slogan with a few pertinent facts, like your phone number, location, and competitive pricing."

His warm hand brushed mine as I handed him the script. A look I couldn't identify flashed across his face.

"That's awesome, Tobi. I'm going to get this to the station as soon as I leave here. It'll run several times tomorrow, and again on Wednesday, Thursday, and Friday, leading up to the Showcase this weekend."

He reached into the inside pocket of his blazer, pulled out a checkbook, and sat down at the table. I watched the pen move across each line of the check, the numbers too small to read from where I stood (not that I was looking or anything). "I'm giving you a little more than we discussed. Call it a bonus for your great work."

I wanted to dance around the room, the urge to fist pump the air nearly overpowering. Instead, I smiled. "Thank you."

"Thank *you*, Tobi. Now, the next thing we need to focus on is a color brochure. I just wish we'd come straight here instead of wasting our time with Beckler and Stanley. If we had, the brochure would have been available for distribution at the Showcase."

I considered his words as he tore my lifeline out of his checkbook. "What we can do is offer a prize drawing of some kind at the Showcase. The entry forms will allow us to collect names and addresses. When the brochures are ready, we've got a mailing list." I pulled the last board off the table and propped it in front of the slogan. "I came up with a few ideas for the brochure."

He stood and walked over to the easel. I watched his green eyes move slowly down the board, only to return to the top as a smile spread across his face. "Man, Tobi, this one is awesome." He pointed to the first idea I'd created with actual photographs of the closet systems rather than sketches.

"I like that one too. Do you think I can get a picture of the system Gary is putting in at the Hohlbrooks?"

"Absolutely. I'll need to double-check with the Hohlbrooks, but if they say okay, would Saturday morning before the Showcase work for you?" He handed me the check he had written and smiled. "Would eight be too early?"

"Eight is fine. I can be there even earlier if you want."

"Let's stick with eight. Mrs. Hohlbrook strikes me as the type who isn't up at the crack of dawn."

I looked down at the check in my hand, at the money that would allow me to pay my rent for the month, buy some food, pay JoAnna, and maybe even buy an outfit that hadn't been worn by someone else first.

I realized Andrew was still talking and forced myself to focus on his words.

"Do you have a photographer on staff? Or do you take the pictures yourself?"

This campaign was a dream come true. I'd created and pitched the slogan completely on my own. It was a feeling I'm not sure I could explain to anyone. Except one person.

By realizing my dream, I could help someone else's come true too.

I smiled. "I've got the perfect photographer for the job. His name is Sam."

Andrew reached for my hand and shook it firmly, my skin tingling against his. "Well then I'll see you and Sam at eight o'clock on Saturday morning."

"Yes. You will." I pushed a wayward lock of hair away from my eye. "Thank you so much, Mr. Zander."

"Andrew—actually, I'd like you to call me Andy. And thank *you*. I think you just saved my company with thirteen words. Thirteen words that are gonna knock 'em dead."

4

I'm not sure what I was expecting when Mitzi Hohlbrook opened the door on Saturday morning. Nicole Kidman perhaps? Maybe Jennifer Aniston. You know, someone who wore their money well. But that's not who was standing in front of me now.

Instead of understated elegance, Mrs. Preston Hohlbrook reminded me of a cross between Kim Kardashian and Kate Upton. Packed into a form-fitting, silver-sequined gown, she sported a set of fake breasts that would make Dolly Parton look, well, small-chested.

If I had any doubt as to whether I was gawking, it was put to rest with an elbow to my side, compliments of Sam.

I gulped.

She squealed.

"Tobi Tobias! I'm the talk of the *town* thanks to you. My phone's been ringing *off the hook*. There's not a day spa *for miles* that hasn't heard my name uttered inside its walls in three days. I am the envy of *absolutely everyone*."

Before I could respond, Mitzi Hohlbrook grasped my upper arms with her long, slender, perfectly manicured fingers and pulled me forward. My face careened toward skin-covered silicone faster than the speed of light.

But just as I closed my eyes and braced for impact, the forward motion stopped. I peeked out through my right eye.

"Isn't it just like them?" she said.

Suddenly free of Mitzi's hands, I tugged my sweater down and tucked a strand of hair behind my ear. "*Them?*"

"Larry and Linda."

She had *names* for her breasts?

I peered at Sam to see if he was having more success in tracking the staccato conversation, but his attention was solely on Larry and Linda. Judging by the look on his teenage face, it was doubtful he was hearing anything. I returned the elbow jab and looked back at Mitzi, her raccoon-rimmed eyes narrowed to near slits as she stared at something behind me.

Curiosity, of course, won. I turned.

A couple, probably in their mid- to late-forties, stood in the street, their heads bent close to each other, their mouths moving a mile a minute as they engaged in a conversation we could not hear. A conversation that was no doubt about us (the finger pointing was kind of a giveaway). Or, more likely, the Hohlbrooks.

"They were so sure their house was going to be the star of the Showcase this weekend. But we showed them, didn't we, Tobi?"

"We did?"

"*Of course.* I didn't see any of *their* contractors on the five o'clock news last night." Mitzi giggled. "That little saying you came up with has the whole city abuzz. Even Preston started salivating over the possibility of a fresh start for the dealerships. In fact, he's been kicking around the idea so much, he hasn't had time to get too upset about— oh, forget it."

I knew my mouth was hanging open, but I was powerless to stop it. Mitzi Hohlbrook was the fastest talker I'd ever met. When, exactly, the woman took a breath was a complete mystery.

"And, frankly, I couldn't be more thrilled with the attention I'm"— she stopped for a moment and smiled—"I mean Zander Closet Company is getting from all of this."

"Really?" I asked.

"Of course. That's what this Showcase is all about. Helping the business community thrive. It's just more satisfying when it's one of the little guys, don't you think?"

I looked back at the couple on the street. "And they're jealous?"

"Jealous doesn't begin to cover it. Their housekeeper, Glenda, told our housekeeper Deserey that the two of them were practically throwing the china last night after that news clip."

"You mean the one about Zander's slogan?"

"Uh-huh." Mitzi bent her fingers inward and moved her thumb across her pinky. "I swear, it is hell to find a decent manicurist these days, you know?" She looked up at me, at my colorless nails and scratched-up hands, and tsked. "Well, maybe you *don't* know. Okay, so what were we saying? Oh, that's right, the slogan. You saw the clip didn't you?"

Saw it? How about taped it in forty different languages? (A slight exaggeration, of course, but I'd be willing to bet every member of my extended family had already received a copy of last night's news, compliments of my mother?) To Mitzi, I said, "Yes, I saw it. They interviewed me."

Mitzi stopped looking at her fingers for a moment, and turned her nearly inch-long eyelashes in my direction. "They did?"

I looked at Sam. He was still gawking.

"Yes. The story focused on the slogan. That I created."

"Oh, that's right. Silly me. That's how I recognized you this morning." Mitzi raised a polished hand to her mouth in feigned embarrassment, but her attention was no longer on me. The finger-pointing neighbors had that honor once again. "Let's go inside, it's a little stuffy out here."

When Mitzi turned, I quietly snapped my fingers in Sam's face then pointed at his camera bag on the walkway beside his feet. Like an obedient puppy, he grabbed the bag and followed his teenage fantasy into the marble foyer of the Hohlbrook mansion. I glanced back at the green-eyed neighbors one last time then followed Sam inside. As I passed Glitzy, I mean, Mitzi, she touched my arm and lowered her voice to a near-whisper.

"I can give you the name of a good plastic surgeon. He can make mountains out of those molehills."

I didn't need a mirror to know my cheeks were a perfect match for Ronald McDonald's nose, but a crowbar would have been nice to pry my jaw off the floor when I looked up and saw Andrew Zander standing in front of me. Good Lord, had he just heard what Mitzi said? I looked down at my newly purchased plum-colored V-neck top and back up at my client. It didn't matter if he'd heard or not. Those emerald-green eyes could see reality all on their own.

"Hey there, Tobi. How're you doing this morning?"

I looped my thumb under the strap of my backpack and tugged it higher on my shoulder. The movement gave me time to find a steady voice—one that wasn't shaky from embarrassment. It also gave me time to note that his sandy blond hair and tanned skin looked pretty spectacular in conjunction with the hunter-green sweater and black slacks he was wearing (not that I was looking or anything).

"Andrew . . . I didn't realize you were here already. I hope you weren't waiting too long."

"Not long at all. The housekeeper just let me in through the back door." He nodded a hello at Mitzi and then extended his hand to Sam. "I see your camera bag so you must be Tobi's photographer. I'm Andy Zander."

Any reservations I may have had about hiring a teenager for this job were whisked away as I watched Sam return Andrew's handshake with a firm squeeze and spot-on eye contact. Mary Fran would be so proud.

"It's nice to meet you, Mr. Zander."

"Andy, please. And if you can get your boss here to start saying *Andy* instead of *Andrew*, I'll buy you lunch sometime."

Sam looked at me, grinned, and nodded at Andrew—Andy. "You're on."

Great, now I was getting ganged up on by—

"Ba-boo."

I sucked in my breath and stared at Sam.

"Ba-boo. Dad-ee."

"Rudder?" I didn't realize I'd uttered his name aloud until I heard Andy's voice.

"Rudder? You mean Rudder—"

Mitzi clapped her hands together. "Oh, it's just Preston's damn bird. I've tried to find a muzzle for it, but no such luck. He talks non-stop most days, and he's so loud we can hear him all the way down here."

She beckoned to us with her finger as she sashayed across the entry foyer and into the living room. We followed.

"What kind of bird is it, ma'am?"

Until now, I'm not sure Mitzi had even noticed Sam's presence. But when he closed his mouth around the word *ma'am* her head snapped to the side and he was the *only* one she saw.

"Manners *and* good looks. Aren't you just a dreamboat?"

Now, I can't be certain, but I'm fairly sure I saw Sam gulp. I definitely saw his cheeks turn the same shade of crimson as the wallpaper. But before I could get him back on track, Andy spoke.

"I asked Mr. Hohlbrook that same question earlier this week. It's an African grey parrot, and his name is Baboo."

"Really? That's cool. My mom's got one at—" Sam looked at me and stopped. "I'm sorry. We're not here to talk about pets."

Andy clapped a hand on Sam's right shoulder. "It's okay. I like animals too. But you're right, we probably should get the show on the road. So, what kind of shots do you want to get today?"

Sam looked at me. "Tobi?"

"What we'd like to get is a few interiors of the closet. Some with nothing in it so we can feature the materials and craftsmanship, and some with clothes and accessories in place so we can demonstrate the organization your system brings." I looked at Mitzi, her attention back on her fingernails. "Mrs. Hohlbrook, will it be okay for us to move things out for a few minutes? We'll get everything back just the way you had it."

Mitzi Hohlbrook waggled her fingers in the air. "That's fine. Just so long as everything is picture-perfect when the Showcase opens at ten."

"That won't be a problem at all." I started for the foyer, Sam in tow. Mitzi's voice brought us to a stop.

"Of course I'll need a few minutes to freshen my makeup for the pictures."

It was my turn to gulp.

"Pictures?" I asked.

"Of course. You *are* planning on having me in these shots, aren't you?"

Sam looked at me. I looked at Andrew. I mean, Andy. We all looked at Mitzi.

She couldn't be serious. Could she?

"Why don't you all sit down for a few minutes. I'll send Deserey in with a plate of muffins. I won't be long. Toodles." In a blur of silver sequins, she was gone.

"Oh man, what do we do now?" Andy dropped onto one of the floral couches and dug his elbows into his thighs. "I don't want her in my brochure, but I can't come out and say that."

"You don't have to," Sam said. "They just don't come out."

Leave it to the teenager to come up with an answer. God, I love that boy.

"They don't come out?" Andy asked.

"Yeah. I take the pictures we want, and I take some with Mrs. Hohlbrook. The ones with her won't come out for some reason. Wrong setting or something like that."

A slow smile crept across Andy's face and he looked at me with those sparkling clear eyes. "Where'd you find this guy? He's good."

"Where'd she find *me*? Nuh-uh. I found *her*. Actually, my mom and I did. We're the lucky ones. Tobi's the best."

I could feel Andy's eyes on me, but I didn't meet them. Instead, I pulled Sam in for a hug and whispered in his ear. "Thanks, Sam."

I was still hugging him when the Hohlbrooks' housekeeper breezed into the room carrying an oval serving tray filled with an assortment of miniature muffins. I heard Sam sniff the air, felt him step back.

At least I knew where I stood. Important, yes. But still second fiddle to food.

"Mrs. Hohlbrook will be down in just a moment. Can I get you something to drink?"

Ever the growing boy, Sam swallowed a mouthful of muffin and said, "Sure. Milk would be great."

The housekeeper nodded and left.

I peered at Andy over on the couch and then shifted foot to foot as I realized he was still watching me. "Muffin?" I asked, my voice a little shaky.

"No thanks." He patted the vacant spot next to him. "Let's talk for a few minutes before the shoot gets started."

I chose a blueberry muffin and left Sam hovering over the tray in search of some flavor I'd never heard of before. I sat down beside Andy and willed myself to focus on something other than his eyes. It didn't work. My willpower stinks.

"I haven't had much of an opportunity to thank you for everything you've done for my brother and me. For our company. We've gotten more calls in the past four days than we've gotten in the past six months. And it's because of your slogan and you. Thank you."

My senses were in overdrive as I sat there, my ears hanging on his every word, my neck conscious of his hand draped across the back of the couch just inches from my skin. And, of course, we can't forget the voice chanting in my head—*You don't date men you work with. You don't date anymore. Period*—chants I couldn't share with Andy Zander. I searched for something else to say.

"I'm glad things are working out. For both of us. Your slogan has helped me too."

"How's that?" he asked.

"The slogan on the radio has gotten so much attention that my secretary has been fielding calls from businesses all over the area. They want a slogan that'll get them the kind of recognition you've gotten this week."

"I'm glad. I know I took a number of calls about you as well. Got one at home the other night from an old college buddy, Craig Miticker. He's the brains behind New Town."

"*New Town?*"

Andy smiled. "Yup. I take it you've heard of it?"

My mouth dropped open and I nodded. "Absolutely. That place is amazing! I read recently that architects from other countries are virtually flocking to New Town to see the concept in person. Beckler and Stanley does their ads. That's their biggest client—the one who keeps their boat afloat."

"Then I think they better start looking for a good bucket."

"Excuse me?"

"To bail out the water."

I stared at him.

"Their boat's about to sink, Tobi."

I blinked.

"What?" Andy grinned. "Craig called and asked me who was doing my campaign. Naturally I gave him your name."

I found my voice, or, rather, a raspy version of it. "You can't be serious?"

"Yeah, I can be. And I am."

"That'd be awesome, but—"

"But what?" Andy looked at me closely as I scrambled to find words to explain my momentary hesitation over the possibility of landing a new client.

"I heard what you said about John Beckler that first day. About his attitude. I understand that. I worked with him for a few years. He's beyond pompous. Looks out for number one at all times. But Mike? He's a good guy. I hate to see his livelihood hurt."

"If it is, maybe he can come work for you." Andy's hand left the back of the sofa long enough to give my shoulder a quick pat. A simple gesture that made me blush. Again. "You've got to take care of yourself and your company. It's the way business works. Competition is the name of the game."

He was right and I knew it. Heck, Mike knew it too. I looked down, pulled a piece of plum-colored lint off my new black slacks.

"You look great, by the way, Tobi."

I swallowed.

"I meant to tell you that when I first saw you in the foyer, but you looked as if you were in a pretty deep conversation with Mrs. Hohlbrook."

A recommendation of implants might not necessarily qualify as deep conversation, but at least it hadn't been overheard as I'd initially feared.

"Thank you."

Andy pulled his hand from the back of the couch and cleared his throat. "So, how did Sam come about?" he asked quietly.

The momentary awkwardness was suddenly gone as I looked at Mary Fran's son. Sam's head was tilted back as he chugged the glass of milk the Hohlbrooks' housekeeper had apparently brought in while I was otherwise focused.

"I've known Sam for about two years. He and his mom live in the two-family house next to mine. I don't know what I'd do without them."

"He sure seems to feel the same way about you."

I turned slightly and met Andy's gaze head-on. "If you're worried about his ability considering his age—"

Andy held his hand up, palm out. "I'm not worried. If you think he's good enough to do this, that's all the endorsement I need."

If I had a nickel for every time I'd blushed so far today, I'd be a rich woman.

"Thanks, Andy. You won't be disappointed. I promise."

"I know I—"

When he didn't continue, I turned to see what had widened his eyes to nearly twice their normal size.

It was Mitzi.

The golden streaked hair that had been in a chignon just twenty minutes ago, was now down, a few stray hairs slightly askew from the rest. Gone was the silver-sequined gown. In its place was a hot-pink, body-hugging satin cocktail dress that emphasized each and every curve on Preston Hohlbrook's wife.

I swallowed. It couldn't *hurt* to write down that doctor's name, could it?

"How do I look? Is this color right for the camera?" Mitzi rose up on the balls of her feet and spun around slowly.

"It's awesome, but you-you didn't have to change," Sam said as he wiped muffin crumbs from the corner of his mouth and reached for the last swallow of milk in his glass. He used the upward motion of his hand to cover the wide-eyed look he shot in my direction. A look I knew all too well. It was the same expression he had every December when Ms. Rapple hired him to take Christmas card pictures of her and Gertrude. In matching holiday attire, of course.

Mitzi giggled. "Oh, but I did. A few of my sequins rip—popped off." She ran her polished nails across her chest. "I think I was just too much woman for those little threads."

Sam coughed.

Andy was still speechless.

Men. You'd think they hadn't seen a woman before. I mean, really, what was I? Chopped liver? I looked down. Looked back up at Mitzi. Okay. So when did chopped liver get such a bum rap anyway?

"It's getting close to eight thirty, and I think we better get these pictures taken so we can be out of here before the Showcase kicks off." I was surprised to hear the words come out of my mouth. I hadn't realized my mind was still functioning in Mitzi's wake.

"That's a great idea." Andy cleared his throat and stood. "Ready to go, Sam?"

"You bet." Sam grabbed his camera bag from the floor, slung it over his shoulder, and then followed Mitzi into the foyer and toward the back of the house.

I walked in the direction Mitzi and Sam had gone, my thoughts running a mile a minute as visions of Zander's print ad danced in my head. As I crossed the foyer and turned down an outer hallway, I nearly smacked into Andy's brother, Gary, coming out of the bathroom, fussing with his belt buckle. When he saw me, he grinned.

"Hey there, darlin'. Don't you look gorgeous this morning?"

Andy skidded to a stop behind me, his hand gently brushing my back. "When did you get here, Gary?" he asked.

Gary hesitated briefly then shrugged. "Just now. But I needed to take a leak first."

"For Pete's sake, Gary, would you cool it?" To me, Andy said, "I'm sorry about my brother. He forgets his professional face—and mouth—sometimes."

Gary waved his brother's words away. "Relax, Andy. The system is in, it looks fantastic, and Hohlbrook is getting tons of exposure. Nothin' I do is gonna ruin that. Trust me. So, where are you two headed?"

"Upstairs. To Mrs. Hohlbrook's room. We need to photograph the closet system for the color brochure," I said.

"Gotcha. Follow me."

Andy and I fell in step behind Gary as we headed toward the back staircase. The hallway or corridor or whatever you'd call this part of the Hohlbrook home was an experience all its own. Each room that branched off was reachable through a stone archway. The walls were wood panel with stone trim. A large picture window ran almost the entire length of the hall and overlooked a bird sanctuary complete with a marble bath and a variety of beautifully painted houses. Cardinals, finches, and hummingbirds could be observed from one of several oversized window seats with thick cushions and fluffy throw pillows. Wrought iron chains hung from the ceiling, each strand of links holding an old-fashioned lantern. The walls, the floor, the framed pictures, the quiet details, all lent a circa 1940's Pacific Northwest feel to the setting—a showpiece that few visitors probably ever saw. I couldn't help but marvel at the waste.

Then I looked at Gary.

Mr. Roving Eyes himself was a few steps in front of me, running a hand through his tousled hair. I bit back the urge to laugh as a fleck of something fell out, shimmered in the morning light as it skirted across one of the window seats, and then disappeared under the fringe of a throw pillow.

I forced myself to focus, once again, on my surroundings by peering into as many rooms as I could as we made our way toward Mitzi's new closet. Every piece of furniture I saw, every knick-knack I spotted, was perfectly positioned, almost museum-like. It was an interesting way to treasure what you had. Sure, I'd like money to be less of an issue. I'd like to know that I could sort through my mail without that feeling of dread when I spied my landlord's handwriting. I'd like to walk into a store and buy an outfit that caught my eye without trying to figure out how many lunches I'd need to brown bag to stay within my budget. I'd like to be able to buy my parents something special for their anniversary—like a cruise. Instead, I made them a pillow with a sentimental slogan embroidered on the front.

But, as I looked around at the Hohlbrook mansion, I couldn't help but realize I was the luckier one. Fancy stuff and large rooms didn't make a home. And a workaholic husband and a near-silent housekeeper didn't make a loving family.

"Hey, guys?" Andy called. "I forgot something in the car. I'll meet you in the room in a few minutes." A smile spread across his mouth as I turned and our eyes met. "You okay 'til I get back?"

Gary's arm slid around my shoulders. "She'll be just fine, bro."

The spasm of anger that flashed across Andy's face was fleeting, but I still noticed. If I took a guess, I'd say that Gary took great delight in pushing his brother's buttons. How and when I'd become one of those buttons was the part that confused me.

"I'll be *right* back."

I politely disengaged myself from Gary's grasp and rounded the corner into Mitzi's—whoa!

I stopped in the doorway, rooted to the polished wood floor beneath my feet. My mouth dropped open and I, well, *stared*. Sure, I know it's not polite. But my mom—who had taught me the golden no-staring rule—had never seen Preston and Mitzi Hohlbrook's bedroom. If she had, she'd be doing a little rule breaking herself.

Palatial was the only word that could describe it. The crown molding, doors, and trim work were all polished mahogany. An enormous royal-blue Oriental rug denoted the room's sitting area—a section with several high-backed chairs grouped around a massive floor-to-ceiling stone fireplace. Thick drapes graced the long windows that framed the hearth, one side pulled back with a tasseled gold cord. A corner cabinet made of mahogany and glass housed the largest collection of Hummels I'd ever seen (an extensive assortment that made my grandma's lifelong collection look like a passing fancy). The wallpaper above the room's chair rail was detailed in velvet, the golden sconces bathed in sunlight from the window wall on the far side of the room.

The bed was canopied by white sheers that hung from the coffered ceiling above. The armoire beside it boasted a silver brush-and-mirror set that could pay my rent for years.

And it was all part of a room that, as gorgeous as it was, simply didn't fit its owner. Not Mitzi, anyway.

I looked at Mrs. Hohlbrook in her hot-pink satin cocktail dress and strappy silver spikes, her hand flirtatiously resting on Gary's upper arm. Come to think of it, nothing I'd seen in the house so far represented the woman in front of me now.

It made no sense.

Why would a man of Preston Hohlbrook's standing be married to a woman like Mitzi? She had to be the laughing stock of the country club community, with her neon-colored eye shadow, caked-on lip gloss, and over-the-top taste in clothing.

I watched as Sam stood beside Mitzi, gawking once again (though, if I was honest, I'm not sure he had ever stopped). Gary Zander was also mesmerized by the scantily clad woman, his eyes noting every curve.

As I looked at them looking at Mitzi, I answered my own question. Preston Hohlbrook liked attention. Liked to be envied. Any one of the dozen commercials currently running for his car dealerships was proof of that. He didn't just stand in front of a camera and ask for your business. No siree. He brought in camels and dancing girls. He wore a king's robe and a gold bejeweled crown (John's contribution to the commercial, no doubt).

Mitzi was his domestic camel. The wife that all the other husbands stared at. The wife that all the other husbands drooled over. Which made *him* the guy that all the other husbands wished they were. She was, in a nutshell, a show piece, not a treasure in the way a wife should be. And because of that, I pitied her.

"Baboo. Baboo Dad-ee. PHhhhtttttt."

"For God's sake, shut up, Baboo!" Suddenly void of its syrupy tone, Mitzi's voice rose to an angry shriek as she shook her fist at the large cage in the back left corner of the room.

As if drawn by a magnetic pull, Sam and I walked over to the bird's cage at almost the same instant. I peered inside. Baboo was smaller than Rudder, his feathers a softer gray.

"He's stressed." Sam bent his right index finger, tucked it between the bars of the cage, and beckoned to the bird with a soft whistle under his breath.

"Why do you say that?" I asked.

"See the feather on the bottom of the cage?"

I looked below Baboo's perch and spotted the soft gray feather Sam indicated. "So? Rudder loses feathers."

Sam took a slow sidestep to his left, his shoulder breezing against mine. "Rudder *loses* his feathers, Tobi. Baboo plucked his out."

I looked again at the feather on the bottom of the cage. Sam was right. The feather looked ripped.

"And that means stress?" I asked.

"Uh-huh. African greys are notorious for being sensitive."

As crazy as Rudder Malone made me with his back talk, imitations, and impersonations, I had grown to appreciate the uniqueness of this particular breed of bird. They were incredibly smart and loyal.

"Okay, everyone, we've got exactly forty-five minutes to get these pictures taken before the Showcase opens—" I spun around at the sound of Andy's voice and met his eyes as he walked into the room and stopped, a small lavender gift bag clutched in his left hand. "Whoa. Is everything okay in here?"

Mitzi sidled up between Andy and Gary and placed a hand on each man's arm. "Everything is fine, handsome. Preston's bird is just demanding attention. As always."

I looked back at Baboo one last time. Sam was right. Something was off. What that was, though, I had no guess.

"Ready, Sam?" I asked softly.

"Sure. But I want to take a picture of Baboo real fast. I want my mom to see him."

I took a step back as Sam pulled out his camera and raised it to his eye. The shutter fired once before I heard him mutter under his breath.

"Something wrong?" I asked.

"Nah, just out of memory on this card. I've got another."

He picked up his camera bag and headed for the double doors to the right of the bathroom, his left hand unzipping the case before he even reached his destination. I followed, my mind shifting from Baboo to the task at hand.

"Since all of the Hohlbrooks' clothing items are already in the closet, let's shoot it that way first," I said.

"Too bad we don't have a Halloween skeleton hanging from one of the bars," Gary chuckled. "You know, to drive the slogan home."

I knew my grin was forced when I looked at Gary. But people who had to take everything so literally all the time drove me nuts.

Andy reached for the doorknob and pulled, revealing rows of beaded gowns, satin dresses, and spandex pantsuits, all hanging from bars of varying heights. Preston Hohlbrook's ties hung from tiny recessed hooks along a side wall. The back row held built-in platforms for hats and purses.

I gasped when I saw Mitzi's shoe collection. Never had I seen so many pairs of sandals, strappy shoes, spike heels, ankle boots, knee-high boots, and thigh-high boots in one place (department stores included).

After fiddling with his light meter and talking through shots with Andy, Sam started snapping pictures. Some of those pictures were with Mitzi posing among the closet's contents, and some, thankfully, weren't.

While Sam concentrated on the hat and purse platforms, I stepped through an arched doorway into a section of the closet that held even more built-ins and secret hiding places.

"Pretty neat, huh?"

I smiled up at Andy and nodded. *Neat* didn't even come close to describing what Zander Closet Company had created here. Unbelievable was a much better description. And it was *that* description that I needed to portray in the print brochure.

I pointed at a relatively narrow floor-to-ceiling cabinet. "What's that for?"

"An ironing board." Andrew Zander walked toward the cabinet, stopped, and placed the lavender bag on the floor by his feet. His emerald green eyes sparkled as he lowered his voice to a near whisper. "Though I doubt Mitzi Hohlbrook has ever touched an iron in her entire life."

I bit back the urge to voice my gut instinct aloud. After all, whether Mitzi had fallen into money or not, really didn't matter. She had it now. Besides, Andy was probably right. The ironing board would have been better suited to the housekeeper's closet than Mitzi's . . .

"So? What will it be? Would you like a vowel or a consonant?" Andy asked.

"Excuse me?"

"Vowel or consonant." Andy gestured toward the cabinet door in a perfect imitation of Vanna White on *Wheel of Fortune.*

I laughed. "Um, well, okay, how much are the vowels?"

Andy smoothed his imaginary dress and fluttered his eyelashes. "For you? Free."

"Then I'll take an *A*, please, Vanna."

I couldn't help but giggle at Andy's dramatic nod as he wrapped his hand around the narrow handle and slowly pulled, a rapturous *ta-da* escaping his lips.

It was probably silly of me, but I actually expected to see the interior of the closet light up and a black letter *A* appear. Or, at the very least, an ironing board . . .

Instead, I got a rush of air in my face as Preston Hohlbrook's body hit the floor.

5

My friends were all assembled in my tiny living room like pigeons around a park bench, impatiently waiting for the next tasty morsel to drop. Any initial concern for my well-being had disappeared, replaced by the overwhelming desire to get as much dirt as possible—the grittier the better.

Fortunately, Sam's animated retelling of the police department's request for his photographs was keeping our resident ambulance chasers happy. For the time being.

With them occupied, I reached for the glass of water Mary Fran had set on the coffee table when I first sat down and took a few big gulps.

From the moment Preston Hohlbrook's body had tumbled from the cabinet, my day had gone to hell in a handbasket. I never knew I had it in me to scream as loud as I had, or that someone could possibly top my shriek the way that Mitzi had.

The moments after we found the body were still jumbled in my mind, a blur of screams, questions, accusations, and disbelief.

"For someone who's been through the wringer like you have, Sunshine, you look as radiant as the brightest, most twinkly star shimmering in the darkest night sky."

Leave it to my upstairs neighbor, Carter, to make me smile no matter what. Forget the fact that his hair color changed with each new stage show he worked on. (I was almost sad to see *Othello* close—the raven-black hue he'd created in Laurence Olivier's image suited him much better than last month's Cinderella-blond.) What I found *most* endearing about him was his attitude. Carter McDade was a true optimist in every sense of the word and delighted in viewing the world as a breeding ground for similes.

"Radiant? You think Tobi looks radiant? I think she looks awful. Look at those circles under her eyes. She doesn't look like any shimmering star I've ever seen."

And leave it to Ms. Rapple to speak her mind. What little was left of it anyway. But if I'd learned anything over the past few years, it was that Ms. Rapple didn't mean any harm by her callous words. She simply told it like it was. Through her bifocal-laden eyes anyway.

Mary Fran, on the other hand, had yet to learn that engaging the old biddy in a war of words was an exercise in futility. "Excuse me for saying this, Ms. Rapple, but how do you expect Tobi to look? Having a body fall at your feet isn't normal, you know." Mary Fran pulled her legs upward, rested her chin on her knees. "Carter was just trying to be nice."

"There's nice and there's stupid. And telling Tobi that she looks radiant when she looks anything but is stupid." Ms. Rapple's voice raised an octave with each word she spoke, her left eyebrow meeting each rise in volume with a lift of its own.

"Is that so?" Mary Fran's chin jutted outward as she dropped her legs back to the carpet and straightened her back in preparation for battle. A battle I didn't need or want today.

"Whoa, everyone. Enough. Please. I'm sure I look like crap. Finding a dead body wasn't on my list of to-dos today. And no matter how hard I try to block that vision from my mind, I still keep seeing Preston Hohlbrook at my feet. It's awful." The words poured from my mouth at Mitzi-speed, but I couldn't stop. Every thought that had teased my subconscious over the past few hours was suddenly playing in real time through my mind. And there wasn't an off-switch to be found anywhere. "Less than twenty-four hours ago I was on an all-time high. My slogan, my company, were being talked about on the news. Then this morning, during what should have been a routine photo shoot, a man's body falls from my client's closet. I'm not sure I'll ever be able to close my eyes and not see him staring up at me."

As my torrent of words came to a stop, I felt Mary Fran's gentle squeeze on my knee, Carter's feather light kiss on my temple, Sam's head on my shoulder. *This* was what I needed. To be surrounded by people who loved and supported me.

"And your slogan was the catalyst for all of it, dear."

I turned my misty gaze on Ms. Rapple, wiped the corner of my nose with my plum-colored sleeve, and waited for her to offer an explanation for her odd statement.

But she said nothing. She simply snapped her fingers at Gertrude and stood. "It's time for Gerty's afternoon nap. She needs her beauty sleep. Something *you* might want to think about, Tobi."

That lesson I'd learned? You know, the one about not engaging my elderly neighbor in battle? Duress has a way of clouding judgment.

"What are you talking about, Ms. Rapple?"

"Oh good Lord, Tobi, don't tell me it hasn't dawned on you? Zander's closet system can find a place for everything. Even a *skeleton*, remember? Or, in this instance, Preston Hohlbrook's dead body."

I opened my mouth to speak, but no words came out. All I could do was sit there and stare at my neighbor as she worked her flappy skin into the sleeves of her Gerty-matching lavender knit sweater.

The silence that met her departure was deafening.

I looked at Mary Fran on the floor in front of me and then turned and met Carter's look of horror behind me as Sam simultaneously lowered his head back onto my shoulder. "Do you think she's right? Are people going to see my slogan as some sort of weird foreshadowing?"

Three voices converged at once, all trying to put my mind at ease.

"Ignore her, Tobi. It's just Ms. Rapple," Sam said, his voice a whisper in my ear.

"Tobi, that woman is sick, you know that." Mary Fran continued softly, fiddling with a loose thread on the front of my sofa. "She doesn't know what she's saying half the time."

"Putting stock in anything she says is like, like, well—" Carter nibbled on his lower lip for a moment and then looked at the floor. "It's just, crazy, that's all."

And that's when I knew Ms. Rapple was right. In the two years I had lived here, I had never known Carter to be at a loss for a colorful simile. Until today.

Why it hadn't hit me until that moment was beyond me. My slogan, coupled with Mr. Hohlbrook's body, was exactly what my advertising professor, Dr. Markum, had called a campaign nightmare. The kind of truth in advertising that could crush a company.

Dr. Markum had found the subject so important that he'd devoted five classes to slogan snafus. When he was done with his instruction, he'd split us up into project teams to create a disaster campaign for a well-known company. My group had found the project silly at first, seeing as how we were focusing on something we were supposed to *avoid*. But we'd given it our best shot and had laughed more on that project than any other we'd done that entire semester.

"Do you think that saying about looking back on things later and laughing can work in reverse?" I heard my voice, felt the words as they left my tongue, but was still taken by surprise that I'd uttered the question aloud.

"What do you mean?" Carter asked.

"Have you ever looked back on something that you found funny at the time only to be horrified later?"

He must have sensed the rhetorical nature of my question because he simply squeezed my shoulder.

I, of course, kept talking. And talking. "I'm going to be a living, breathing example of a campaign nightmare in Dr. Markum's future classes. I'll be dubbed the former student who failed—who didn't heed his advice. I'm going to be mocked by advertising students for years to come."

"No, you won't," Mary Fran offered on the heels of an audible gulp.

My babbling turned to out and out rambling. "It's like a lightbulb company saying they'll light up your world, and then someone electrocutes themselves twisting it into the socket. Or a burger company claiming their hamburger is so good you'll never eat another, and then the customer drops dead of a heart attack."

I was ruined. Plain and simple.

"Pretzel?" Mary Fran lifted the bowl off the coffee table and shoved it in my face. I shook my head, pulled back the sleeve on my left arm and noted the time on my watch: 4:58. I picked the remote off the armrest of the couch and aimed it in the general direction of the small television cart I'd assembled on one of a string of dateless weekends.

Dirk Winter's voice filled the room. "The metro St. Louis community is reeling this evening over the death of one of its most prominent citizens. Preston Hohlbrook—of Hohlbrook Motors—was found dead in his Chesterfield home this morning. The same home he had graciously offered to the small business community for its annual Home Showcase Weekend. Among the many contractors who had been brought in to update various aspects of his home was Zander Closet Company—a company we highlighted on our newscast last night for its extremely creative slogan. A slogan that is now being hailed as an eerie premonition for the murder of Hohlbrook Motor's owner and C.E.O."

I had to be imagining this right? Surely yesterday's slogan of the year hadn't become today's recipe for murder.

"Let's go to Gwen Roberts at the scene for a live report. Gwen?"

The perky redhead with a reputation for getting to the heart of a story, appeared on my screen, her eyes filled with an anticipation one might find on a child's face at Christmas. Only her anticipation had nothing to do with wrapped packages under a tree and everything to do with digging around in other people's misery.

"Good evening, Dirk. It started out as support. Support for new business owners hoping to gain exposure for their companies. In fact, it was a cause near and dear to Preston Hohlbrook's heart. A cause that ultimately resulted in his untimely demise."

Mitzi Hohlbrook appeared on my television, her eyes puffy and swollen, her spoiler heaving with each labored breath from beneath a sheer black V-neck sheath. I felt Sam sigh next to me.

"I don't know what I'm going to do without Preston. He was the love of my life. He understood me like no one else." Mitzi hiccupped as fat, black crocodile tears ran down her cheeks. She dabbed at her eyes with a silk handkerchief and spoke into the camera in a raspy, choked-up voice. "All I've got left of him now is this big, empty house, a fleet of car dealerships, and our sweet little Baboo."

Sweet?

Sam shifted on the couch next to me. "Did she just call Baboo *sweet?*"

"She sure did," I said, the surprise in my own voice a near perfect match to that of Sam's.

"Who's Baboo?" Mary Fran asked.

"Mr. Hohlbrook's African grey parrot." Sam stood and walked over to his bag, unzipped the top compartment, and retrieved his camera. Turning it over, he opened a small door on the side and inserted a flat square cartridge that he'd pulled from his pocket. After pressing a few buttons, he handed the camera to his mom. "See?"

"I thought the cops took your photos, Sam," Carter said from his spot behind the sofa.

"They did. Sorta. I shot this picture before I realized my memory card was too full for the photo shoot. The new card I dropped in is the one the cops took."

Mary Fran looked into the back of the camera and studied the shot of Baboo in his cage. "This bird isn't well. Do you see the feather he's pulled off?"

"I know. That's what I told Tobi." Sam sat back down on the cushion beside me. "Remember, Tobi?"

"Yeah, I remember. You said it was a sign of stress."

Mary Fran spoke, her voice firm and steady. "This was *Mr.* Hohlbrook's bird?"

We nodded.

"Yup." Sam pointed to Mitzi on the television screen. "And she hates him. She screamed every time he spoke this morning. I wanted to take him home with us the second I saw him. But I figured he'd be okay when Mr. Hohlbrook came home."

"Only he already *was* home." I heard the disbelief in my voice as I forced my attention back to the screen once again.

Gwen Roberts was still speaking, her hands gripping the microphone much like I held a piece of chocolate. "This shocking death has reverberated through this quiet, posh neighborhood in Chesterfield, leaving residents fearing for their safety."

The reporter turned to a man and woman in their mid-to-late forties. I recognized them as the couple who had been pointing at Mitzi Hohlbrook and me just that morning.

"How are you coping with this tragedy?" Gwen Roberts asked.

The woman, a petite blonde, spoke first. Her name, Linda Johnson, and her affiliation as a Hohlbrook neighbor, appeared on the bottom right corner of the screen.

"It's just awful. But, as you know, our home is featured in the Showcase this weekend as well. And while my husband and I struggled with the decision to continue our participation in light of this tragedy, we've come to the conclusion that Preston would have wanted this."

"You lying little—"

The off-camera ranting was cut short as Gwen Roberts stepped in front of the camera. "Back to you in the studio, Dirk."

I sat and stared at the television, not really seeing or hearing anything as the news anchor repeated his comment about my slogan serving as a premonition for Preston Hohlbrook's murder before moving on to the next story.

"Was that Mitzi's voice in the background?" Sam finally asked.

"It sure was." I pushed the red button on the remote and watched the screen go dark.

"So, let me get this straight." Carter walked around the sofa and started pacing in front of the coffee table, his left hand holding his right elbow as he used his index finger to tally some sort of score. "Mitzi Hohlbrook hates her husband's bird. *And* she hates her neighbor?"

"Yep," Sam said.

"I tell you, these rich people—they portray this glam world of fancy houses and glittery dresses as some sort of holy grail. But they aren't happy. In fact, I'd venture to say they're no happier than a vegetarian at a steakhouse." Carter grabbed his denim jacket off the coatrack in the corner and blew me a kiss. "Cheer up, Sunshine, it'll all work out."

I raised my hand in a wave as he headed out the door, but my thoughts were focused elsewhere. As blurry as everything seemed at that moment, one thing was crystal clear: The popularity of my slogan and its perceived foreshadowing of Preston Hohlbrook's murder was a dream-come-true for the local media. It was an angle they would mercilessly hammer until everyone in the metropolitan St. Louis area was convinced my agency was taboo.

It was up to me to provide a new angle for them to chew on. Like the truth. . . . If I didn't, Tobias Ad Agency would be as dead as the Car King himself.

6

That morning I'd dressed carefully in a burgundy-colored pantsuit, white camisole top, and black sling-back heels. It was one of my all-time favorite ensembles. The jacket's fitted waist and sleek lines did an awesome job of: a) finding my figure (shocking, I know); and b) enhancing what it found (wonders never cease).

I had chosen the effect as much for myself as the potential clients JoAnna had lined up for me to woo. The most recent issue of *You* magazine had promised that if I looked put-together on the outside, it would impact my inner confidence.

I hoped—no, needed—*You* magazine to be right.

JoAnna had been out of town all weekend, visiting her newest grandchild in southern Illinois. But as of her final voice mail on Friday, I had two meetings set for this morning: A-1 Garage Door Company at nine, and Murphy's Bar & Grill at eleven. Two accounts I was determined to land.

I crossed the corner at Maryland and Euclid and walked three blocks south to the brick storefront that housed Tobias Ad Agency. *My* agency.

It's funny, but after six months it still didn't seem fathomable that I owned my own business. Probably because I'd done very little "business" prior to Zander Closet Company.

I waved at Mr. Houghtin and Sandy on the other side of the street, but didn't stop. I wasn't in the mood.

I'd always enjoyed my walk to and from work. I loved basking in the sun's rays on the beautiful days, dodging rain drops on the not-so-beautiful days, and talking to neighbors along the way, regardless of the weather. But not today. It was hard to engage in idle chitchat when my mind kept replaying the events of Saturday morning. In particular, the discovery of Preston Hohlbrook's body.

My determination to uncover the truth was as strong as it was after the Saturday evening newscast, but now it was sharing mental space with another emotion: regret.

I hated the fact that Zander Closet Company had gotten caught up in this whole mess. And if Ms. Rapple was right, I was partly to blame.

Andy Zander had given me my first real break. Sure, my slogan had been good—damn good. But if he hadn't hired me (and given me that nice big paycheck), I'd be living on the street by now. Me, my Cocoa Puffs, and I.

I was so engrossed in my thoughts that I completely missed my door. Doubling back, I went inside and headed for JoAnna's desk at the end of the hallway.

"Good heavens, Tobi, what's going on?" JoAnna came from around her desk to give me a quick hug. Her normal easygoing sparkle was noticeably absent, replaced by a worry that extended beyond her eyes to her mouth and stance.

"Going on?"

"I've gotten calls from WKTS-5, WJRT-4, Fox-2, and some ham radio operator up north. Moscow Mills, I think. They all want to speak to you. And some of them were rather rude and pushy."

I peeled off my thin, black leather coat and draped it over the crook of my arm. "Oh. That."

"*Oh that*? To-bi!"

I sunk into the metal-framed upholstered chair across from her desk and pulled my coat onto my lap.

"I guess I never stopped to think you wouldn't know." I nibbled the inside of my left cheek for a moment then went the way of a rhetorical question. "You didn't read the paper this morning, either?"

JoAnna shook her head slowly, leaned back against her desk, and waited for me to continue.

"When did you hit the road on Friday?" I asked.

"As soon as I left here at five."

"So you didn't see the newscast that night?"

"No. How did the segment look?"

"Great. Corrine Martin, the reporter for Channel 2, started the story outside the Hohlbrooks' home with a Zander truck in the driveway. She interviewed the president of the Home Showcase who used the popularity of our slogan to entice people to the event. And she talked to Gary on-camera too. He was fun to watch because he was so jazzed about everything. It was all very exciting."

JoAnna smiled at me. "And you? How did you look?"

"Okay. Professional."

"You didn't snort, did you?"

I leaned my head against the wall behind my chair and looked up at the dot pattern on the drop ceiling. "No, I didn't."

JoAnna laughed. "Good. Did you tape it for me?"

"Of course. And if my copy breaks, my mom's got about fifty more."

"So? What's happened since?"

I forced my gaze off the ceiling and back onto my secretary. "You really want to know?" At her raised eyebrow, I filled in the dreaded blank. "Well, I guess you could say my slogan hit a little too close to home."

JoAnna stared at me, her eyes squinting as she appeared to process my words. "How so?"

"Remember the skeleton part?"

"Yes . . ."

"Well, apparently a Zander closet can actually, in fact, house a dead body. In some of their taller, more expensive cabinets, of course."

Seeing the confusion on her face in the wake of my half-story, I cut to the chase. "While Sam was taking shots of the Hohlbrooks' new closet, I asked Andy about a particular cabinet. He said it was for an ironing board but when he opened it, Preston Hohlbrook's body fell out."

JoAnna gasped. "You can't be serious."

I looked at the floor and nodded, tried to think of something else to talk about. Of course, there was nothing. So I offered a few more revelations.

"He was strangled with a drape cord. Sometime between Friday evening and when we found him."

"Strangled by whom? And why?"

I shrugged. "All good questions. As of now, there are no answers."

"So why are the stations calling here?"

I dug my fingers into the glass jar on JoAnna's desk and slowly unwrapped a mint. My mouth was dry, real dry. "The media is having a field day touting my slogan as some sort of foreshadowing."

She gasped again. Only this time it wasn't a gasp of surprise.

"Oh, come on. They can't possibly believe—" JoAnna's pallor drained to the color of chalk as she covered her mouth with her hand.

"JoAnna? Are you okay?"

"It makes sense now." She pushed off her desk, walked around to her chair, and peeled a pink while-you-were-out sticky note off her calendar.

"What makes sense?"

"These."

"What is it, JoAnna?"

"When I came in this morning there were messages from both A-1 Garage Door Company and Murphy's Bar & Grill."

I saw the way she looked at me, saw the pity where disbelief had been just moments earlier. "And?"

The quick jump of her throat told me what I needed to know. I gulped as tears sprang to my eyes. "They've canceled, haven't they?"

JoAnna reached across her desk and patted my hand while I fought the urge to bawl like a baby. How could things go from so awesome to so crappy in such a short amount of time?

We sat that way for a long time. In silence. Each of us deep in thought and at a loss for how to fix something so far beyond our control.

In fact, it's how we still were when the front door opened ten minutes later. I looked up, hoping to see one of our canceled appointments with a change of heart. Instead, I caught a glimpse of a crew cut behind an enormous floral arrangement the likes of which I'd never seen.

"Can I help you?" JoAnna asked while I continued to stare.

"Uh. Yeah." The twenty-something male set the cardboard-protected vase on a corner of JoAnna's desk and reached for the delivery slip in his back pocket. He pulled it out and turned it over. "Yeah. These are for some guy named Tobi. Tobi, uhhhh, Tobias. He here?"

I shook JoAnna off. The assumption that I was a man was something I'd dealt with since childhood, thanks to my parents. The fact that my first name was simply a shortened version of my last name just made me even more of a curiosity. How my parents could have been so clueless to the hell that awaited me on the school bus, and in the lunchroom, and on the playground, was beyond my ability to comprehend. But somehow, along the way, after years of taunting by my elementary school classmates, and inaccurate profiling by most of the colleges I'd applied to, I'd gotten to a point where I actually liked my name. It suited me.

I reached up, pulled the French clip from the back of my head and let my blond hair fall onto my shoulders. I ran my tongue over my lips to moisten them and stood.

Delivery Guy looked up from his sheet and met my eyes. I saw his Adam's apple move up and down while his eyes ran from the top of my head to my sling-back shoes. Slowly.

Then, just as that look of male appreciation crept across his face, I spoke. "I'm Tobi Tobias."

The look that followed was one I knew well—surprise fused with a mixture of embarrassment and posturing. The fact that I took such great enjoyment in it these days was simply a commentary on my current pitiful existence rather than any residual childhood trauma.

Delivery Guy coughed, swallowed, and coughed again.

"Mint?" JoAnna offered.

Judging by the way his face reddened, Delivery Guy knew he was being mocked. And, being the lightweight that I am, I finally let him off the hook. "It's okay. Really. I've gotten that my entire life. It's not your fault. It's my parents'."

He nodded slowly. His caught-in-the-headlights expression slowly faded. "I bet I looked like quite the idiot just now, huh?"

"Really, it's okay." I pointed at the arrangement on the desk. "Those are really for me?"

"Uh-huh." He handed me the delivery sheet and then slapped his hands against the pockets of his jeans and coat.

"Pen?"

He flashed a sheepish grin in JoAnna's direction and took the ballpoint from her outstretched hand. "Thanks."

I signed my name beside the black X and handed the pen back to JoAnna. "They're beautiful."

"It's one of our nicest arrangements." Delivery Guy gave me the once-over one more time. "You must be pretty special."

I waited until he left before I pulled the card from its plastic fork-like holder.

"Did something *else* happen while I was away this weekend?" JoAnna asked.

"You mean did I find a man and fall in love sometime between discovering Preston Hohlbrook's body and walking in here this morning? Um, that would be a no."

I tore open the tiny white envelope and stared at the inscription.

> *It's time for you to go back to school, little one.*
> *You've got a lot more learning to do.*
> John Beckler

Now I'm not one for cursing. Really. I see the use of obscenities as a reflection on the lack of literary creativity in our country. But, like all things in life, there's an exception to everyone's personal beliefs. John Beckler was mine.

When I was finished with my diatribe (which, in all fairness, would have made a career-curser laugh) I looked at JoAnna, her mouth open wide enough to catch a swarm of summer flies.

I apologized and then handed her the card.

I watched her eyes scan the note. I watched her lips tighten in disgust. And then, shock of all shocks, she let her own string of obscenities fly. Only the career-cursers would have applauded *her* effort.

"Who the hell does he think he is?" she asked.

I took the card back, placed it on top of the envelope, and shoved it between the plastic fork thingy. "Who he always is. A boil on the backside of mankind."

JoAnna grabbed the arrangement off her desk and started for the back door.

"Wait. Where are you taking that?" I asked.

"The dumpster."

"No. Don't."

JoAnna spun around, her mouth wider than it was during my verbal descent. "Good heavens, Tobi. Why on earth would you want to keep them?"

I tugged my jacket down and squared my shoulders. "Motivation."

"Motivation?"

"That's right. Motivation. John Beckler would love nothing more than to see me fail. And the weekend's news tying my slogan to Preston Hohlbrook's murder had to be music to his ears. I should have known the flowers were from him. It's got his MO written all over it. He takes great pleasure in pouring salt in people's wounds. Especially people who threaten his ego by daring to think they can make it on their own without him." I took the flowers from JoAnna and headed down the hall toward my office. "Don't you see? Our success the past week has gotten to him. Gotten to him good. So I'm going to put these on a shelf where I can see them. Where they can motivate me to make Zander one of a long list."

I didn't need to look over my shoulder to see JoAnna's smile. I knew it was there. I was just glad she couldn't see my shoulders slump when I walked into my office and out of her line of vision.

As true as the whole John Beckler motivation thing was most days, today it was different. I'd gotten in his head all right—for a grand total of four days. And then reality dropped in.

I set the arrangement on my bookshelf and glanced at my desk. The pile of bills had definitely shrunk over the past few days, thanks to my first Zander check, but it wasn't completely gone. In order to accomplish that feat, I needed to hold on to them *and* secure more clients.

My mind wandered to Mitzi's living room and the conversation with Andy. Specifically, the part about Craig Miticker and New Town. Landing a powerhouse account like that would mean the end to virtually all my money worries.

But Beckler and Stanley wouldn't give up their bread and butter without a battle—a battle that would be a lot easier to engage in without the *deadly premonition* tag hanging over my latest work. In a parallel universe, I would pick up the phone and call Mike. After all, he was my first and only mentor in this business. But since the universe I resided in had me wanting to swipe one of his company's biggest clients, I knew that option was off the table.

Instead, I grabbed a pen and some paper from the top of my filing cabinet and walked over to my window. You'd be surprised what lines in a parking lot can do for one's thoughts.

Okay, maybe not.

But it didn't really matter because my creativity was somewhat stifled at the moment. A dead body and less-than-desirable news coverage had a way of inhibiting stuff like that.

My intercom buzzed.

I walked over to my desk and pressed the black button atop my phone. "Yes, JoAnna?"

"Mr. Zander is here to see you."

I gulped.

JoAnna, being JoAnna, anticipated my mental question and answered it with finesse. "Would you like me to settle *Andrew* in the conference room or send him to your office?"

My gaze flew around the room, skirted my relatively clear desk (JoAnna had been busy before I showed up), and rested on the decorative mirror to the left of my fake—but tasteful—silk palm tree. I spread my fingers, worked them up my hair to the roots, and gave a gentle tug upward (gotta love Carter and his grooming tips). I puckered my lips and was pleasantly surprised to see that the soft champagne hue I'd forked over six bucks for did, indeed, live up to its claim of unsurpassed staying power. Unfortunately, nothing in my makeup bag had worked on the dullness in my eyes. I mean, really. When are these cosmetic firms going to wake up and create something to reverse the effects of finding a dead body? Sheesh. Other than the absence of a sparkle, though, I was pleased enough with the face I saw looking back.

"My office is fine, JoAnna, thank you."

Now that he was on his way, I allowed my mind to process what this unexpected meeting could mean. And I didn't like where my thoughts jumped.

A soft tap at my door coincided with the sudden thumping in my chest. He wasn't coming to fire me, was he?

I swallowed. Hard. Forcing a smile to my lips, I pulled my door open. "Good morning, Andr—Andy."

The deep voice and boyish smile that greeted me caught me off guard, and I lost all business acumen from that moment forward. He, in turn, stood awkwardly in the doorway, a small lavender gift bag clutched in his left hand. "Can I come in?"

Good, Tobi. Real good. Professional . . .

A quick flash of warmth spread across my face, and I motioned him into my office. "Of course. Come in. Make yourself comfortable."

As he passed, I poked my head into the hallway and made a face at JoAnna's eye roll.

I shut the door of my office and studied Andy Zander for a moment as he peered at the various framed photographs on my shelves. He didn't look tense like I'd imagined he would if he'd come to fire me. In fact, he looked rather relaxed in a pair of khaki slacks and a navy polo, his tanned chest visible through the unbuttoned neckline.

"This is Hawaii, isn't it?"

I pulled my gaze off his body and moved closer to the shelf, our shoulders brushing against one another for a brief but wonderful moment. "Yes. That's my brother and his wife."

"Have you been?" he asked.

"To Hawaii?" I laughed. "I wish."

"It's beautiful. You'd love it." He moved a centimeter to his left, our shoulders touching once again. He pointed to a five-by-seven print in a delicate silver frame with tiny hearts woven into the wire. "Is that your sister?"

I looked at the picture of the barefoot brunette clad in Bohemian garb. "Yes, it is. How'd you guess?"

"She has your nose and cheekbones."

I stood there for a moment, uncertain how to respond. But of course that didn't last long. "She's a hippie."

"Oh?"

"Yeah, like I'm not sure she owns a pair of shoes. Unless you count the rubber thing she ties to the bottom of each foot."

Andy laughed. (Have I mentioned the fact that his laugh starts somewhere deep in his chest and makes my heart skip a beat?) "You've *met* Gary. So you know I get the whole different-as-night-and-day sibling thing."

I grinned and pointed at the picture of my sister. "My brother and I used to tell her she was adopted all the time. We even had a certificate we showed her as proof. But she never quite believed a judge would sign a document like that with Crayola's Screamin Green."

"Purple Mountains' Majesty didn't work with Gary, either."

I think we stood there and laughed for five minutes before I finally got with the program and realized he hadn't come to discuss my family tree, or Crayola's wide assortment of colors for that matter. So I motioned to the set of chairs in front of my desk.

"What can I do for you this morning?"

He strode over to the chair and sat, placing his bag on the floor beside his feet. "Things didn't exactly go as planned on Saturday."

So he *was* here to talk about my slogan. My *deadly* slogan. I sat down behind my desk and leaned forward. Despite the confidence I hoped to convey with my voice, all I could find was a single, husky word. "Yes."

Good answer, Tobi. Confident. Reflective . . .

He looked at me curiously. "Are you okay?"

I wasn't sure how to answer that. I mean, if I went with the truth, I'd be babbling on and on like an idiot. If I said I was fine, he'd see right through my shaky voice and sparkle-less eyes.

So I opted for the truth, buffered with a little Tobi-esque confidence (that's what I call that strange calm that envelops me at the oddest of times). "I will be. Once I get the media latched onto the truth."

He nodded.

"I'm so sorry about all of this, Andy. If I'd known this would happen I'd have taken the slogan in a different direction."

Andy held up his hands, palms out. "Please. Your slogan is dynamite. It was the talk of the town last week."

"And all weekend," I said quietly.

"Well, yeah. But I predict the negative aspect will fall by the wayside as the truth comes to light. I'm just hoping for sooner rather than later."

"I wish I could share your optimism, but our slogan timed with Preston Hohlbrook's murder is a reporter's dream come true." I picked a pen out of the rectangular holder and tapped it gently on the desk. "But I plan to change all that."

His eyes narrowed. "How?"

"By finding the killer."

"Whoa. No way. You concentrate on my print brochure and creating a commercial script. I don't need to be worrying about you, okay?"

My face grew warm again. Worry? Did he really say *worry*?

Seeming to sense the sudden charge in the room, Andy leaned quickly to his side and plucked the lavender bag up off the floor. He set it on my desk and smiled. I remembered that bag. It was in his hand when he returned from his car just before the photo shoot we never finished.

"What's this?" I asked.

"My way of saying thanks. For all your hard work."

He could have knocked me over with a feather at that moment. *Andy* was thanking *me*? I sat there, dumbfounded.

He scooted the bag closer. "Open it."

I always wondered what it meant in all those novels when a character swallowed around a lump in their throat. Now I knew. I had a lump. And I swallowed around it.

I reached into the bag and pulled out a small wooden box.

"Turn it around," he urged.

I shrugged my shoulders and turned the box around to reveal a glass front. Beyond the glass was a miniature closet system with a tiny skeleton neatly stored inside an opened cabinet. Across a gold plate at the bottom, engraved in cursive, was my slogan: *Zander Closet Company. When we're done, even your skeletons will have a place.*

I swallowed around that same lump. Only the lump had grown bigger. I blinked quickly against the sudden moisture in my eyes.

"I wanted to give this to you on Saturday, but never had the chance. For obvious reasons." Andy shifted in his seat, his eyes never leaving my face. "Then I debated all weekend whether I should still give it to you. I was afraid the skeleton would upset you. But then I decided that would be letting the media win. Your slogan was, *is*, dynamite. And you have a right to be proud of it."

My voice was barely audible when I spoke, the emotion running through my body like none I'd ever experienced. "Thank you. I love it."

Tiny red points spread across his cheeks as he smiled. I caught sight of a dimple in his chin I hadn't noticed before, and my heart sunk. "Again, I'm so sorry about this whole mess, Andy. I really am."

He reached across my desk and patted my hand, my skin tingling at his touch. "Tobi, none of this is your fault. Put that out of your mind. Okay?"

How could I argue with those eyes? That dimple?

"Okay."

He rose to his feet. "I guess I should leave you to the onslaught of prospective clients who want a piece of what Zander has."

I didn't have the heart to tell him the truth. Not now.

I pushed my chair back and followed him to the door. "Thanks for stopping by, Andy."

"My pleasure." He took a step toward me, his breath warm against my skin. I stifled a shiver as he continued. "Now remember, no snooping into Hohlbrook's murder, okay? Let the cops do their job."

I think I nodded. I'm not exactly sure. I was still focused on the warmth of his breath and the scent of his cologne. Yet, as he turned and left my office, I knew I couldn't honor his request.

7

Most of the time my decision to be car-less wasn't an issue. My neighborhood offers virtually everything I need (a market, Laundromat, coffee shop, restaurants, and a quaint little mystery bookstore to satisfy my unhealthy reading addiction). And what *isn't* right around the corner can be reached from the bus stop that *is* right around the corner.

Unfortunately, today wasn't most of the time.

If I was at my apartment, I'd hit up Carter or Mary Fran. Sometimes the decision on who to ask was based purely on who was home when I needed wheels. Sometimes it was based on my mood. Mary Fran's car was classy—a bright red Beamer she'd been nursing for fifteen years. It was fanatically clean and turned heads. Carter, on the other hand, drove a 1975 Ford Granada (surely the only remaining one left on the road) that had been repainted a powder blue and boasted a set of coordinating throw pillows on the back seat. It, too, turned heads, but for a very different reason.

But I wasn't home. I was at the office. Which left me just one viable option: JoAnna.

In theory she should be easy since she adores me. But I'd never asked to use her car before, so I wasn't certain what she'd say. In order to increase my chances for success, I opted to try a few of my best begging faces in the mirror before asking. There was the *don't know what I'm gonna do* face. That required the corners of my mouth to droop and my eyes to well, just a little.

I tried it out. Not horrible, but I could do better.

There was the *my business is about to go belly up if we don't fix this face.* All I needed for that was a majorly stressed-out look, complete with hand wringing and a little stuttering.

Nah, not right either. Too dramatic.

There was always the *how can you tell someone with freckles no* face. It was the same one that had gotten me away with murder when I was growing up. But would JoAnna fall for it?

I tilted my head to the right and flashed my biggest smile with a few extra blinks thrown in for good measure.

"If you need my car that bad, why don't you just ask?"

I gulped, turned, and met JoAnna's amused expression with what I imagine was a variation of the infamous *completely caught in the act and now I feel like a fool* face.

She smiled.

"How on earth did you—" I stopped, shook my head. "You scare me sometimes, JoAnna. Do you know that?"

"Thank you. I think."

I grabbed my coat and backpack and turned off the overhead light. "So it's okay? For me to use your car?"

"Of course." JoAnna followed me out of my office and down the hall. "Does this have something to do with the body in the closet?"

"It's got everything to do with the body in the closet." I pulled my jacket on and hiked my purse onto my shoulder. "It might be a few hours; is that okay?"

"How long is a few hours?"

I looked at the clock on her desk. It was almost eleven. "Back by three?"

"That's fine." She looked at me, her eyes studying my face intently. "He sure is cute."

"He?"

"Mr. Zander. *Andy* Zander."

"Oh. I hadn't noticed." I grabbed a mint from her jar and unwrapped it quickly.

"Denial is always a sign." JoAnna walked around her desk and pulled out her chair.

I started to pop the mint in my mouth but stopped. I was sensing a trap but, as always, I stepped right in anyway. "A sign? Of what?"

"That you've got it bad."

I snorted. Minus the laugh.

"Don't you snort at me, Tobi Tobias. Don't think I wasn't aware of the faces you were trying out before I sent him down to your office this morning," JoAnna said, her eyes trained on my face like a dog waiting for a treat to emerge from its owner's pocket.

"So much for your psychic ability. I didn't try out a single face thankyouverymuch."

"Okay. Bad choice of words. But you did *examine* your face from top to bottom."

"I . . . wanted to make sure I didn't have anything stuck in my nose."

JoAnna sat down, opened her filing drawer, and pulled out a folder marked *Invoices*. "Why don't you just admit you think he's cute? I mean, after all, the man brought you a gift."

Was there anything that got past ol' eagle eyes?

"Gift?" I tried for a hint of surprise in my voice but got something closer to a coughing choke as the last of my mint got sucked down my throat. I grabbed another mint and undid the wrapper.

"The purple bag, Tobi. He had it when I sent him down to your office, he didn't when he left." She opened the file, thumbed through the outgoing invoices (which, of course, consisted of two—Zander's slogan and the photo shoot), and then carefully stamped each sheet with a single red word: *Paid.*

I thought of the shadow box Andy had given me, my slogan cleverly depicted behind the glass. Truth be told, a dozen roses wouldn't have meant as much as that box did.

"Okay. Okay. Yes, he gave me something. It's on my desk. Take a peek when you get a chance. It's very cool. But it was merely his way of saying thank you for the slogan. Really." I dropped down onto the edge of the nearest chair. "I just wish it hadn't brought him so much grief."

JoAnna looked up, her eyes solemn. "Your slogan?"

I nodded.

"What happened at the Hohlbrooks' is not your fault. You know that, right?"

Twirling the mint between my thumb and index finger, I pondered JoAnna's words for a moment. "I *want* to know that. And I *do* know that, most of the time. But it doesn't necessarily make things any easier. Some people are going to forever associate Zander's slogan with a dead body if I don't do something to change their perception. That's why I'm heading out to the Hohlbrooks' house now. Because there's got to be something that will get everyone's focus off me and onto the truth."

JoAnna separated the correct key and handed me the ring. "I just filled the tank this morning, so you're good to go. Just be careful, okay?"

I jumped up and headed toward the back door, talking over my shoulder as I walked. "Thanks. I will. Don't you worry."

My hand was on the door when she threw her final shot. A three pointer from way outside the line . . .

"Oh, and Tobi?"

"Yes?"

"I'm well aware of the fact that you dodged the whole *cute* thing."

I didn't look back. I mean, why bother? That woman knew me inside out and backward. In just six months. Besides, now was not the time to remind her of Nick's betrayal. Nor was it time to fill her in on Andy Zander's ultra-cuddly roommate. I had a murderer to find.

JoAnna's car wasn't hard to spot in the lot. In fact, even if it had been a huge parking garage I could still pick it out. Because it was, well, *JoAnna*—hip and fun. Pressing the button on the key fob in my hand, I unlocked the driver's side door and slid into the black Miata, my knees practically cutting off air flow in and out of my mouth. I pushed the seat back a few inches and turned the key, the engine and radio springing to life simultaneously.

I cringed as a medley of elevator music surrounded me from all sides. Everything about JoAnna was fun *except* her choice in music. It simply didn't fit. Which is why I was always half expecting to walk into the office some morning and find her listening to, I don't know, something from the last couple of decades? But no such luck. I'd yet to catch her doing any closet bebopping.

Closet. Ugh.

I slid the car into reverse, backed out of the parking spot, and headed toward Kingshighway. A few traffic lights later, I merged onto Highway 40, westbound. Of course, this was when I decided to change stations. But I was at my best when I was multitasking. That and I was going to go loopy if I had to listen to beat-challenged music for another nanosecond.

A Bruce Springsteen tune came on (doesn't matter which one, because, after all, Bruce is Bruce) and I started belting out the lyrics at the top of my lungs. I opened the power moonroof with my right hand while I tapped out The Boss's rhythm on the steering wheel with my left.

The parking lot of the St. Louis Zoo was packed when I drove by. School buses, mini vans, and SUV's were jammed together like sardines in the North lot, everyone—young and old—eager to enjoy some of the last decent days before winter rolled in.

I'll admit, the car had serious thoughts of getting off the Brentwood exit for a pit-stop at the Galleria Mall (Dillards was having a shoe sale that would blow your mind), but I resisted with all my might and kept us moving in the right direction. Fortunately, at this time of day, traffic was virtually nil, which meant I crossed over the 270 loop without stopping and encountered smooth sailing all the way to the Woods Mill exit.

And that's when I started to panic.

What exactly did I think I was going to find? The killer as he snuck out of the house after hiding in an empty room for two-and-a-half days? Since the likelihood of that happening was, well, *impossible,* I needed a plan. Fast.

I headed down the same tree-lined roads and winding curves that I'd driven just two days earlier in Mary Fran's Beamer, with her son riding shotgun. Things were good then. Hopeful. Exciting.

As I pulled the Miata into the Hohlbrooks' circular drive, I was aware of three things. First, the contractor vehicles that had been scattered around the neighborhood in preparation for the Home Showcase were gone; in their place, a series of white panel vans representing every news station in the metropolitan St. Louis area. Second, Larry and Linda Johnson were no longer standing at the end of Mitzi's driveway, pointing. They'd changed geography and were now sitting on their front porch sharing what appeared to be a tiny pair of binoculars trained in the direction of the Hohlbrooks' home. Third, a Zander truck was parked behind the house.

I pulled to a stop near the front steps and climbed out of the car, unsure of what I was going to say and how I was going to explain my being there. I suppose that's why I was mumbling as I climbed the stone steps. I tend to mumble when I'm thinking. Drives JoAnna nuts.

And then it hit me. Or, rather, I should say, Rudder-inspired genius hit me.

God, I love that bird.

I pushed the doorbell and waited as a series of chimes sounded throughout the house—low, booming ones that I could hear from the doorstep. Less than five seconds later the door opened, and I came face to face with the Hohlbrooks' housekeeper, Deserey.

Truth be told, I hadn't really paid much attention to Deserey on Saturday, what with my mind focused on the photo shoot and drooling over the possibility of landing New Town as a client. But today I studied her.

Deserey was a beautiful woman in an uptight, almost stern way. Tiny lines around her eyes and mouth did hint at a sense of humor and an easy smile, but neither were present at the moment.

"Good afternoon, Miss Tobias, what can I do for you?"

I straightened my shoulders and tried to look formidable. Well, maybe not formidable so much as confident. Okay, I was shooting for simply looking like something other than a freckle-faced late-twenty-something-year-old who was grasping at straws to explain her presence at a murder scene.

I eked out an answer. "I was hoping to check on Mrs. Hohlbrook. See how she's doing. And to offer my help with Baboo."

"Mrs. Hohlbrook is at the gym. She's not due back for about an hour."

I suppose I should have thanked the woman and left. But I didn't. I think I was more dumbfounded than anything else. The victim's widow was at *the gym*? Shouldn't she be picking out caskets? Selecting flowers?

"Do you think it would be okay if I waited for her?" Where that question came from, I had no idea. But I went with it and waited for Deserey's reply.

The housekeeper nodded, stepped back, and motioned me into the house.

That was easy . . .

"The police just finished up about thirty minutes ago. The bedroom is a mess from that black fingerprint stuff."

I tried not to gawk as I looked at her. After all, just because I hadn't heard her speak more than a handful of words on Saturday didn't mean she couldn't.

"I can imagine," I said.

"It's funny you mentioned Baboo when you arrived. The poor

thing hasn't been himself since . . . well, Mr. Hohlbrook. He just sits in his cage and plucks his feathers. He makes a sound every once in a while but, for the most part, he's silent."

Deserey led me into the living room and then stopped. The stress of the past few days showed in her tired stance and weary eyes. My heart ached for the woman.

Without really realizing what I was doing, I reached out, touched her forearm. "I'm a good listener if you need someone to talk to."

I saw the tears well in her eyes at my words, heard her gulp as she worked to keep her emotions in check. When she finally met my gaze, she nodded and forced a smile. "I'd like that. I really would. But I'm pretty sure Mrs. Hohlbrook wouldn't like the idea of a guest hanging out in the kitchen with the housekeeper."

"Don't you worry about that. I'll tell her it was my idea."

She pulled a handkerchief from the pocket of her apron and dabbed her eyes quickly. "Are you certain?"

"Yes." I followed her down the hall and into the ceramic-tile— whoa. It was like seeing the master bedroom all over again. Never in my life had I ever seen a kitchen so large, so grand. The cooking area had two refrigerators that didn't look like refrigerators. They boasted cabinet fronts rather than the steel or fiberglass doors native to the rest of the world. There were two sinks, one in the corner with a beautiful bay window above it, the other in the center of the island— only this island was a good six by eight. Two ovens were built into the left wall; a third was housed in the right. The fixtures were all copper, the countertops a marbled mixture of hunter green and brown. A see-through fireplace denoted the separation between the working-area of the room (read: Deserey's side) and the eating-area of the room (read: everyone else's side).

I plopped onto an upholstered barstool next to the island and caught my breath. This house was incredible. Selling cars must be big money—money I wouldn't mind getting a chunk of at the agency. But, as always, the big accounts seemed to flock to Beckler and Stanley. Proof once again that money didn't mean brains.

I cleared my throat and forced my attention onto the Hohlbrooks' housekeeper. Her eyes were red-rimmed, her mouth turned downward.

"How long have you worked for the Hohlbrooks?" I finally asked.

"I started with Mr. Hohlbrook eight years ago." She busied herself with a cookbook, her fingers skimming the list of required ingredients. "He was a good man. A hard-working man."

I nodded. She moved effortlessly between the cookbook and the pantry (an offshoot room that, from where I sat, appeared to be bigger than my living room and kitchen combined) retrieving the items she needed. I was reminded of a saying my Grandpa Stu always spouted. Something about the doers and the watchers. Deserey was a doer.

"So you've known them for eight years. Wow, that's a long time."

Her head shot up from the cookbook. "I said eight years with *Mr.* Hohlbrook."

I straightened on the stool at the blatant animosity in the woman's tone. "Oh, I'm sorry. I just assumed that would mean Mrs. Hohlbrook too."

Deserey snorted and rolled her eyes.

I was torn on what to think. Part of me couldn't overlook the fact that Deserey was obviously not a fan of Mitzi's. The other part of me was focused on the fact that someone other than me snorted.

Deserey grabbed a mixing bowl from a cabinet below the island and plunked it on top of the counter. "Mrs. Hohlbrook—*this* Mrs. Hohlbrook—has only been here for two years."

Did she just say *this* Mrs. Hohlbrook? I needed clarification in case I was hearing things. "Was there *another* Mrs. Hohlbrook?"

Deserey nodded, her lip trembling as she measured out flour, sugar, and cinnamon. "Alana. She was Mr. Hohlbrook's first wife. A woman of class in every sense of the word."

I sat on the stool for a moment, the housekeeper's words washing over me with a host of implications I couldn't even begin to comprehend. Yet.

"What happened to her?" I asked.

"Breast cancer. Took her in less than a year." Deserey walked over to the first of the two refrigerators, extracted a carton of eggs, and carried them to the island. "Mr. Hohlbrook was devastated. He left the country for a while. Ran his company from overseas. Made a few conference calls from time to time to make sure things were on track, but for the most part he left everything in the hands of a few trusted employees here in town."

I considered my next question as she cracked each of the three eggs she'd set beside the bowl, her technique flawless.

"If the first Mrs. Hohlbrook was so classy, then—" I stopped.

Deserey was sharp. She followed (and finished) my train of thought. "Then how did he end up with *Mitzi*? Is that what you were going to ask?" Deserey dropped the egg shells into a trash compactor that looked like an ordinary cabinet from the outside. "Grief? Desperation? The painful knowledge he could never top his wife, so he didn't even bother trying? I don't know. Maybe a combination of all of those." I sat perfectly still as Deserey continued to speak—her words wooden and void of any discernible emotion. "But whatever it was that made him marry her couldn't hide reality."

"What do you mean, Deserey?" I asked.

"I mean he made a mistake the day he married Mitzi Moore. *I* knew it. His *friends* knew it. His *co-workers* knew it. Even *Baboo* knew it. In the end, I suspect he knew it too."

8

I'm not exactly sure what I said when Deserey dropped her bomb regarding the Hohlbrooks' marriage, but I do know one thing. Stools should have sides. Like a chair. You know, to hold a person in place when a possible motive hits them between the eyes.

Why do I say that? Because it was the sound of me falling off my stool that snapped the housekeeper out of her stream of consciousness and into the present. No matter how hard I tried to pick up where she left off, Deserey wasn't talking. So I tried another approach.

"It's possible I need my eyes checked, but when I drove up it looked as if the next-door neighbors were using binoculars to look over here." I ran my index finger along the island's countertop and waited to see if my effort would stick. I could almost hear the sound of the reel spinning as the woman's stance relaxed and her mouth started moving again.

Thank you, God.

"You mean the neighbor on *this* side?" Deserey pointed to her right, her eyebrows quizzical.

I turned around on the stool to get my bearings and nodded. "Yes. Those neighbors."

Deserey crossed the kitchen to the copper baker's rack and pulled a 24-cup muffin tin from the lowest shelf. "I figured that's who you meant. That's Larry and Linda Johnson. They're the old money on the street." She walked back to the island, popped open a tub of Crisco, and began lightly coating the bottom of each muffin holder. "He inherited his father's business, who inherited *his* father's before that, and so on down the line."

My stomach churned to life as I watched the housekeeper grab a bag of miniature chocolate chips and sprinkle them into the batter bowl. It took everything in me not to reach across and pluck a stray chip off the island.

"Are they the *only* old money on this street?" I noted the oven in relation to the island. Deserey would have to turn around in order to put the tray into the oven, leaving me a clear shot at the chip. I bided my time and waited for her answer.

"Yes. Everyone else got theirs the old fashioned way."

I grinned. "They earned it?"

"That's right."

As Deserey filled the final muffin cup with batter, I leaned forward on my stool, ready to move as quickly as possible in my pursuit of chocolate. But I was thwarted. Instead of putting the muffins in the oven and *then* cleaning up, Deserey set the batter-filled tin off to the side and grabbed a damp wash rag from the sink. My heart sank into my empty stomach as she caught the chip up with the stray sprinkling of flour and sugar that had missed the bowl.

So much for lunch. My stomach gurgled.

"The funny thing is, it's not the ones who bust their backs for this lifestyle that walk around with the sense of entitlement. It's always the ones who were handed it on a silver spoon. Isn't that strange?" Deserey dropped the wet rag into the sink and carried the tin over to the oven. "Even Mr. Hohlbrook used to say rich folks didn't make much sense."

I eyed the housekeeper as her voice faltered when she spoke of her late boss. "You two were close, weren't you?"

She nodded slowly, her eyes moist once again as we made eye contact across the island. "He never treated me like his employee, never talked down to me. Nor did Mrs. Hohl—I mean the *first* Mrs. Hohlbrook."

I leaned forward against the island and lowered my voice to a near-whisper. "Mitzi talks down to you?"

"Talks down to me?" Deserey echoed, cocking her left eyebrow at me. "How about *looks* down at me? *Snaps her fingers* at me? *Glares* at me? Take your pick."

I sported what I hoped was my best mortified expression and threw in a snort of disgust to boot. "So why are you still here? Making muffins? Cleaning up?"

"Out of loyalty to Mr. Hohlbrook. If I ran out now, before the facts are found, I'd feel like I was dishonoring his memory and letting the little hussy win."

Hussy? Did she say hussy?

I took a moment to compose my thoughts. "I imagine it must be awfully hard to remain professional when you have such strong feelings against one of your employers."

Deserey nodded. "It is. But I still have it better than Glenda does."

"Glenda?" I asked, searching my memory back for an explanation as to why that name sounded vaguely familiar.

"Larry and Linda Johnson's housekeeper."

Ah. That was it. Mitzi mentioned Glenda when we stood out front Saturday morning. Something about the Johnsons and a jealous china-throwing hissy fit.

"They treat her badly?" I asked.

Deserey laughed, rolled her eyes, *and* threw her hands up. I was impressed. "Like yesterday's trash."

That would certainly qualify as badly.

I got down off the stool, wandered over to the window, and looked out at the stone patio that sported the kind of uncomfortable backyard furniture I doubted anyone ever actually used. I found this whole lifestyle unsettling, I really did.

As I gazed past the patio to the squirrels darting up and down the trees, I found myself voicing questions for which I had no answers. "Then why does she work for them? Can't she find a different family? One who would treat her like a human being?"

"They pay better than the devil."

I tried that statement on for a while as I caught sight of a pair of cardinals peeking out from atop a low-lying branch. The male cardinals were always breathtaking with their flaming-red feathers and regal faces. The females were so drab, decked out in a muted brown with just a hint of red. It was funny how the males were always the best looking in the animal/bird world. Of course, they didn't have couches and remote controls to upset *their* beauty regimens . . .

"Mrs. Hohlbrook said the Johnsons were jealous of the attention she and Mr. Hohlbrook were getting after my slogan took off." I leaned my forehead against the window and peered at Larry and Linda's backyard. They had traded their lookout spot on the front porch for a pair of chaise lounges in their French garden out back. "Is that true?"

"Was it ever. They got so upset after that feature story on the news Friday night—you know the one, you were on it—that they started screaming about the Hohlbrooks and how they have the entire town in their pocket." Deserey came up behind me and lowered her voice. "Glenda said Mr. Johnson called Mr. Hohlbrook a no-good, lousy upstart. Can you imagine?"

I eyed Larry Johnson in his perfectly pressed khaki trousers and starched, white, button-down dress shirt as he lounged in his chair, his arms bent behind his head, his gaze trained in my direction.

"What difference did it make?" I asked.

Deserey laughed. "Difference? It's the difference between being noticed first and being noticed second. And between the Hohlbrooks and the Johnsons, that difference was everything."

But was it enough to murder someone?

It was a valid question. Especially when its answer could be the thing that saved my agency. However, in the interest of keeping our gabfest on track, I opted to let it go. For now.

"Does Mr. Johnson have a temper?" I asked instead.

Again, the laugh. I was beginning to realize that the housekeeper had a few distinct laughs. The most notable, by far, was the stupid-question laugh. I'd gotten it a few times now.

"Mr. Johnson apparently got so upset at the prospect of the Hohlbrook house being the talk of the Showcase that he destroyed an entire Limoges service for ten," Deserey said.

Ahhh, yes. The china-throwing incident . . .

I turned my gaze onto Linda Johnson. She had a brittle, uptight look with facial features that were too rigid to be natural.

The timer sounded, and Deserey headed toward the oven. "According to Glenda, a new set arrived by limo the next day. While the coroner was *here*."

"Do you think I could meet Glenda one day?" The question surprised me. But I let it hang out in the air anyway.

"I don't see why not. We have the same night off each week. Wednesday. If Mr. Hohlbrook's body still hasn't been released—and I'm not knee-deep in preparation for a memorial reception—you can find us at the Car Crash in Westport. Do you know it?"

I turned from the window and gawked.

Deserey at the Car Crash?

And that's when I really looked at the woman. If she released her hair from that tight bun and put on something less, well, *maidish*, Deserey would not only be pretty, but younger than I realized. Mid-forties at the absolute oldest.

Interesting.

"I know the place. I'll be there. Sounds like a great stress-reliever." I returned her smile and then looked back outside. The Johnsons were gone—their previous Hohlbrook watching spot abandoned in favor of another, no doubt. I moved my gaze across the backyard to the driveway and the Zander truck parked under a leafless Bradford pear.

"Is Andy here?"

"Who's Andy?"

I turned from the window and walked over to Deserey. "Andy Zander. The owner, well, actually he's *one* of the owners of Zander Closet Company."

Deserey mumbled under her breath as she yanked open a smaller pantry door and extracted a mop and bucket. "*That* sleaze?"

She may as well have hit me with a left hook the way her words blindsided me. Andy, a sleaze? Sure, my good-guy radar was still missing parts, but had I missed the boat again?

She had to be wrong.

I tried again. "Andy. Tall. Sandy-blond hair. Emerald-green eyes. Dimp—"

"Ohhhh. No, not him. He's sweet. And oh, so cute." Deserey waved her hand in the air. "I'm talking about the other one. The sleazy one that has the hots for Mrs. Hohlbrook."

I thought about that for a moment as my heart rate returned to normal. And then I remembered. The cell phone call that very first day. Mr. Hohlbrook had been complaining about Andy and Gary's cousin, Blake. Gary wanted to fire him, take over the closet installation himself.

"You mean *had* the hots, right?" I looked back at the truck quickly and then met Deserey's darkened eyes as she straightened up, the mop handle clutched in her hand.

"No. I mean *has* the hots. As in ongoing. As in reciprocated."

"They have a thing going on?" I heard the disgust in my voice, felt the sympathy for Andy as the meaning of what was being said hung in the air like a storm cloud waiting to break open and unleash its fury.

"You bet they do!" Deserey picked up the bucket, dropped it into the corner sink, and flipped up the faucet handle. "And you wanna know the worst part? Mr. Hohlbrook *knew*."

9

My Grandpa Stu taught me a lot of things when I was growing up. Because of him, I know to give up my bus seat to anyone older than me. Because of him, I can distinguish between a phone solicitor and a legit call before a single word is uttered. And because of him, I had always known to tell my grandma her cooking was the best even when it wasn't. I listened to everything he told me and committed it to memory, certain that what he had to say was akin to the Gospel. But, of course, there was one lesson he desperately tried to teach me that I just couldn't master. The poker face.

If I had a secret, everyone knew. If I aced a test, everyone knew. If I had a crush on someone, everyone knew. Grandpa Stu, being the smartest man I know, recognized a lost cause when he saw one and adjusted his teaching accordingly. Which, simply put, means he taught me ways to compensate for my shortcoming.

Today's compensation? A sudden coughing fit the likes of which would have made him beam with grandfatherly pride. I almost felt sorry for Deserey as her eyes widened in worry. But I didn't stop coughing. I almost cried uncle at the way she pounded my back in case I was choking (on what, I have no idea since the chocolate chip I'd been eyeing was in the trash can instead of my stomach). But I didn't stop coughing.

It worked like a champ.

I'd created such a commotion that all talk of jealous neighbors, cheating wives, and suspicious husbands flew out the window as I excused myself to the bathroom. Once inside the same room from which Gary had emerged with unbuckled pants just two days earlier, I looked at myself in the mirror. Thankfully, the two-minute coughing spell had left me no worse for wear (probably because it wasn't real—but we won't dwell on that). I splashed a little water on my face to complete the show and then killed a few more seconds (dotted with a stray cough or two, of course) by freshening my makeup and hair.

But even as I did that, my thoughts were on the enlightening conversation with Deserey. I had come here hoping to unearth something—a few clues, a possible motive, and yeah, a killer. Deep down inside, though, I'd known the likelihood of that happening was pretty nil.

Now I wasn't so sure.

I had known Preston Hohlbrook was a wealthy man. I had known he had a strong footing in the local community, thanks to a number of placards and bricks in many of St. Louis' most beloved locations over the years. I'd known that his fleet of car dealerships represented an advertising empire for one lucky local firm (*not* Tobias Ad Agency).

But now, thanks to Deserey, I knew a few things I hadn't known before. Like the fact that Preston Hohlbrook was in a less-than-ideal marriage in more ways than one.

Granted, it didn't take a rocket scientist to see Mitzi wasn't in Hohlbrook's league. I knew that the second she opened the door Saturday morning. How he couldn't have realized that from the get-go was beyond me, but I suppose grief and loss could create a rose-colored desperation. And it certainly sounded as if the death of his first wife had been truly devastating for the poor guy.

I leaned against the wall and coughed a few times as a picture began to form in my head. If Preston Hohlbrook had finally gotten himself to a point where he could see that his marriage to Mitzi had been nothing short of a badly fitting Band-Aid, what did that mean? For him? For Mitzi?

More importantly, did Mitzi know? Was that why she had developed a thing for Andy's cousin, Blake? Or was Blake just the most recent in a long line of play toys for a woman who so obviously didn't match her surroundings?

And if she *did* know, was Blake her only revenge? Or was murder? I shivered. Mitzi Hohlbrook wasn't the only one with a motive. Blake Zander had one as well. Humiliation and a change in job status had certainly driven people to kill before, right?

I closed my eyes and steadied my breathing. Coming here, to the Hohlbrook house, had been a good call. It had given me a chance to place a piece or two in the Who-Killed-Preston-Hohlbrook puzzle. But I needed more. A lot more.

I pulled open the bathroom door and stepped into the hallway. It was time to start wrapping up my visit to the Hohlbrook mansion. I had a cousin to meet. A Zander cousin.

"There you are. Deserey said you weren't feeling well." Mitzi Hohlbrook came sauntering down the hallway in my direction. She wore spandex workout shorts and a sports bra that did little to corral her superstructures. Of course, the shorts and bra were black, lest anyone forget the wealthy widow was in mourning . . .

"Are you okay?" she asked as she came to a stop between me and the window. I was just about to utter something about allergies when the sound of a car engine rumbled to life.

I stepped to my left, peered around Mitzi, and strained to see past the flaming red sugar maple that blocked my view of the service driveway. But it was too late. The white truck was gone (and, with it, any visual confirmation of Blake Zander's inappropriate behavior).

"Damn."

"Excuse me?"

I hadn't realized I'd voiced my frustration aloud. But I had. And now, thanks to my inability to censor myself, I was on the receiving end of what looked to be curiosity seeping through the widow's caked-on mascara.

"Oh, don't mind me. I was trying to figure out what got me coughing." I marveled at my ability to lie as the words flowed from my mouth. "I'm allergic to maple trees. And sure enough, you've got a big one right there."

I raised my hand to point at the gorgeous tree just outside the window and then peeked at Mitzi out of the corner of my eye to see if she'd taken the bait. Based on the way she nodded and tsked, I'd pulled it off. Point for me.

"Allergies are awful, aren't they? They make your nose red and your eyes puffy." Mitzi leaned toward me. "But you look okay."

I gulped.

"I react differently. I just cough. A lot. Even sneeze sometimes. But I don't get all red and puffy." I made a mental note to visit the confessional the next time I was at church and then waited to see if Mitzi would accept my latest fib.

She took hold of my wrist and led me down the hallway and toward the back staircase. "I think I've got some over-the-counter antihisti-whatever upstairs in my bathroom. That should help, right?"

Now I'm not a fan of medicine. Never have been. The dislike (okay, hatred) of the stuff dates back to my childhood when I used to run from my mother every time she pulled out the Robitussin. I never understood why, when you felt lousy to begin with, you had to endure stuff that smelled so bad your eyes watered and tasted so bad you were sure you'd vomit. Even now, as an adult, I still balked at taking any medicine unless I had one of those infrequent (thank God) sledgehammer headaches.

But I'd walked myself into this situation. Or, rather, lied myself into it.

"Okay . . . sure. Thanks." I hoped I sounded believable.

I followed Mitzi up the stairs, my throat tightening with each step. The thought of going in that room again was unsettling at best, and that was *before* Preston Hohlbrook's eyes flashed through my mind. I wiped my palms down my slacks and forced myself to keep walking, to ignore the pounding in my chest.

Mitzi, on the other hand, seemed unfazed. She simply breezed into the room without hesitation and peeled off her sports bra as she headed toward the armoire on the other side of the bed.

Three distinct things struck me at that instant as I watched Mrs. Hohlbrook yank open a drawer: 1) she seemed oddly at ease in a room that had held her husband's dead body just two days earlier; 2) she seemed perfectly content to strip down to nothing in front of a complete stranger; and 3) implants left a person rather, um, perky.

The workout queen-in-mourning uttered a few choice words. Nothing horrible, but enough to get my attention off the boob-building doctor that would soon be on speed dial at the office.

"The police cleared the room over an hour ago, but would you look around this place?" Mitzi groused. "Black dust *everywhere*! And is the overpriced maid cleaning it? Nooooo. She's making muffins in the kitchen because that's what Preston liked. Never mind the fact that Preston won't be eating them anytime soon."

I stood perfectly still. Afraid to move. Afraid to cough. Afraid to have Mitzi snap into reality and realize I was standing there, listening.

She continued, her ramblings growing more bizarre with each word. "I can't tell you what a pain it was not being able to get in here the past few days. I had to use back-up clothes—*back-up clothes* from the guest room." Mitzi pulled a black satin shirt over her head, the fabric clinging to her body like a second skin. "Of course, they were *last year's* clothes."

I tried not to take offense at the way she curled her lip in disgust at the travesty of wearing last year's styles—after all, most everything I owned was either last year's or somebody else's or, in most cases, both. Instead, when I spoke, I opted to take the old buttering-up angle.

"You look great in whatever you wear, Mrs. Hohlbrook."

It worked. Mitzi grinned from ear to ear, the antihistamine forgotten.

"Aren't you sweet?" She pulled her hair into a low ponytail and swooped it upward with a clip. "I can't wait to get my hands on this room. Get rid of all this mahogany stuff. I want modern and new. Not old and stuffy. It was always a sore point between Preston and me. He refused to change it. Because it was what *Al-a-na* liked. And God forbid her tastes be allowed to die *with* her."

My mouth dropped open, my nostril flared. Mitzi Holbrook had been a widow for, what, a little over forty-eight hours and she already had plans to redecorate?

The woman pulled off her black spandex shorts and left them in a heap at her feet. "The only time that man ever let loose was in his ads. And that was thanks to me."

"*You*?"

"That's right. When his ad guy told him the camel idea, Preston nearly flipped a gasket. But I liked it. I thought it was fun and different. I encouraged him to try it, to let his hair down. And he got a lot of attention because of those spots."

I considered trying to debunk the whole bad-attention-is-better-than-no-attention myth, but I let it go.

"Who was the rep on your husband's account?" I asked instead as I shifted my weight onto my left leg and tried not to tug on the stray thread dangling down the side of the Hohlbrook's bedspread.

"Originally it was the one partner. The one that starts with S."

I stifled a laugh. Mike would be mortified. "You mean, Mike *S*tanley?"

"Yeah, that's the one. Preston liked his ideas, said they were well-suited for him. But the head guy? John? He stepped in with the camel idea. The first guy—Mike, you said?—he wasn't thrilled. Kept insisting it wasn't the best choice. That Preston would be unhappy pretty quickly unless he took a classier, more refined approach. I mean, puhleeze. Classy? Refined? Give me a break. I wasn't going to sit by and watch my husband put the greater metropolitan St. Louis area to sleep every time his ad came on. So I spoke up and agreed with John on the camels. And naturally I won. Preston gave in to me a lot."

Sounded like John and Mitzi were cut from the same cloth in a lot of ways. Their way or the highway . . . I sighed as I looked around the room. Grandpa Stu's voice echoed in my head: *Whatever you do in life, Tobi, make sure you enjoy it. Because no amount of money will bring you happiness. True happiness.*

I made a mental note to call my grandfather when I got home. My life had gotten so out of hand that I found myself craving a dose of his wisdom.

Ba. Boo. Dad. Ee. PHhhhttttt.

I gasped. I'd completely forgotten about Baboo amid my snooping and lying. My heart ached as I reached Baboo's cage and saw the pile of feathers at the bottom.

"I swear, I am so done with that thing. I hate it. At least in the beginning, he was kind of pretty. But now he's just plain ugly without his feathers."

I didn't turn to look at Mitzi. I simply couldn't pull my attention from Baboo. It was hard to believe this obviously sick bird was the same breed as Rudder Malone. Rudder was always ready to kick some, well, you know. But not Baboo. Baboo looked as if he wasn't too far off from meeting his little bird-maker in the sky.

"Let me take him home with me. I know a little bit about African greys. I think I can help." I bent my index finger and pushed it between the bars of the cage while I waited for Mitzi's reply, unable to take my eyes off Baboo.

"Would you? Oh, Tobi, you're a lifesaver." She clapped her hands together and giggled. "*His* lifesaver, that is."

10

I never realized just how small a Miata was until I tried to cram a bird cage inside one. Baboo, though, didn't seem to notice. Not that I was surprised. He was pretty out of it.

I tried to keep my eyes on the road as I darted in and out of traffic, but it was hard. My interest in Preston Hohlbrook's murder was no longer about saving my agency. It was about finding the truth no matter where it led. A lot of people had been hurt by what happened. I peered over at the passenger seat and the silent animal who had retreated into himself, as much a victim in all this madness as anyone else.

I'd been wrong. Preston Hohlbrook had been a good man. I could tell that by the things that Deserey had said, sense it in the emotion she struggled to keep in check, and feel it in his love for the birds that flocked to his backyard and his beloved Baboo beside me.

I reached behind my seat for my purse. In my haste to rescue Baboo from Mitzi's clutches, I had overlooked one tiny fact. My landlord despised pets. *All pets.* No exceptions. Which meant I had to find another home for Baboo. Fast.

My hand closed around my cell phone and I pulled it onto my lap. The pet store was number five on my speed dial.

"To Know Them Is To Love Them Pet Shop. This is Sam; how can I help?"

"Shouldn't you be in school?" I asked as I came to a crawl just west of the Brentwood exit.

"Tobi? Is that you?"

"Yup. Sorry."

"It's four-fifteen. School's been out for almost two hours."

I glanced at the clock on the dashboard. Crap. So much for having JoAnna's car back by three.

"You okay, Tobi? You sound funny."

I pressed down on the accelerator as traffic finally began to open up again, anxious to get my copilot on the road to recovery. If it wasn't too late. "It's Baboo."

"Is he okay?" The concern in Sam's voice was unmistakable. An emotion I knew would be matched by his mom as well.

"No, Sam, he's not. And we're no longer just talking about a few plucked feathers, either. He's almost bald. And, other than three quick words an hour ago, he hasn't said a thing. Nada. Zip. I think he's in really bad shape."

"Let me talk to Mom, see if we can call Mrs. Hohlbrook and offer some tips."

"No, Sam."

"Why not?"

"Because I have Baboo." I looked over at the African grey as he hunched over in a corner of his travel cage. His mouth was moving, but no sound came out. He reminded me of a person in shock, unable to cope with a tragedy.

A horn blared and I looked up, my gaze coming to rest on the car in my rearview mirror.

"What do you mean, you have Baboo? Have him how? Where?"

"In my car—I mean, JoAnna's car." I hurried to explain. "I was at the Hohlbrooks' today to try and dig up . . . well, that's not important. What matters is that I was there and Baboo was in bad shape. Mitzi was droning on about how much she hated him, and I couldn't take it anymore. I offered to take him under the guise of helping get him back to normal. She, of course, was elated at the prospect of getting rid of him."

Sam released a sigh in my ear. I smiled. The kid got it.

"Anyway, I'm heading back now and it hit me. My landlord would have a cow if I brought Baboo into the house. So that leaves only one option."

"I'll give Mom a heads-up, and we'll be waiting."

It was my turn to sigh. And did I ever. Getting Baboo out of that house and into the loving care of Mary Fran was the first truly right thing to happen all day.

"You're the best. Thank your mom for me, and I'll be there soon. Just need to call JoAnna and explain why I'm late."

I flipped the phone shut and waited a second. Yeah, I know there's a button on the phone somewhere that will end a call, but I can't seem to find it. So I flip it shut instead. End result is the same, right?

JoAnna was number six on my speed dial. Though, I really should think about moving her up to number one. She's kinda like my own personal little angel.

"Are you okay, Tobi?"

"Sorta." I slid into the right-hand lane as I approached the Kingshighway exit. "Look, I'm so sorry that I've been gone longer than I said. But things got interesting and sad and—"

"It's okay, sweetie. I've got nowhere to go tonight. Take all the time you need."

I stopped at the top of the ramp and waited for the light to change. Baboo sat wordlessly in his cage. I wondered if he was listening to my conversation. "I'm almost back. I just need to stop at the pet shop for a few minutes. Then I'll be back and can fill you in on everything."

"Okay. Fair enough." JoAnna's voice, calm and cool, always made me feel as if I could get through anything.

And I could. So, too, could Baboo.

"Thanks, JoAnna. For—well, for everything you do. And for being you. I'm truly blessed." I pressed on the gas as the light changed, turned left, and headed toward the Central West End—my home in more ways than one.

"As am I, Tobi."

I flipped the phone shut and blinked against the tears that stung my eyes. My world was topsy-turvy right now in so many ways. I still hadn't gotten to a place where I was ready to share my heart with another man. Not sure that day would ever come, thanks to Nick. And the career I was supposed to be able to throw myself into? That wasn't going any better.

In the grand scheme of things, though, it didn't matter. None of it did. Sure, losing the agency would be hard. When is the death of a dream not? But there was one thing I had that made the heartache more bearable and the lifelong dream less of a be-all and end-all: Friends. True friends.

I found a parking spot half a block from the shop and did my best to back into it with no more than two corrections. I succeeded. Mostly. Grabbing my purse from the floor behind my seat, I got out of the car. Sam appeared like magic beside the passenger door, opening it and reaching for the cage before I made it around the car.

"Hey there, Baboo. How was the ride, big guy?"

For a moment, I simply stood there and watched as this teenage boy, who had more confidence and poise and heart than men twice his age, focused all of his attention on the traumatized animal. It was beautiful to see.

When I felt my eyes beginning to burn, I made myself step forward.

"Hi, Sam." I gave him a kiss on the side of his forehead. "We made it."

Sam nodded, his eyes filled with worry.

"Sam? What's wrong?"

He hoisted the cage onto his right forearm and made a beeline for his mom's shop. "He's not good, Tobi. Mom's gonna freak."

I didn't say anything. Instead, I fell into step with Sam as we headed toward the shop.

Mary Fran was waiting. She pulled the door open as we approached and plucked the cage from Sam's arms. Lovingly, she set it down on the counter and pulled her favorite stool beside it, her eyes never leaving the occupant inside. "Hi, Baboo. I'm so very sorry you lost your special friend."

I accepted the tissue Sam held out for me and dabbed at the tear that ran down my cheek. Mary Fran had a heart bigger than the entire universe. She loved with every inch of it—which explained Sam.

When I found my voice, I spoke slowly so my choked-up words could be understood. "He called Preston his daddy."

Mary Fran met my eye quickly and nodded. She looked back at the parrot. "Your daddy loved you very much, and he wants us to take good care of you."

"Good-Good care."

Rudder. I'd forgotten all about him.

I tugged at Sam's sleeve and jerked my head toward the corner. He followed me there. "Is there gonna be a problem having two of these birds in the same place? Any weird domination thing?" The question was probably stupid, but I had to ask.

"Nah. Rudder's cool. You know that."

Yeah, I did. I squeezed Sam's arm and made my way over to Rudder's perch, careful to avoid Sadie's empty cage. I simply couldn't handle not having her right now. As wonderfully loving as Mary Fran and Sam were, as supportive as JoAnna was, as loyal as Carter was, there was just something powerful about my connection with Sadie. Odd, I know, to say that about a cat. But she knew my secrets. She knew my fears. She knew my heartache. She knew *me*.

And God help the guy who took her if he didn't treat her right.

I stopped next to Rudder's cage and poked my finger inside.

"I like your blue bandana, Rudder. It's a good color on you."

"Snort-Snort!"

Sam laughed from across the room.

I didn't.

I wiggled my finger at Rudder. "Okay, wise guy. I get it. I snort a lot. And *you* stutter. But do I mock you? No, I don't."

"Snort-Snort!"

Sam *and* Mary Fran laughed. And, I swear, the hamster did too.

"You be nice, Rudder. If you can't be nice to me, then be nice to Baboo. You got it, buster?"

"Nice-Nice to Baboo."

"Thank you."

I turned away from the cage and headed back toward the counter and Mary Fran. If there was a chance for Baboo to regain his strength, this was where he would do it. I was confident of that.

"Is it really okay if he stays here?" I meant to look at Mary Fran as I asked, I really did. But my visual attention was, once again, back on Baboo, his heartache palpable.

"I wouldn't want him anywhere else." Mary Fran pulled her gaze off Baboo and fixed it on me. She slid off her stool and gave me a big hug. "He'll be okay. It's gonna take some time. He's suffered an awful loss and you know how loyal these birds can be. But I think we can turn him around."

There was something uplifting about Mary Fran's hug and I needed that desperately right now.

"It'll be okay, Tobi," she whispered in my ear.

I nodded as she stepped back and reclaimed her spot on the stool.

"I better return JoAnna's car." I tugged my backpack higher on my shoulder and pulled my keys from my jacket pocket. "How long will you be here tonight?"

"I think it will be best if I sleep in the back room tonight. Just so Baboo knows he hasn't been abandoned in an unfamiliar place." Mary Fran kept her voice quiet and calm as she spoke, every inflection of her voice carefully chosen to make Baboo feel safe.

"Then I'll bring a pizza by when I'm done at the office." I pulled the door open and looked over my shoulder. "Thanks Mary Fran, Sam. I don't know what I'd do without you guys."

"*Snort-Snort-Snort!*"

11

I'm not sure how long it took before I finally heard the tapping. A minute. Maybe two. But it's a miracle I heard it at all with the stuff rumbling around in my head.

I set my Cocoa Puffs down on the coffee table and walked quietly over to the window. At the risk of sounding awful, I simply was in no mood for Ms. Rapple and her directness. My nerves were shot.

I pulled back the curtains, grateful for the fact that I'd chosen to sit in the dark to eat. No light, no shadow. Not that Ms. Rapple didn't already know I was home. Despite two years of smelling my smells and hearing my noises, Gertrude still acted like I was an escaped convict from death row every time I came up the shared sidewalk between our buildings. I suspected Ms. Rapple got a kick out of it. Or rather, a kick out of the way I jumped out of my skin each time the damn thing barked. (The woman really needed a man, or a job, or an institution—something.)

The old-fashioned street lamp, ten feet away, cast a faint glow across the back of my mystery tapper, illuminating the person's wiry build and clown-red hair. Carter.

I pulled open the door and poked out my head.

"Your door is that one." I flashed a grin at my upstairs neighbor as I yanked my head to the right.

"I know which door is mine, Sunshine."

"Oh." I pointed at his head. "Let me guess. *Annie*?"

There was little need for a nod, but he did anyway.

"The kid they cast in the lead has jet-black hair. A challenge, sure, but not one I can't conquer. Started messing with different shades tonight and got this." He ran a finger through his hair as if touching a

Van Gogh. "Ended up a bit redder than I wanted, but I like it. It's zippy."

Note to self: Stay away from zippy.

"You want to come in?" I backed up and motioned inside, surprised at how much I hoped he'd say yes. Five minutes ago the last thing I wanted was to make conversation with another living soul. But Carter was different. He listened better than anyone I'd ever met. And when he spoke (similes and all) he always made me stop and think. And boy, could I use some of that tonight.

"I was hoping I could." He stepped past me, strode halfway into the living room, and then pointed at the darkened overhead light. "Dodging Ms. Rapple again?"

"Who? Me?"

"That's what I thought." Carter unzipped his leather coat and hung it carefully over the back of the couch. He picked up my bowl and looked inside. "Let me guess. Broccoli Soup? Salad? No, wait. It can't be. You love your greens as much as CEOs love trailer parks."

I laughed (and snorted).

He ignored me. "Really, Tobi, *Cocoa Puffs? Again?*"

I pulled my bowl out of his hands. "You're darn tootin'. Breakfast of champions. Want some?"

"I'll pass. Besides, it's ten o'clock at night, if you didn't notice." He dropped onto the nearby armchair and crossed his legs, his moccasin dangling from his big toe. "Just tell me this isn't your *dinner*, okay?"

I hated statements like that. I mean, he obviously didn't want to hear that it was indeed dinner, but did he want me to lie? Pretend I hadn't passed on the pizza I brought to Mary Fran and Sam after work?

I shoveled a spoonful of cereal into my mouth and shrugged. It would have to do. If I tried to talk around my Puffs, I ran the risk of one escaping. And I'd lost one piece of chocolate already that day. I couldn't stomach the thought of another.

"Tobi, what am I going to do with you?" We both knew it was a rhetorical question because he'd go nuts without me. Who wouldn't?

I sat down, tucked one leg under me, and replayed the day at a speed that would impress Mario Andretti.

When I was done, Carter simply nodded.

"That's it? A nod? Where's your thought-provoking reply? Where's your simile? Where's your—" I stopped, leaned my head against the back of the couch, and sighed. How could I really expect him to make sense of this mess any better than I could?

"Seems to me you've uncovered some good stuff. A possible affair between Mitzi and the contractor's cousin, a jealous neighbor with a nasty temper, and a dead husband who not only knew about his wife's inappropriate behavior but also had come to realize she wasn't up to his standards. That about sum it up?"

"Uh-huh."

His moccasin finally lost its will to hang on and dropped to the ground. He kicked the other one off and leaned all the way back in his chair. "I wonder where all that money is gonna go."

I stopped chewing and stored the unswallowed Cocoa Puffs in my left cheek like a hamster. "What?"

"The money. There were no kids, right?"

Somehow, the Puffs found their way down my throat unassisted. What did I tell you? Carter is a genius. An absolute genius.

"Oh my God, you're right! If there was any kind of a prenup, Mitzi likely would have been out on the street if Preston left her. If he'd truly found out about her and Blake, if he'd simply gotten past the pain of losing his first wife and realized the mistake he'd made with Mitzi . . . Wow. Mitzi may have gotten hosed in a prenup, but maybe not in a will."

Carter held up his hand in the same way he did when we played Red Light, Green Light that one time (don't ask—long story). "Slow down, Tobi. It's a *possibility*. Something to think about. But sometimes the truth isn't that easy. It takes a keener mind."

I ignored the keener mind comment. But, in all fairness, I'd completely overlooked the fact that Preston Hohlbrook was a very wealthy man.

"How long does it take for a will to be read? Any idea?" I asked.

"Probably depends on a lot of different circumstances. But I'd imagine pretty fast in this situation. A lot of people count on Hohlbrook Motors for their paycheck."

I considered his words, played them out in my mind. It was time to do some more snooping.

"Want to go check out The Car Crash with me on Wednesday night?" I asked.

"Now, Tobi, tell me you can find better entertainment than watching a bunch of beer-bellied men high-fiving each other after someone wrecks a car. Tell me that breaking things off with Nick hasn't made you resort to *that*."

I laughed. "No. *The Car Crash*. It's a bar over in Westport."

The words had no sooner left my mouth when Carter started coughing and smacking himself on the back. (It was really an impressive display of theatrics for a guy who works *behind* the curtain.) "Me? In a traditional singles' bar? With people who can't dance . . . and who sing even worse? That's like, like, like expecting Ms. Rapple to . . . to be *nice*."

If Rudder had been in the room, I'd have let him take it away. But since he wasn't, I snorted all on my own. Loudly.

Miraculously, Carter didn't seem to notice. Or, if he did, he'd heard it enough that he accepted it as normal. I suspect the latter.

I pushed off the couch and picked up my empty bowl. "That's okay. I think I can handle a bar on my own."

"You finally ready to meet someone, Sunshine?"

It's a good thing my mom had included a few of those melamine bowls from my childhood in her last care package—she calls it a *care package*, but it's really a way to get my crap out of her house—because I dropped my bowl.

"Good Lord, no!" I hissed. "Who are you? *Mary Fran*?"

Carter jumped to his feet and retrieved my bowl. He held it up and turned it toward the small sliver of light streaming in from the still-open curtain. *"Bugs Bunny?"*

I grabbed the bowl and headed to the kitchen, my hands still shaking at the thought of going to a bar to find a new guy. I mean, please, as if I needed *that* headache on top of everything else in my life right now. "Yeah, Bugs Bunny. Got a problem with that?"

Carter shrugged. "No. I'm just more of a Porky Pig fan, myself. Think about it. He was a trailblazer. A pioneer. A trendsetter. I mean, that pig did for stuttering what Superman did for spandex and Lycra."

I thought I'd swallowed the last of the Cocoa Puffs, but apparently I hadn't because when I started to laugh, I began choking. Really choking.

Carter was at my side in a split second. "Arms up, Tobi."

Oh God. Visions of childhood dinners flashed before my eyes. My mom was (and still is—trust me) a firm believer in the "arms up" de-choking method. Never mind we all felt like idiots at the height of our discomfort when she insisted on it. But it was the only way to stave off death by choking in her book, a book that Carter obviously owned as well.

I did as I was told and shot my arms up, wincing as he thumped the same spot on my back that Deserey had pounded repeatedly just eight hours earlier. Note to self: Find a new way to compensate for my lack of a poker face *and* refrain from eating when Carter was around.

Sure enough, it worked. Always did.

"Yet another reason why you need a little variety in your diet, Sunshine." Carter kissed my forehead, picked up his coat, and headed for the living room, me in tow.

"That had absolutely *nothing* to do with my choice in food. It had *everything* to do with your similes and analogies. Do you think you could do something about those?" It was odd, but I was genuinely disappointed to see him slip into his coat. Life was so much more fun with Carter in it. Without him, I had too much time to think and no one around to set me straight.

He stepped into his moccasins, turned, and looked me straight in the eye. "If I *did* something with those, as you say, you would lose one of the things you love most about me. My essence. My sparkle. My shine."

I didn't argue. He was right.

Carter pulled open the door. "Wednesday night, you say?"

Yay! I had a victim—I mean, an accomplice. I grinned. A big goofy grin that I could feel spread across my face from one end to the other. "Yeah, Wednesday night."

He mumbled something under his breath about checking his schedule and needing to buy earplugs to block out the singing, but I knew I had him. Carter was a sucker when it came to anything me-related.

"Oh, and Carter?"

"What is it, Sunshine?"

"It'll be okay. Really. After all, you know what they say, right?"

Carter turned, his brows furrowed, obviously clueless to what I'd been waiting to say all night.

I couldn't resist, I launched into the song "Tomorrow" from Annie.

And once I started, I broke out into full song and couldn't stop. I kept on singing despite his pleas for me to stop. I kept on singing despite the fact that lights were turning on in homes all over the block. And I kept on singing loudly despite the fact that I knew darn well my voice would rival one of Carter's Gertrude-waking sneezes.

It was official. I'd lost it. I knew better than to poke a stick in Ms. Rapple's cage. Yet I didn't care. In fact, in a strange and twisted way, I think I even welcomed it.

When he was finally gone, backing his way into his door with his hands tented in prayer to the Patron Saint of Mutes, I would have traded just about anything to have that fun back. Because when I shut the door I was alone with visions of a dead man, a growing list of motives, and the very real image of a heartsick bird named Baboo. Not a fun place to be. Trust me.

I leaned against the door and closed my eyes. The bar would be a great place to try and pump Deserey for any thoughts she might have on Preston Hohlbrook's will. Carter, when clued in, would come in handy for getting some information out of the Johnsons' housekeeper, Glenda. He could make a rock talk. It was a gift.

But that was two nights away. Plenty of time to do a little snooping at Zander Closet Company first.

I opened my eyes (not much different considering the lights were still off) and pushed away from the door. What did I know about Blake Zander?

Not much.

He was Andy's cousin. The labor side of the business. Or *was* until Gary got the call from Preston Hohlbrook demanding Blake be removed from the job site. Gary wanted him out right away, even volunteering to take on the task of completing the closet himself, despite the fact that the Showcase was days away at the time. Andy had wanted Blake to have a chance to defend himself, but Gary had shot that down.

Did they verbally reprimand him after that call? Did they dock his pay? Did they fire him?

I didn't have a clue. The subject hadn't come up since the phone call. And I hadn't thought to ask. Until now.

Making a mental note to pay a little visit to my newest (and only) client, I picked up the phone and punched in my office line. Friday had been so crazy, with the television interview and JoAnna leaving early for her trip, that I had only listened to voice messages that had been tagged as urgent—a prearranged indicator JoAnna and I had worked out to ensure I was on top of things at all times.

I'd intended, of course, to listen to the rest over the weekend, but hadn't. For obvious reasons, like a little thing called *murder*. And then today I'd gotten a little sidetracked by a floral arrangement, a gift from a guy who made me feel kind of funny inside, a snoop-fest at the scene of the crime, an animal rescue by way of a Miata, a horribly delayed car return, a pizza delivery, and an honest-to-goodness choke-a-thon (punishment, no doubt, for faking the first one).

I mean, really, who had the time to listen to voice messages with all that going on?

The first message was from my mother. She left it Friday morning at ten. As soon as I heard the words *Sunday dinner* and *Uncle Fred*, I cringed and skipped ahead.

The next message came in about an hour later. It was from Gary. He'd just finished his interview with Corrine Martin from Channel 2 and wanted to share every last detail. I could picture him puffing up his chest and flexing his arms as he spoke, his ego bursting through every word.

The third message was my mother again. Something about chicken parmesan (she was pulling out the big guns by mentioning my favorite dinner). I pressed skip again but not before my stomach gurgled.

The fourth message was a voice I was unfamiliar with.

"Ms. Tobias? My name is Charlotte West. I work with Preston Hohlbrook at Hohlbrook Motors." I pulled the phone closer against my ear as the woman continued. "Mr. Hohlbrook would like to set up an appointment to talk with you one day next week. My number is 555-CARS. That's 555-CARS. We look forward to hearing from you."

The phone slipped inside my grasp, a casualty of my sweaty palms no doubt.

The woman continued. "By the way, we're all very impressed by your creativeness around here."

I didn't hear the next eleven messages. Instead, I listened to Charlotte West's again and again. The words never changed. The tone never changed. I learned nothing new no matter how many times I pressed replay. But, for whatever reason, I kept on doing it anyway.

When my finger got tired of pressing repeat, I put the phone down and glanced at the clock. It was eleven-thirty. The morning loomed ahead of me with places to go and questions to ask. I needed sleep. Desperately.

Still, I grabbed the phone and pressed the first number on my speed dial. It was never too late to call my Grandpa Stu.

12

I'd been up for hours. Not a hard thing to say when you never went to sleep in the first place. But my late-night talk with Grandpa Stu left me thinking. And plotting. And staring at the ceiling above my bed.

I suspect he didn't sleep either. You see, my grandfather hated being left out of things. It drove him nuts, batty, cuckoo. And the thought of me knee-deep in a Hardy Boys novel without him had to be absolute torture for a man who owned every mystery party game out there. He'd gotten so proficient at naming the killer within the first three pages of the script that his cohorts from the Sexy Seniors Single Group had sworn off his parties. Permanently.

Fortunately for me and *unfortunately* for him, Grandpa Stu lived in Kansas City, a four-hour drive away. Doable? Sure, under normal circumstances. But as far as I knew, he hadn't gotten his driver's license back after the last speeding ticket.

I leaned closer to the mirror and applied a little concealer under my eyes to offset the effects of my murder-induced insomnia. Sometime during the night I'd left a voice mail for JoAnna telling her I'd be out of the office most of the day. Gathering data.

On Blake Zander.

How I was going to get the answers I needed without tipping my hand to Andy was beyond me. He'd been fairly adamant I not get involved with Preston's death, but what he didn't know wouldn't hurt him, right? Besides, when you think about it, why should he care? As long as I met my campaign obligations, what difference should it make if I were to sneak around in the hopes of catching a killer?

I pulled the tan cinch-waist jacket off the hanger and slipped it on over my dusty rose cami and jeans. My hair always looked good in two French braids, and today was no exception. With any luck, if

Blake wasn't into answering routine questions I could use my feminine charms on him.

I bypassed the kitchen on my way to the front closet. I was a little Cocoa-Puffed-out at the moment, and my stomach was a little too squirrely for anything else. Maybe I'd try to grab a bagel or something at St. Louis Bread Company later. Or maybe I'd just make this a one-meal day. Certainly wouldn't be a first.

As I pulled my ankle boots from the closet, I peeked out the window. Ms. Rapple was already heading inside after the first of Gertrude's two morning pees, so I was safe. Leaving the house an hour before normal had its definite advantages.

I grabbed my backpack and a bus schedule and yanked open the door. Glancing to the left to ensure a clean getaway, I stepped onto the front stoop, the heel of my boot pushing down on something crinkly. An envelope with pastel lettering had been left on my door mat, a rock placed on top to keep it from blowing away. I bent down to grab it and recognized the handwriting in all its flowery glory. Carter.

I ripped open the envelope and pulled out a piece of lavender note paper.

> *Good morning, Sunshine!*
> *I know you've got big plans today. Plans that will be a lot tougher to implement while working around a bus schedule. So take my car for the day. I don't need it until tonight. If you're not back when I need to leave, I'll walk. It's good for me.*
> *Go get 'em, Tobi. But be careful!*
> *Carter*
> *P.S. Let me do your hair tomorrow night before we go to that nightclub. It's been a while since you've let me.*

I blinked against the sudden mistiness that clouded my vision. How I got so lucky to have these people in my life was impossible to comprehend. But I knew one thing for sure: When this whole mess was cleaned up, I was going to throw a party—a big party—to thank them. And yeah, I'd even invite Ms. Rapple. As much of an irritant as she was, she'd still kind of grown on me. Like a bunion.

The key was at the bottom of the envelope. The car was even easier to find. I walked down the sidewalk and crossed the street, the powder-blue paint job glistening in the early morning sun. It was really a pretty color—for a little boy's nursery. Or a sweater. But a car?

I unlocked the driver's side door and tossed my purse across the seat. Powder blue or not, it was transportation that didn't involve incessant stops and body odor. Yet it was big enough to hold a bird cage if need be (not that I expected to be rescuing anymore birds today). Most importantly, it would get me where I needed to go.

Zander Closet Company was located on Brentwood Boulevard, just down from the Galleria Mall. How Andy and Gary could afford a lease in that neighborhood was a mystery all its own. How I was going to keep from pulling into the mall parking lot was an even bigger one.

Willpower, Tobi. Willpower...

I turned the key in the ignition and pulled away from the curb, the homes of my neighbors and friends disappearing into my rearview mirror. Carter's car was old. Really old. Crank windows, manual door locks, no power steering, and no cassette deck or CD player. It did, however, have a fairly decent radio if you could get the knobs to move.

When I was stopped at a traffic light on Brentwood Boulevard, about three blocks from the office building that housed Zander Closet Company, "Dancing in the Dark" came on. Bruce.

I, of course, started singing. And dancing. As usual, I was completely oblivious to my surroundings, with the exception of the circular red light in front of me. If I missed its change to green, though, I was fairly certain the brick-foot behind me would let me know.

While I waited, I grabbed a pen from the center console and sang into the tip with gusto, bopping my shoulders and my head to the beat. Yet all dancing and singing ceased the moment I looked to my left.

Andy Zander (sitting in a very nice black Avalon) stared back at me from the turning lane, pure enjoyment covering every square inch of his face. I sat there, stunned. The idiot behind me honked.

I would probably still be sitting there if it weren't for Andy's sweet smile and encouraging thumbs-up. The guy had class. He made me think, albeit briefly, that what I'd been doing was completely normal.

A burst of rare flirtatious confidence made me wink across at Andy just before I engaged the gas pedal and continued on my way.

I drove four blocks, turned left, and pulled into a parking spot in front of the three-story brick building just as the song came to an end. I was relieved to realize that wherever Andy was headed, work was not it. It was easy to be playful when you were separated by metal and glass, quite another to be facing each other on an elevator and having to explain what the heck you were doing while sitting at a traffic light in a borrowed 1975 powder-blue Ford Granada.

The building itself was fairly nondescript. It was obviously home to a number of tenants as the wooden sign outside the door held at least a dozen names. Zander Closet Company was located on the third floor in Suite A. (Probably the only time they were listed first.)

"Hey good looking, finally came to your senses, huh?"

I spun around.

Gary.

I hoped my cringe wasn't too obvious. After all, he'd be signing some of my paychecks. But could he be any more forward? And what was with the hairy chest and gold chain?

"Hi, Gary." I mustered a smile and held out my hand. He kissed it.

"To what do we owe this honor? And I hope you realize how sexy you look right now with that jacket and your hair like that. *Grrrr.*"

I was so glad I'd passed on the Cocoa Puffs. I was fairly certain they'd be on his shoes by now if I hadn't. I shivered.

"You cold?"

"No. I'm okay. I just do that sometimes. Bad habit or something." I tugged my backpack higher on my shoulder and shifted foot to foot. "I was hoping to check out your office. Get a better feel for what the clients see." Point for me. I was getting really good at fibbing.

Gary shrugged and reached around me for the door, his arm brushing against my back. "Sounds good to me. Come on in. We're on the third floor." His eyes moved slowly down my body as I crossed in front of him. "It's a really nice, quiet elevator ride. Very private."

My palms moistened, and I wiped them on my jeans. He was harmless, right? Just a playboy with a really huge ego. And it's not like I had the kind of body guys like Gary went after. So there was nothing to worry about.

I pointed to the door at the end of the hall. "I'll meet you up there. I didn't have a chance to exercise this morning, so I'll take the steps." I didn't wait for a reply. I simply walked—okay, so it was closer to a run—to the stairwell and took them two at a time. I knew I was sufficiently unnerved when I found myself wanting to go back to the embarrassment I'd felt when I spied Andy watching me at the traffic light. Gary made me want to scream for help.

When I reached the top level, I stopped. From what I'd seen and heard that first day, there was some serious bad blood between Gary and his cousin. If I played my cards right, I could use that rift to my advantage. I took a deep, cleansing breath and pulled the stairwell door open. Gary was waiting on the other side. I gulped out a smile. He winked. I shivered again.

"C'mon darlin'." He draped an arm across my shoulders and led me down the hall. I, of course, wanted to elbow him in the gut, but was afraid I'd ruin my chances of getting the dirt I needed if I did, so I restrained myself.

When we reached Suite A, he pulled a key from his pants pocket and inserted it into the lock. "Andy's got an appointment with a buyer, so we've got the place all to ourselves." He stood in the doorway and motioned me inside, his body pressing against mine briefly as I moved past him. "Wanna see my office? It's real quiet."

I stepped to the right and dropped into a chair in the tiny reception area. "That's okay. I don't want to infringe on your space."

"You can infringe on my space anytime you want, Tobi."

I set my purse on the ground and steadied the shake in my hands. "Um, so when does your secretary come in?"

Gary ran a hand through his hair and moistened his lips with his tongue. "Next week. She's on a cruise with her husband and kids."

I dug my palm into my right thigh in an effort to stop the shake that had traveled from my hand to my leg. It was guys like this that needed to be corralled in a pen like pigs and slaughtered once a year . . .

Focus, Tobi.

"Look, I just need a few minutes of your time. It's about Blake."

Gary's eyes widened in surprise then narrowed to near-slits as he locked his gaze on mine. He leaned against the wall and crossed his arms against his chest. "So you've got the hots for Blake?"

I feigned a laugh. "Of course not. I've never even met him. I'm just trying to learn as much about your company and your employees as I can so I can better serve you in this campaign."

He seemed to accept my answer, if the wink he shot me was any indication. "That's better. I can think of *lots* of ways you can serve me quite nicely."

It's tough to keep one's eyes from rolling when they are hell-bent on doing so, but I tried anyway. It didn't work. Gary Zander was a piece o' work. I chose to ignore his latest innuendo.

"When you were in my office that first day, you got a call from Preston Hohlbrook. He wanted Blake off the project because of what he perceived to be inappropriate ogling of his wife, Mitzi." I leaned forward in my seat, intrigued by the way Gary's eyes clouded over. "You took the labor on yourself in order to get the job done and accommodate Mr. Hohlbrook's wishes, isn't that right?"

He pushed off the wall and started sifting through a pile of papers on the secretary's desk. His search seemed aimless, but what did I know? "You bet I did. Blake certainly wasn't up to the task."

I chewed the inside of my cheek and considered his words. "So what happened to Blake? Did you guys fire him?"

Gary laughed. Not a happy-go-lucky laugh but, rather, a sarcastic, edgy one. "Oh, I wanted to. I've hated that guy since we were teenagers and he stole my . . ." His words trailed off momentarily, his gaze focused someplace far away. After a few silent, tense-filled moments, he shook his head and continued. "Bringing him into this company was a mistake. But it wasn't my idea. That moment of genius belongs to my brother. He's a sucker for family loyalty and all that happy feel-good crap. A real wimp."

I was surprised at the flash of irritation I felt at Gary's use of the word *wimp* in reference to his brother. Andy Zander was more of a man than Gary could ever hope to be. But instead of lashing out in defense of a man I shouldn't be thinking of, I focused on the task at hand: Blake.

"So where is he?"

"Who?"

"Blake. I'm assuming, based on what you said, that Blake is still employed here? Am I right?"

"Unfortunately. Andy is too damn soft. And more than a little gullible, if you ask me."

Since Gary didn't seem to want a response, I took a moment to absorb my surroundings. To the left of the sitting area was a hallway with a series of doors. From where I sat, I could tell that at least one of the doors didn't lead to an office as one might expect. Instead, it led to a closet decked out in a Zander system. Smart move on Andy's part. Any time you could provide customers with an up-close-and-personal look at your work was invaluable. I made a mental note to bring Sam in for some pictures.

"Does he have an office here?" I asked as I trained my focus back on Gary.

"Blake?" He answered my nod with a shake of his own head. "Nah. He works from home. We dispatch him as needed."

"Where's home?"

Gary pulled open the secretary's top drawer and helped himself to a stick of gum. "I'm in Ladue. Blake is out in St. Charles County. The Weldon Spring area." He unwrapped the foil and crammed the stick into his mouth. "And to think, back when my aunt owned the place, I actually liked going out to Duggan Road."

"Duggan Road?"

"Where Blake lives now."

13

Duggan Road was—*hmm*, how shall I say this?—interesting. The houses were old and rundown, yards littered with automobiles that hadn't seen pavement in decades. Any individuality in exterior decorating rested solely on the color of the appliances that had trick-led onto the front porch (eggplant purple being my favorite).

I, of course, spent so much time gawking at "country living" I drove right past Blake Zander's home. Truth be told, I simply hadn't seen it. Which, in and of itself, wasn't a big deal until I saw the drive-way I needed to use for my turn-around.

Perhaps it was the faded sign that hung from the barbed wire fence—the one that threatened to shoot trespassers. Or maybe it was the matched set of Doberman pinschers with spiked collars that ran to-ward me (and my powder-blue car) with teeth the size of cinderblocks.

My heart pounded as I shifted the car into reverse and then headed back in the direction from which I'd just come. This time, I was care-ful to note each and every mailbox I passed until I found one marked *Zander*.

Blake's home was, in a word, charming. Canopied by golden-leaved ash trees, it was the epitome of the white-picket-fence dream every little girl harbored inside. The cornflower-blue shutters and window boxes were freshly painted, their contrast against the white clapboard siding both calming and alluring. A high-backed swing hung from the rafters of the front porch with an Adirondack chair nearby. Star-gazing nights and lemonade-sipping days hung in the air with an undeniable presence.

And there wasn't a sign threatening bodily harm *anywhere.*

I pulled into the driveway, parked, and reached for my backpack on the passenger seat. It always struck me as odd when a person or place didn't match the image I'd created in my mind. Like the world had slipped off its axis somehow.

The midmorning sun blinded me momentarily as I stepped out of the car and prevented me from seeing the identity of the person whistling an Eagles tune to my left. I raised my hand to block the light and quickly looked around.

A tall man, clad in jeans and a white T-shirt, set his tools down on a sawhorse-propped board and waved at me. I waved back.

"What can I do for you this fine morning?" He walked toward my spot on the driveway, a wide grin revealing an expanse of perfectly straight, white teeth. "I'm Blake Zander."

The world hadn't just slipped off its axis. It had tumbled.

"I'm Tobi Tobias."

"Hey I know you! You're the gal who came up with that dynamite slogan for our company." He shook my hand, a hint of admiration rippling across his face. "Man, I wish I could be that clever with words. I try. I really do. But they never come out the way they should."

Blake pointed up to the house. "Thankfully, God blessed me with a wife who appreciates the *thought* behind my notes. Good thing or she'd have left me long ago."

I suppose I should have assumed there was a wife when I saw the house, but I hadn't. Maybe that's because Blake looked like the kind of guy who'd take pride in his home and his work, with or without a wife.

I shifted my stance and repositioned my hand on my forehead. The glare was still bad, but from this angle I could see a little of what Blake had been working on when I drove up.

Dollhouses. Breathtakingly detailed dollhouses.

"You built those?" By the time I heard the surprise in my voice, it was too late to call it back. But he didn't seem to notice.

"Yes, ma'am. This new design is a tough one. C'mon, take a peek."

My boots crunched along the gravel driveway as I followed him toward the tiny workshop (also white with cornflower-blue trim). When we reached his workbench, I instinctively bent over and peered into the miniature home he'd been tinkering with.

"See that side of the house?" He pointed at the half he'd yet to finish. "It's gonna have those half-rounded rooms. You know, like they have in those country inns sometimes."

"Turrets," I whispered, my eyes riveted on the exquisite detail of the portion he *had* completed.

"See? You know words. Me? I just know how to build 'em." He gestured toward the wood piece atop the sawhorse. "Getting that rounded quality is tricky. But I'm not gonna give up."

I looked to my left and my right, my attention coming to rest on a dollhouse with a cock-eyed front porch and uneven windows. I considered asking if he was making a replica of the Doberman pinschers' house, but thought better of it. "What happened to that one?" I asked, leaning in for a closer look.

He laughed. "I'm still trying to figure that out, myself."

"Well, everyone has to start somewhere, right?" I moved on to the dollhouse on its right, the two-story Victorian with gingerbread trim and tall windows nothing short of breathtaking. "I wanted a dollhouse just like that when I was a little girl."

Blake nodded his interest. "You didn't get one?"

"No. My sister wanted our dolls to live in a tent—to be one with the earth and buck normalcy."

"Let me guess, a hippie?"

I smiled. "Yeah. So, anyway, my parents made us compromise."

Blake's eyes sparkled as they met mine, his amusement poorly disguised behind twitching lips. "Let me guess—a plain Jane one-story ranch?"

"Nope. We got a camper. That way *my* dolls could feel like they had a house, and *my sister's* dolls could commune with nature."

His laugh was deep, hearty, and extremely contagious.

When we finally stopped, I thanked him.

"What are you thanking me for?"

"For making me laugh at a memory I've always hated."

He shoved his hands into his pockets and leaned against a workshop wall. "I don't know a lot of fancy words, and I certainly can't come up with clever slogans and stuff like you can, but yeah, I guess I can make people laugh. And I build stuff."

"Sounds to me like you've got it pretty good." I heard the awe in my voice as I straightened up and looked—really looked—at Blake Zander.

Now I'm not the best visual judge when it comes to a person's weight or even, sometimes, their height. But Blake was easy. Leaving a two-year margin of error on either side, I guesstimated him to be about twenty-eight, like me. He was tall and lean like Andy, his eyes a softer green. The skin around his mouth creased when he smiled, something I suspected he did often.

It was a good thing I'd not met him when he was single. I'd have pegged him as a nice, honest, sweet guy. And I'd have been wrong—just like I was with Nick. What an idiot I was.

He seemed to sense the shift in my mood. "So what brings you out here?"

"I'm getting ready to put together a commercial for Zander Closet Company and thought it might be helpful to talk to the man who installs the systems. You know, get a better feel for what you do, how you fit into the company, that kind of thing." If God did occasional liar-surveillance, as my mother always claimed, I was in big trouble.

"Not sure how much help I can be. I've been temporarily removed from closet installations, thanks to my cousin and his overactive imagination."

Hmmm. I wondered how he justified the same overactive imagination in both Preston Hohlbrook *and* the man's housekeeper? Were they all wrong in his eyes too? Typical.

I played dumb. "Overactive imagination?"

"Wait. My bad. What's that word when someone takes on the quality of someone else?" His eyes narrowed as he looked up at the sky, his question so soft that I wasn't sure if he was even asking me.

"Transference?"

He snapped his fingers and pointed at me. "Yeah. Transference. Gosh you're good with that stuff. I bet you were real smart in school, huh?"

I shrugged an answer while my mind worked feverishly to catch up with what he was saying.

"Let's just say that my getting sidelined from closet-building duty had a lot more to do with that transference stuff than an overactive imagination."

Okay, so now I was really confused. Understandable when you considered the amount of sleep I'd gotten the night before.

He motioned me toward the house. "Why don't we go inside and sit down. You can meet Peggy. She's the best."

The wife . . .

The poor, unsuspecting wife . . .

I had a sudden urge to scratch Blake's eyes out but I resisted. For the moment. Instead, I followed him across the top edge of the driveway and up the three steps to the front porch.

"Peg? We've got some company, sweetheart." He held his hands up, binocular style, to the outer door and peered inside. "It's Tobi Tobias. The slogan gal."

The slogan gal. I liked that. Had a nice ring.

A petite strawberry-blonde came to the door, a dishtowel in hand. She was tiny, maybe five-foot-one and had a slender build. She opened the door and kissed Blake on the mouth. A sweet, tender kiss that made me look away. I wanted that so badly. But not with a guy like Nick. Or a guy like Blake, for that matter.

Peggy stepped back, her ocean-blue eyes lingering on her husband for a brief moment before turning to me. "Hi, Tobi. It's nice to meet you. We're sure impressed by what you've done for Zander so far."

I liked her instantly. There was a sweet, nurturing goodness about this woman that was as tangible as the flowered shirt she wore. It made my pity for her so much deeper.

"Thanks. They've been good to me too." I walked through the open doorway and stood in the small living room, the aura created on the outside of the home duplicated tenfold on the inside. Photographs filled nearly every square inch of wall space. "Do you mind if I look? I love pictures."

Peggy grinned. "Of course not. It's why I put them up. I love them too."

I crossed the room and looked at the first of three collage frames. This one held pictures of a little boy with a face-splitting smile in every shot. I recognized the shape of the face, the set of the eyes. It was Blake.

"See that one right there?" Blake pointed to a photograph in a rectangular-shaped hole. "That's me and Andy. I was probably five. He was nine. He came and stayed with my mom and me for a few days. They only lived about ten miles up the road, but having him under the roof was special. We caught an awful lot of frogs in the creek that week."

"Are you two still close?" I asked.

"As close as brothers. Actually, even closer. He comes out here on Saturdays sometimes. When it's Gary's turn to man the office. He's not real good with his hands like I am, but he wants to learn so he keeps trying. Remember the lopsided dollhouse? That was Andy's attempt at building one. He put himself on painting duty after that one."

My heart fluttered, and I forced my gaze onto another picture. Somehow it felt like I was violating Andy's privacy by seeing pictures of his childhood without him knowing.

The second frame held pictures of a young girl. Peggy, I assumed. The strawberry-blond hair grew in sometime after her birth, replacing the original dark shade. By the time she was four, the light color cascaded down her back in ringlets. I looked from one picture to the next, each shot depicting a happy and self-assured young girl.

And then I saw it.

An oval slot near the top of the collage contained your typical frou-frou backdrop native to all prom pictures. Peggy wore a satiny blue dress with capped sleeves and a cinch waist. Her hair was styled in a bun with strawberry tendrils making a choreographed escape from the left side. But it wasn't Peggy that made my skin clammy. It was her date. The tousled-hair brunette with the killer smile.

"Is that Gary?" I heard myself ask.

Peggy moved in beside me and nodded. "Uh-huh. We dated in high school. That's the picture from our junior prom."

"The last prom she ever went to with my cousin." Blake's voice boomed across the room from the spot he had taken up on the couch.

"Oh?" I asked, curiosity coursing through my body at such a rate I thought I would explode if someone didn't explain. Soon.

"That's right. It was that very night—at a party in this house— that Peggy and I met. And we've been inseparable ever since."

Talk about being bowled over. I felt as if I'd been hit by a two-ton ball. But any speechlessness was quickly replaced by questions. Lots of them. "How'd he take that?"

Peggy shook her head and cast her eyes down toward the ground. "Hard. And I felt just awful. I never wanted to hurt him. But I truly believe that Blake was—is—my one and only. I tried to break it to Gary gently. Tried to explain that it wasn't him. But he never forgave me for that."

Blake strode over to where Peggy stood, and wrapped his arms around her. "It's not *you* he can't forgive. You know that. It's me."

I tried to process what was being said, the possible implications that were running through my head. But when I tried to speak, nothing came out.

"Gary hasn't spoken to me since that night. Drove my mamma nuts. But no matter how many times I tried to explain, or how many times my mamma or his mamma would try to help him understand, it didn't matter. He saw my relationship with Peggy as a betrayal. And he's been out for revenge ever since."

Revenge. It was a word I understood all too well. I'd dreamt of ways to exact revenge on Nick for breaking my heart. Relieving him of his manhood was my personal favorite. But I also knew I'd never follow through on any of the plans I concocted. It just wasn't in me. Besides, if he was destined to be a cheat, it was better to know it sooner rather than later. At least that's what I kept trying to tell myself.

So I understood Gary. A little.

"What kind of revenge?" I closed my eyes and willed myself to absorb the present conversation instead of traveling down a littered road of painful memories.

"You name it, he's tried it. He let the air out of my tires every night for the next month. My mamma sat on the porch one night and saw him doing it. But he denied it anyway. Then, he tried to convince me Peggy would find someone else when she went away to college, but I didn't take the bait. I knew my Peggy." He lingered, his lips on his wife's forehead for a brief moment, before he continued. "He tried to keep me out of the company. Even succeeded in the beginning by finding and hiring a carpenter before Andy knew what was going on. Gave the guy an iron-clad contract that didn't benefit the company. Fortunately, the guy's wife got a new job in Florida, and he had to quit."

Peggy picked up the story. "Andy called Blake right away. Wanted him in the company, installing the systems like he'd intended him to do from the start. Gary went nuts. Only his mother stepped in and demanded Gary stop acting so childish. So that's when Blake started."

"Gary was fit to be tied. I'd see him at the office, for meetings, and he'd act like I wasn't even there. Which, to be honest, is fine by me. I think it's sad, sure. But it's been eleven years. Eleven years! Isn't it time he got himself a life?"

God, how I hoped I wasn't still bitter and alone eleven years from now. I balled my hands into fists and nodded. I needed to remember this conversation, needed to avoid repeating the same mistakes in my own life. Nick wasn't worth that.

"He's been hell-bent on smearing me. In front of family. In front of my best friend. In front of my wife. And he finally found a way to do it."

Peggy reached up, cupped Blake's chin in her hand, and lowered his face until their eyes met. "No. He didn't."

I was confused. Did Peggy know about Mitzi? How could she be so willing to forgive him?

Blake stared at his wife for several long moments, moments that blanketed the room in a peaceful silence. Odd when we were dancing around an ugly little fact like infidelity.

"That's right. He didn't." Blake's voice was quiet yet sure when he finally spoke, his words filled with a passion I couldn't ignore. "Lord knows he tried. But Peggy knows I only have eyes for one woman and it's her. Even if by some cruel twist of fate Peggy wasn't in my life, Mrs. Hohlbrook would be the last woman I'd ever look at. Too showy. Too fake. I like real. Genuine. Like my Peggy."

I didn't know what to say. Didn't know what to think. So I stood there, doing nothing. When I finally found my brains, I asked a question that was screaming inside my head. "Did you tell Andy about this?"

Blake shook his head. "No. Can't do that. They're brothers. I can't mess with that relationship. It'd be the final straw between those two, and it would break my aunt's heart."

As I stood there looking at Blake, I knew I had a lot to figure out. Like Preston Hohlbrook's irate phone call and Deserey's unbridled hatred for the Zander employee. But whatever the truth was, I was confident it didn't point in this direction.

Maybe I was being naïve. But I didn't think so. I actually felt as if I was seeing clearly for the first time in days.

What had started out as a simple visit for confirmation purposes (and, yeah, a little snooping too), had turned into an eye-opening experience in more ways than one. I thanked Blake and Peggy and headed out to the car, my mind replaying the visit in slow motion, pointing out every single instance where I'd let a stereotype or gossip blind me to true goodness.

As I backed down the driveway, I took one final look at 95 Duggan Road. I wanted what Blake and Peggy had. I wanted that unwavering trust. I wanted that unshakeable love that blanketed a home in sweet memories and bright tomorrows. But it was clear I had a lot to learn before that day came.

14

They say that an apple doesn't fall far from its tree. And, in most cases, it's probably a fairly accurate statement.

Take my sister for example. Although she's taken her hippie-ness to extremes (in addition to the odd choice in footwear I already mentioned, she's taken up residence in an actual hippie commune) Danielle has acquired most of her bohemian garb from an old trunk in our family's attic. *My mother's* trunk.

My brother, Caleb, is a professional surfer. He's been fascinated with ocean waves since he got smacked in the face with one at the tender age of two. My mom, however, blames his career choice on *her* brother Frank who, she claims, was born with a skateboard under one arm and a pair of roller skates under the other.

Now, let's imagine what would happen to that tree and its apples if a group of first-grade boys paid a visit during apple picking season. They'd pick some. They'd bite some. And, yeah, they'd kick some into the next grove—usually the ones that didn't taste quite right.

That's what happened to me.

The closest commonality I can find between my love for advertising and anyone in my family is Uncle Frank's obsession with Super Bowl commercials and my dad's never-ending vocabulary. And while the once-a-year ads were amusing, I was more fascinated with my father's love for words. In fact, I kept a journal that I used solely for recording whatever unusual gems he'd utter on a given day. My favorite? *Discombobulated.* Don't ask me why, but that word always made me giggle. I could never say it right, and I couldn't have imagined using it to describe myself. Oh, how I miss the naïveté of youth.

I paused at the end of Duggan Road and tried to focus on the things I still needed to do. Like check on Baboo, touch base with JoAnna, and pay a visit to Charlotte West at Hohlbrook Motors. But no matter how hard I tried to wrap my mind around any one of those tasks, my thoughts were completely . . . discombobulated.

I eyed the dashboard clock. Eleven-thirty. No wonder my stomach was flipping and flopping.

The fact that it was almost lunchtime put an immediate hold on all three of my plans. I couldn't call Mary Fran now because she was hustling around the pet shop feeding the animals and placating Rudder while she cut his kiwi. I couldn't call JoAnna because she went out to lunch on Tuesdays with her best friend. And I couldn't walk in on the late Preston Hohlbrook's secretary when she was nibbling bites of a salad over her keyboard.

A check in my rear view mirror showed no one behind me, so I sat at the stop sign a few moments and looked around. This part of St. Charles was still fairly quiet. Sure, the homes were going in fast and furiously, but Weldon Spring officials were playing hardball with many of the builders—insisting on things like trees and green space (a novelty in other areas of the county). I flipped open the glove box and pulled out a box of granola bars that Carter kept there for emergencies. And if I was hungry and desperate enough to eat a granola bar, you knew it was an emergency.

A Green Day tune came on and I began humming as I looked at a series of billboards that ran along the west side of Highway 94 South. The one for New Town caught my eye.

The picture showed one of the development's beach cottages in one corner, a beautiful brick row house in another. In the middle were the words *A Home Not Like Any Other.*

Really? That's all John and Mike could come up with? I could do so much better than that. I'd read everything I could get my hands on about New Town, and giving them one simple slogan was highway robbery in my book. An innovative community needed an innovative slogan—a *series* of innovative slogans. Each one building on the one before it, all coming together to create a sense of heaven on earth.

But New Town wasn't my client. It was Beckler and Stanley's. For now, anyway . . .

My mind made up, I flipped my right blinker and pulled onto the northbound lane of 94. Curiosity had gotten the best of me and my competitive nature. I mean, just because my slogan for Zander had kind of come true didn't mean I'd never hear from Craig Miticker, right?

As I continued north, my mind started doing what it always did when I got in that strange little world I referred to as Slogan Land. The few people I'd told about Slogan Land over the years looked at me like I was nuts. But I didn't care. It was my happy place, and we all need one of those.

When I finally reached my destination, I slowed to a crawl as I tried to absorb the shift in my surroundings. With just a simple left turn, it was as if the St. Charles I'd been driving through for the past fifteen minutes had simply disappeared off the face of the earth, replaced by a world—*a retreat*—of its own. In the first section, gorgeous brownstones lined a street-bordered canal. In the next section, beach cottages along a sandy-beached lake made me feel as if I'd somehow landed in the middle of Cape Cod. On and on it went, with each new area of the community making me feel as if I was in a different part of the country or the world.

I wiped the corners of my mouth with the granola wrapper and pulled into a parking spot that bordered a large grassy area with a stage-like platform. Grabbing my backpack, I stepped out of the car and stopped, my mouth dropping open once again. A few yards from where I stood was a brand-new mom-and-pop market, a town hall–looking building, a hot-dog stand, coffee shop, book store, and a lake that invited an ocean-like breeze in the middle of Missouri.

The buildings were cool, the set-up creative as all get out. But what stuck in my mind most were the people walking around. Sure, I saw people walking to and from work down in the Central West End every day. I saw people carrying their heavy baskets home from the Laundromat at night, and I saw them walking their dogs down to Fletcher's Newsstand in the mornings. It was that connected-neighborhood feel that kept me living close to the city even though my money would go further out in the suburbs.

I'd seen enough burb-living during visits to my parents' home about twenty miles west of here. The houses were big, the yards tiny. My dad joked that their next-door neighbor should be paying him for yard maintenance since every time he cut the grass he invariably got some of the neighbor's too. But despite how close the houses were, my parents could go months without seeing another living soul in their cul-de-sac. Sad, but true.

New Town was different. People were out and about, walking, biking, running, meandering. They didn't seem to be going anywhere in particular. And they actually stopped and chatted with one another.

As I stood there and continued to gawk, one coherent thought kept running through my mind: *I can do a much better job than Beckler and Stanley.* At least the Beckler half, anyway. It still drove me nuts thinking Mike's paycheck would be affected by any move I made to win over New Town, but Andy was right. This was business.

I reached into my backpack and fished out the little blue notebook I carried with me at all times. I felt around for a pen, then started jotting down impressions—some sentences, some single words. Everything and anything that came to mind while standing there, absorbing life in this master community.

I knew I still had to figure out who killed Preston Hohlbrook— and I would. The list of suspects and motives was growing on an almost hour-by-hour basis, with each addition proving more bizarre than the one before it.

Yeah, the primary reason for catching the killer had shifted from saving my company to finding justice for a man who couldn't find it for himself. But I'd be lying if I didn't also acknowledge the fact that fingering the bad guy would (hopefully) erase away any perceived foreshadowing in my Zander slogan *and* renew any interest Craig Miticker had expressed in working with Tobias Ad Agency.

Besides, I owed John Beckler a gift, didn't I?

15

Guilt, of course, won out over business savvy. Which meant I called Mike when I was leaving New Town and asked if we could meet for a quick lunch at McDonalds. (The stale granola bar had failed miserably in its assigned task of placating my stomach.) I pulled into the parking spot next to Mike's shiny, silver sports coupe and peered into the front seat. Empty.

I'll admit, I was oddly relieved to see he'd opted to wait for me *inside* the restaurant. How much of that relief was due to the shake in my hand, and how much was due to the fact that I hated to hurt people I cared about, I didn't know. Most likely, it was a mixture of both.

But Andy was right. This was business. And competition was part of business.

I pushed my driver-side door open and stepped onto the pavement, pulling my backpack with me.

After locking the car, I cut across the line of cars in the drive-thru lane and spotted Mike's stocky frame and salt-and-pepper hair through the glass door. He waved and held the door open. The aroma of hamburgers pulled me through the opening with an invisible leash and the promise of calories.

"Hey, Tobi. I'm glad you called."

"I am too. It's been too long." I returned his hug and then followed him into the line at the cash register. I didn't need to look at the menu. I'd been craving Big Macs since I was a year old (which is when, I believe, my penchant for slogans kicked in for the first time). I placed my order, paid, and nearly ripped the tray from the cashier's hands. (Okay, so I was a little hungry—sue me.)

I found a table near the sunniest window in the place and motioned Mike over with his tray.

"Still eating Big Macs, huh?" He thumped his tray onto the table and dropped into a swivel-back chair.

"Uh-huh." I bit into the subject of one of the all-time catchiest slogans ever. "Can you still say it? Without missing any of the ingredients?"

He grinned. "Of course. Which isn't too bad for an old guy, if I must say so myself."

"Old?" I repeated. "Since when do you call yourself old?"

"I've been feeling old lately. Washed up."

I stared at my first and only on-the-job mentor. And that's when I noticed the shadows under his hazel eyes, the way his mouth seemed void of its usual trademark smile, and the absence of a familiar bulge inside his lower lip.

"Something wrong? Is Ginny okay?"

He nodded as he played with a French fry in front of him. "Ginny's fine. Work's just been a little stressful. John and I have been arguing a lot lately. Finances mostly. He has a way of forgetting my name's on that door too."

"He always did."

"I think we need to smack it out of the ballpark *every* time. He used to agree with that basic theory, although we didn't always see eye-to-eye on execution, as you well know. But now I don't know what the hell he's doing, I really don't. He basically handed Zander Closet Company over to you by being unprepared and lazy."

"Yeah, I need to thank him for that. It definitely gave me a chance to show all the little guys out there what I can do for them." I took another bite of my Big Mac.

"Not just the little guys, Tobi." Mike made a figure-eight on the table with the same French fry he'd yet to eat. "As for John, of course he gets it now. That's why he suddenly wants new clients, no matter how big or small just to make sure *you* don't—"

"Don't what? Make a living? Use my talent? Leave him in the dust?" I heard the change in my pitch, felt my teeth clench around my words. "He *had* a chance at a new client. But Zander wasn't exciting enough for him. His loss, my gain."

"It was sure looking that way, wasn't it? The loss potential there was enormous," Mike said as he heaved his shoulders upward. "Don't pay him any mind. Just do your thing."

I plucked a sesame seed off the top of my bun and popped it in my mouth. It stung to hear him refer to the loss potential in the past tense. "He's having a field day with the media's spin on Preston Hohlbrook's murder, isn't he?"

"Do you really have to ask?"

I grabbed my water and took a huge sip. My hand was still shaking. Only this time it was powered by anger and resolve rather than guilt. "I'm going after New Town, Mike."

He didn't answer. Didn't react. He simply sat there and played with the same fry, its innards turning to mush the harder he pressed down on it. I'd never seen him quite like this before. Then again, whenever he'd been stressed in the past, he'd shoved a wad of chew inside his lip and spent the next thirty minutes spitting it into a cup. Or, if he was done with the cancer causer, he'd react to stress with what I'd always called his "air-spit." He definitely didn't cope with issues by playing with a French fry. But I guess when in Rome and out of chew in a crowded restaurant . . .

"You understand, don't you? *This* is what you taught me, Mike. To have a plan. To go for it. I'm just trying to do that. To figure out what I want and let nothing stand in my way."

When he finally spoke, his voice was surprisingly calm with the same even (albeit monotone) cadence I'd listened to for years. "Can *you* still say it backwards?"

"Say it?" I echoed. "Say what?" And then I figured it out. "Sure, I can still say it. Bun-seed-sesame-a-on-onion-pickles-cheese-lettuce-sauce-special-patties-beef-all-two."

He smiled. "That's my girl. May the best man, *or woman*, win."

16

Charlotte West was your classic office secretary. She held court behind her desk with an air of quiet authority, the go-to person that corporate America seemed to take for granted these days. Her navy suit was carefully pressed, her blouse crisp and white. A pair of eyeglasses straddled her nose temporarily, while the gold chain tasked with keeping them close hung around her neck, waiting.

I stood in the doorway for a few minutes and watched as she moved between duties with the kind of efficiency that was born from discipline, motivation, and pride. She answered questions on the telephone with a calm voice and scrolled through her emails at lightning speed. Yet every motion she made, every word she uttered, carried an aura that went far beyond thoroughness and expertise to settle somewhere in a realm much closer to autopilot.

The phone rang just as I was about to make my presence known.

"Good afternoon, Hohlbrook Motors."

I took a step back, out of her line of sight, and tried to busy myself with the countless plaques and recognitions Preston Hohlbrook had earned from the St. Louis business community over the past ten years. Many of the awards were accompanied by a photograph that depicted the moment the honor was received. The mayor's face changed a few times along the way, but the recipient's never did. There were no stand-ins sent to the event, no poor middle-management guy stuck with the task of humoring the press.

"Oh, hello, Mr. Stanley, what can I do for you?" The initial cheeriness of Charlotte West's voice slipped away, replaced almost instantly by a tired, guarded tone.

Mr. Stanley? *Mike* Stanley? Holy mackerel, he was taking this competition stuff seriously.

Naturally, my ears perked up and I sidestepped closer to the open doorway.

"No, Mr. Stanley, nothing has been done. No changes have been implemented. I'm sure you can understand we have more pressing matters to attend to at the moment."

I wondered if the secretary could hear my heart pounding, sense someone lurking outside her door listening.

"I don't know who will make the decision. But I'm sure, when we do, that someone will contact you."

So much for being the proverbial fly on the wall. What I really needed was access to a phone and a common extension. Not that I'd actually pick it up and listen. Sheesh.

"Look, I'm fairly certain we won't be making any major changes right now. It's not the time—excuse me? I'm not sure why you think that, but Mr. Riker isn't in position to decide that at this time. But if you feel better having some alternate plans in place, I'm sure the board will listen. Yes, yes, I will make a note and be sure to give it to—"

I think I leaned forward a little too far because I ended up face first on the carpet (Berber, I think) in Charlotte West's office. And unlike the movies, it was anything but slow and graceful.

"Mr. Stanley, I have to go." The secretary slammed the phone down and jumped to her feet, a look of surprise etched in every facet of her face. "Are you all right, miss?"

I tried to smile, but found it rather difficult with my right cheek pressed against the floor. I pushed off the ground with my hands and rose to my feet, my face toasty warm. "I'm so very sorry. I think I tripped on my own two feet as I was approaching your door just now. It's why my mom is always calling me a klutz."

She seemed to buy it—or at the very least, agreed with my mom. Either way, she flashed a smile and then motioned me to a chair. "Can I offer you a cup of coffee? A soda?"

Truth be told, I wasn't terribly thirsty. I'd just left Mike less than thirty minutes ago, and I'd refilled my cup three times while I was there.

I nodded, my mind already calculating the time it would take for the secretary to walk down the hall and retrieve a drink. A minute? Maybe two? Surely enough time to scan any notes that happened to be lying around after the phone call she'd just taken. "That would be wonderful. Thank you."

"Water? Pepsi? Coffee?"

"Water would be great." I smiled an extra thanks at her as she patted my arm and turned toward the doorway. My gaze flew to the desk in front of me, briefly rested on the pad of pink paper beside the telephone, and widened at the sight of the notations written in red ink. My heart rate accelerated as I looked back at Charlotte and stopped dead.

In all my snooping, falling, and calculating, I'd completely missed the small refrigerator and coffee station recessed into the back wall. Nancy Drew I wasn't.

"Here you go."

I accepted the bottle of water from her outstretched hand, my mind rapidly searching for a plan B.

"Thanks." I twisted open the cap, took a few slow sips, and used the momentary silence to think of words that sounded semi-intelligent. When I was fairly certain I had some, I set the bottle at my feet, stood, and extended my arm toward Charlotte. "I'm sorry. I just realized my grand entrance didn't include an introduction. I'm Tobi Tobias of Tobias A—"

That's all I managed to get out before her eyes widened to the size of dinner plates—okay, so maybe not *that* big but it was close—and her skin drained of all color.

"*Tobi Tobias?*"

I wasn't sure how to take her reaction. I wasn't sure if I was seeing simple recognition, anger, or, worse yet, fear. So I just nodded. And waited.

The woman ignored my hand and covered her mouth with her own, her struggle for appropriate words evident in the pained creases near her eyes and the downward tilt to her lips (what I could see of them behind her hand). When she finally spoke again, her tone was that of a woman who'd lost her autopilot façade to the shock that had been lurking below the surface all along. "Isn't it just awful?"

Now I might not always be the sharpest crayon in the box, but I do pretty well. I'm the anti-blond bimbo (except for when it comes to noticing details like small refrigerators) and have always taken great pride in that fact. But at that moment, I was utterly clueless. Not a place I like to be.

Fortunately, I didn't need to say anything because the woman continued speaking, though her voice was still hard to hear without straining (which, of course, I did). "We're all in shock. I've never seen this building so quiet. So void of energy."

Ah yes, Preston Hohlbrook, of course. She'd heard my name and, rather than think of the message she'd left me, she thought of my slogan's tie-in to the death of her boss.

"I'm so sorry about Mr. Hohlbrook. I can't even begin to imagine how you're feeling in all this."

The woman nodded, reached for a tissue from the box on her desk, and blew her nose—a long, slow sound that more closely resembled a foghorn than the cliché trumpet.

"It's been awful. We all found out on the news which made it even harder. I understand you were there? That you're the one who found him?"

I nodded.

She reached out and grasped my hand, held onto it for a long moment. For some reason I didn't mind. It gave me as much comfort as I suspect it gave her.

"Was he—was he still breathing? Did he say anything?"

The question took me aback at first, until I realized that she'd have no way of knowing the answer. The news didn't report stuff like that. And regardless of our sorrow, human beings had an almost predictable need for facts no matter how bizarre or hurtful they might be.

"No. He was dead when I found him." I squeezed her hand gently then released it so she could grab another tissue. I hoped that the information would eliminate any concern she might have regarding her boss's suffering. How much of the actual strangulation he felt, I couldn't tell. But at least he hadn't suffered in agony for hours and hours before his death.

"Thank you." Charlotte dabbed at her eyes with the tissue, her voice raspy and unsure. "The police were here this morning—asking questions and looking through Mr. Hohlbrook's office. I asked them whether he suffered. They just said they weren't at liberty to discuss specifics about the victim. *The victim!* They didn't even call him by his name." The woman walked around the desk and dropped into her chair. "I saw him Friday night, not more than twelve hours before you found him."

"How was he?" I knew, from what the police had said to one another at the crime scene that morning, that Preston Hohlbrook hadn't been dead long when he fell at my feet. Maybe five or six hours at the most. Something about body temperature and the absence of rigor mortis. So I knew it would be doable for someone to have seen him the night before. But still, I found the information worthy of goose bumps.

"He was fine. A little on edge, but that was to be expected. He was dealing with a lot. Personally and professionally." The woman raised her head in response to the ring of her phone. She straightened in her chair and reached for the handset, her efficiency reset to autopilot once again. "Good afternoon. Hohlbrook Motors."

I tried not to listen (really, I did) as Charlotte handled a few questions, opting instead to look at the assorted frames on the woman's desk. There were the usual family photographs of the man I assumed to be her husband and their young son, a US Marine. My gaze traveled up the shelved cubby that ran along the short side of her L-shaped desk, and I scanned the assortment of pictures that graced that section. When I came to a close-up shot of Preston Hohlbrook, I stopped and stared.

The man I had seen in each of the hallway pictures, and in mementos throughout his home, looked virtually the same—except for the smile. Always an enthusiastic subject, Preston Hohlbrook boasted a different level of happiness in this picture. The sparkle in his eyes and the pure joy in his smile were different than any other I'd seen thus far. At his side was a diminutive woman with auburn hair styled in a neat bob. Her hazel eyes had tiny flecks of gold that shimmered in the late afternoon sun. They were wrapped in each other's arms, privy to an inside joke or wonderful memory that the photographer and casual observer could only guess at. My skin tingled.

"They were an amazing couple. The kind of love story that most of us only dream of."

I'd been so busy absorbing the picture in front of me that I hadn't noticed Charlotte West conclude her phone call. I simply nodded and continued to stare.

"That was Alana. Preston's wife."

"You mean his *first* wife, right?"

A sound that resembled a snicker escaped from the secretary's lips, and I turned my gaze just in time to see the disgust zip across her face.

"Technically, yes. His first wife. But Mitzi Moore was nothing more than a diversion. Someone to take the edge off Mr. Hohlbrook's loneliness."

"Did it work?" I followed Charlotte West's gaze to the photograph and then looked back at her once again, her reply coming after a long pause.

Her voice was quiet, distracted. "Did *what* work?"

"Did marrying Mitzi take the edge off the loneliness?"

The woman shrugged, her eyes still trained on the photograph. "I don't know. Maybe. Briefly. Mitzi Moore and Alana Hohlbrook were as different as night and day. Alana was demure, classy, generous, loving, and so much more. Sure, she came in to see him—they met for lunch at least three times a week—but she never insinuated herself into the company. She was Mr. Hohlbrook's support system— his personal cheerleader, if you will. But the company was his to run, and she trusted him to do so. She preferred, instead, to focus her days on the foundation."

"Foundation?"

"Yes, the Loving Hands and Helping Hearts Foundation. Alana started it up about three years before her death."

The name sounded familiar and, after a moment, I was able to fill in my mental blanks with details I'd read in a feature story at some point. Loving Hands and Helping Hearts was an organization that provided accommodations to families of terminally ill children. It allowed them to stay closer to their hospitalized children without worrying about the cost of rent. The group also provided care for siblings when parents craved time alone with their sick child.

"I've read about that group. Alana Hohlbrook really started it?" The more I heard about the first Mrs. Hohlbrook, first from Deserey and now Charlotte West, the more I could understand the tremendous void Preston Hohlbrook had been so desperate to fill.

"She most certainly did. She was an amazing woman. Everyone loved her." Charlotte West grabbed a tissue from the box and dusted the frame, her tone tensing as the focus of the story changed. "Mitzi, however, was a different story. A *very* different story."

I shifted foot to foot and tried not to dwell on the fact that my mouth had gone dry and I desperately wanted to sit down and retrieve my water bottle. I was afraid that if I moved, the conversation would stop. And I couldn't let that happen.

"From the day they got back from their honeymoon, she was in this place. Every day. All the time. Reprimanding employees for lingering in the hall, taking part in board meetings, sticking her two cents in regarding the ad campaign, and overseeing the selection of any new secretaries."

"She was in on the hiring?" I asked.

Charlotte West nodded, a sarcastic set to her face. "To make sure no one was hired that would threaten her reign."

"Did the employees like Mitzi?"

"Good Lord, no. They despised her."

"Yet everyone adored Alana, right?"

The secretary's eyes clouded over, her mouth dipped. "You couldn't not love Alana. She was the epitome of grace and class."

Everything Charlotte said so far had been confirmation of what Deserey had told me the day before. But one statement she'd made kept tugging at me.

"You said earlier, before the phone rang, that Mr. Hohlbrook had been dealing with a lot both personally and professionally. Was his marriage one of those issues?"

The woman nodded, her gaze fixed on Mr. Hohlbrook's door. "Yes. I think he'd finally realized that marrying someone as different from Alana as possible wasn't the way to move on and forget. It's been—I mean, it *was* heartbreaking to watch him accept that, but we all felt he'd be better off in the long run. Losing a loved one is not something you ever get over. It's something you learn to live with."

My Grandpa Stu had said the very same thing after we lost Grandma. Even now, five years later, he still shed tears when he recalled certain memories. But he said the tears were good tears. Because as painful as it was to lose her, having had her in his life had been an honor and a blessing.

I backed away from the desk, sat down, and grabbed the water bottle beside my feet. A few short gulps later, I lowered it down to my lap. I wanted to know what the professional issues were but wasn't sure when Charlotte might see my questions as what they were—pure grilling. So I took a different tactic.

"I'm sorry that I'm just now getting back to you. I was busy on Friday when you called and then after finding Mr. Hohlbrook's body on Saturday I wasn't able to think of anything else all weekend. I planned to call you this afternoon but decided to stop by since I was in the area anyway."

She shot a confused look at me. "Getting back to me?"

"Yes. You left a message on my voicemail Friday. You said Mr. Hohlbrook had wanted to set up a meeting."

I saw the light bulb go off behind her eyes a split second before the slow nod. "Of course. I'm sorry. I think I was just so focused on the fact that you found his body." The woman pushed her hands upward as if trying to ward off an invisible weight. "He asked me to contact you—which I did—but then he must have changed his mind based on the note he left on my desk."

"A note from Mr. Hohlbrook?"

"Yes. It was written at—let me see." Charlotte reached into a small inbox beside her phone and rifled through a pile of pink notes. "Here it is. It simply says to hold up on talking to Tobias Ad Agency until next week. He wrote it Friday night at eight o'clock."

"Did he often stay that late?" My curiosity was in overdrive. I tightened my hold on my water bottle and tried to steady my breathing.

"It was happening more and more lately."

"Business picking up?" I asked.

"No. Business is always good. I think it was more a case of a safe refuge."

"But I thought you said his new wife came in all the time. Didn't she just track him down here?"

"Her visits had dropped off. She was . . . rather busy getting ready for the Showcase." I didn't miss the sarcastic laugh that accompanied the *busy* tag. But I let it go. I was more intrigued by the fact that Preston Hohlbrook had expressed an interest in talking to me and then later changed his mind.

"So he didn't realize that you'd already called me?"

Charlotte West shook her head. "No. Though, if he had given it much thought, he should have. I didn't sit on his requests."

That didn't surprise me. It fit the efficiency aura that had screamed at me from the first moment I saw her. "May I ask why he had wanted to see me?"

"I don't see why not. He was impressed by your slogan for that closet company. He found it energetic and intelligent, fun and creative. All the things that he wanted in an ad campaign but hadn't had in a while."

Despite the fact that my water bottle was now empty, I still gulped. Loudly. Yes, I knew I was talented, but Preston Hohlbrook had noticed? Wow. Just wow.

I might have said that wow thing out loud because Charlotte leaned toward me. "Have you *seen* his ads? He hated them."

I tried to focus on the conversation at hand, tried to keep myself from visiting Slogan Land right there in the middle of Charlotte West's office, but it was a struggle. Her last sentence finally filtered its way through my ego trip and got me back on track. "If he hated his ads so much, why'd he keep running them?"

"Because Preston Hohlbrook was a good man. He took his wedding vows seriously and tried hard to include Mitzi in his life. She thought the camels were funny. Encouraged him to try it. To liven up his conservative image. And for some unexplainable reason, Tom Riker agreed." Charlotte West picked up her pen and started doodling on her empty pad. "But the camels and the robes and the crown never suited Mr. Hohlbrook and he knew it."

Everything she said made sense, and I listened (I really did), but the name she mentioned grabbed my attention immediately. It was the same name I'd heard her say during the phone conversation with Mr. Stanley—Mr. Gonna-Give-Me-a-Run-for-My-Money *Mike* Stanley.

Curiosity got the best of me, and I asked the million-dollar question. "Who is Tom Riker?"

"The vice president."

"Of Hohlbrook Motors?"

Charlotte West nodded sadly. "A nice man. But no Preston Hohlbrook."

I fiddled with my sash belt and considered a shift in questions until I glanced at my watch and realized how late it had gotten. I still had to check in at the office and look in on Mary Fran and Baboo. Grabbing my backpack, I stood and walked to her desk.

"If I could ask one more question before I go: Why do you think he decided to hold off on talking to me? What changed?"

Preston Hohlbrook's secretary shrugged her shoulders. "I don't know. I wish I could answer that. But, unfortunately, your guess is as good as mine. Nothing in this awful mess makes sense to me."

I thanked her for her time and expressed my sympathy once more. But it was what she said as I left that made me shiver.

"The biggest consolation for everyone here is that Mr. Hohlbrook is finally at peace in the arms of the only woman who *truly* loved him in return."

17

I was relieved to see JoAnna's empty space when I pulled into the parking lot behind the office. Although I adored her, JoAnna wasn't big on letting me decompress.

She'd start with the look—the one that hovered somewhere between worry and curiosity. The questions would follow, pointed and probing. If I got the slightest bit misty-eyed as I had over a number of things the past six months—my failing agency, the mounting bill pile, my broken engagement, you get the point—she'd move in with a hug. And then I was a goner, reduced to a blubbering ninny incapable of stringing together a coherent sentence let alone a list of viable murder suspects.

I suppose I should have welcomed her questions now as I always had, view them as an opportunity to organize my thoughts into some sort of cohesive order, but what I really wanted—*needed*, in fact—was to be alone. Tracking a killer was taking a toll I never expected.

Preston Hohlbrook was dead. I'd never met the man, never saw him anywhere other than atop a camel in one of John Beckler's idiotic commercials. I had assumed he was shallow simply because of the way he was portrayed in the ads. His quick speech, in-your-face delivery, and ridiculous royal attire had created an image in my mind that was both wrong and unfair. A *staged* image, I now realized.

In fact, I'd allowed that commercial persona to color many of my observations. I'd assumed he had married Mitzi because he was an attention seeker. I was wrong. He'd married her because he'd been desperately lonely, yet so in love with his late wife that he couldn't take the chance of eclipsing her memory. I'd assumed he liked his name on park benches and other visible places purely for self-promotion. Yet, I never knew his money was behind the Loving Hands and Helping Hearts Foundation.

The saddest part? Preston Hohlbrook wasn't the only person I'd misjudged. I'd also made an assumption about Blake and Peggy Zander based on the neighborhood they lived in and a one-sided cellphone conversation between Gary Zander and Preston Hohlbrook. Pathetic, huh?

What I needed to do more than anything else was stop assuming. I needed to look at the facts and come up with viable motives. It was the only way to save my company. And, more importantly, it was the only way to right an egregious wrong.

I deliberately ignored the light switch in my office (a reflection of my blahness, no doubt) and tossed my backpack onto the draft table under the window. JoAnna had put my stack of mail where she always did, a hairbreadth left of the phone. A quick check of the phone itself showed a numeral one next to the message indicator.

It's funny how things can change so quickly. A month ago—heck, *five days* ago—I would have jumped across the desk to see who'd called. And while jumping, I'd be praying that it was a call from a potential client—someone wanting my creative genius who would, in turn, *pay* me. Today, I simply stared at the light and contemplated the many benefits of turning a blind eye.

But I was Tobi Tobias, owner and president of Tobias Ad Agency. This company was my responsibility, my livelihood, my dream. Ignoring the message was really not an option. Not a smart one, anyway.

I grabbed the phone, punched in my code, and waited for the caller's voice in my ear as I poked at the stack of bills.

"Hey, Tobi. It's Andy. Andy Zander." I tightened my grip on the phone, forgetting all about the money I didn't have. "Sorry I missed you at the office this morning. Gary said you stopped by. Anyway, I want to proceed with the color brochure right away. I know we can't use the shots from the Hohlbrooks' closet—but I'm sure you noticed the closet demos I have in the office. I was wondering if you think those would work for the brochure pictures? We can bring in shoes and clothes to make it more real."

Nodding into the phone, I jotted a few quick impressions based on the demos I'd seen from the waiting room that morning. The idea might actually be better than simply using a single customer's closet.

This way the brochure could depict several models that would appeal to a broader segment of the population.

Andy continued. "If you think it would work, could we get Sam in here on Saturday? If we did it first thing, before we open, we wouldn't have to worry about shooting around customers."

I made a note in the upper right corner of my paper to call Sam. If I was able to reach him at the pet shop, I could kill two birds at the same time. As busy as I'd been all day, my mind still wandered to Baboo.

Andy yawned into my ear and I laughed. Maybe I wasn't the only one who didn't sleep last night.

"Excuse me. I've been yawning all day. Just when I thought my new roommate was getting used to things, she started waking me up again. She craves attention like you wouldn't believe."

I rolled my eyes upward. Yeah, I liked Andy. He seemed like a nice guy (okay, he seemed like a really, really nice—and extremely cute—guy). But I had no desire to hear about the attention-starved maniac he was shacking up with. I mean, really, can we not keep *some* things to ourselves? Men.

"Anyway, give me a call when you can. I'll be around until seven or eight tonight. Or you can call me at home. That number is 555-4232."

I pulled my gaze off the ceiling and deliberately kept my pen-holding hand still. There was no way I was going to call Andy at home. I simply had no desire to talk to his nocturnal roommate. Glancing at the clock, I realized I had at least a full hour to reach him at the office. That would give me time to sketch out some ideas and talk to Sam . . .

"Well, that's about it, I guess. I look forward to hearing from you, Tobi."

My grip on the phone loosened and my shoulders sagged. The sudden loss of any remaining energy had nothing to do with the end of the message. At least that's what the little voice in my head kept saying. It was 5:45 in the evening. My food intake for the day had consisted of an old granola bar and a McDonald's hamburger. That was it. I was hungry, that's—

"Oh, and Tobi? Before I forget, you're a good dancer. Wish I could have heard the words."

I barely heard the automated voice that announced the end of the message and the various options (replay, save, delete) available to me. The only thing I was aware of was my body sinking down into my seat, my cheeks warming to near-tropical temps, and the overwhelming gratitude I felt toward JoAnna's dentist for the follow-up appointment that had left me in the office alone.

Somehow between my visit to Blake's house, the stop at New Town, lunch with Mike, and the talk with Charlotte West, I'd completely forgotten about the way my morning had started. In particular, dancing and singing at a traffic light on Brentwood Boulevard with my one-and-only client looking on.

I allowed myself a moment to pout, a moment to squirm, and a moment to berate myself before sitting up tall and reaching for the phone book. I didn't need to look up the number for the pet shop; I had that committed to memory. But I did need to look up the number for Joe's Chinese Food.

After I placed my order, I pressed the button on the top of the phone and punched in the number for the To Know Them Is To Love Them pet shop. Mary Fran answered.

"Hi, Mary Fran. How's Baboo doing today?" I leaned back in my chair and looked out at the streetlamp and the shadows it created against the neighboring buildings.

"Hey, Tobi. Baboo is doing better. Still hasn't uttered a word yet, but he seems more settled. Less stressed. Sam and I are actually going to sleep at home tonight so they can have a chance to bond without us bothering them."

"Them? Who's them?"

"Baboo and Rudder."

I pulled my gaze back into the office and fixed it on the phone. "Rudder's behaving himself, right?"

Mary Fran's smile was audible through the phone. "Rudder's been the perfect host. He's been telling Baboo all of the same things he's heard me say over the past twenty-four hours. Anytime I leave the room and then walk back in, there's a strange hush that falls over the shop. Like I'm interrupting some private discussion between the two of them. It's a hoot."

It's funny how you can picture certain scenes without being present yourself. I could actually see Rudder in his bandana-of-the-day teaching Baboo the ways of the shop. You know—where the kiwi was kept, when feeding time was, how best to ignore the yappy dogs, and which employee snorted.

"So you think there will be a party going on at the shop tonight?" I switched the phone to my left hand and then froze. "Wait. We *do* know they're both males, right?"

"Yes, Tobi, they're both males."

I mouthed a *thank you* into the air. The last thing this world needed was for Rudder to sire a child. "And you're positive?"

"Positive." Mary Fran made a few crunching noises and then swallowed. "He came in again today. Around noon."

I grabbed the stack of mail and rifled through to the bottom. Yup, all bills. Save, of course, the advertisement for breast implants. Mitzi must have added my name to some list in the hopes a referral would gain her a free nip or a half-price tuck. "He? He who?"

"The guy. The cute one."

"You mean the grungy one?"

"That's right."

"And? Is he still grungy?"

"Actually, no. He was stylin' and profilin' today."

Stylin' and profilin'? Mary Fran had truly lost it. Inhaling all those animal scents had finally done her in.

"Okay . . ."

"He came in to get some food for Sadie."

It's a good thing my envelope-slicer opener-thingy was in the process of being used because I'm fairly sure it would have ended up being thrown across the room. A temper is one thing I don't have. I rarely raise my voice and have virtually no thoughts of inflicting bodily harm on anyone (Nick doesn't count) but losing Sadie had upset me so much more than I ever thought it would.

"How is she? He treating her well?" The words were spoken so softly that I had to repeat them in order for Mary Fran to hear.

"She's fine. Stop worrying. Why don't you focus that energy on getting yourself all dolled up and letting me fix you up on a date with this guy?"

My dear friend Mary Fran was akin to a pit bull with its teeth clamped onto some poor defenseless kid's pants. She simply wouldn't give up. Which was kind of funny when you stopped to consider the way she'd sworn off men in her *own* life.

"Hey, is Sam around?" I asked.

"You can change the subject all you want, Tobi. But one of these days you'll be working in here when he shows up, and you'll be *begging* me to introduce you."

I laughed. "And if that day comes, you'll introduce me anyway."

"You're right, I will." Mary Fran's voice muffled momentarily, only to return to its normal volume in short order. "Sorry. Rudder was being inappropriate."

I didn't ask. Didn't want to know. Instead, I repeated my earlier question. "Sam working today?"

"Yes he is. You want to talk to him?"

"For a minute, if you can spare him."

"Sam!" I held the phone away from my ear and cringed. Why she was yelling, I didn't know. The shop was small. Real small. Then again, if Rudder was talking, you could barely hear yourself think let alone hear someone calling your name from across the room. "Here he is."

"Thanks, Mary Fran. For everything."

"My pleasure. Baboo is great."

"Hey there, Tobes. What's going on?"

If anyone else had given me the nickname *Tobes*, I'd have put the kibosh on it from day one. But Sam was different. From him, it was cute—like a pet name. "Work. You free for a photo shoot this Saturday? Around eight?"

"Sure! More closet shots?"

"Yup. We need to get moving on this brochure."

"Okay. But I got my memory card back from the cops today if you want to use those shots."

I twirled the phone cord around my index finger and tried my best to ignore the insistent gurgling in my stomach. "You saw the police today?"

"Uh-huh. They came to the shop. Said they copied the pictures onto their hard drive and that I could have the originals back."

"Okay, but I think it would be best if we took all new pictures."

"Makes sense. So where are we gonna shoot the new ones?"

"Andy's office. He has closet demos."

"But if they're demos, won't they be empty?"

"They will, but I'll bring some outfits, some shoes, some purses, and Andy will bring some of his stuff. We'll stage the shots."

"Sounds good as long as I'm back to help Mom before things get busy around here."

The busiest time at the pet shop was from eleven until about two on Saturday. That was the day everyone seemed to stock up on their pet supplies or opt to bring their pet in for a bath and groom. "That's not a problem. We'll make a point of being out of there by ten and back at the shop by ten thirty."

"Cool! I'm pumped."

I couldn't help but smile at his choice of words. Most guys his age reserved those words for passing their driver's test or landing the girl they'd been drooling over for weeks. But not Sam. He had a two-track mind. Photography and helping his mom. And in staying true to those tracks, he inspired *me*. Pretty neat trick.

"Thanks, Sam. So am I."

"Mom says we can use her car on Saturday."

I made a mental note to add *accommodating* and *selfless* to my list of Mary Fran's amazing attributes. "That's awesome. Tell her thanks for me."

"I will, Tobes. See you soon."

"Say hi to Baboo for me and—" I felt mischievous-me rearing its head and decided to go with it. My energy was returning along with my almost insatiable desire to torture Mary Fran with the unknown (purely in fun, of course). "And tell your mom I'm going out tomorrow night. To a night club. I'll see you soon, hon."

Then I ran over to my backpack, pulled out my cell phone, and set it to ring straight to voicemail. I suppose, on some level, I should feel a little guilt, but I didn't. Mary Fran, after all, was responsible for foot-fetish guy, wasn't she? I allowed myself the shudder that always accompanied that memory and then dialed Andy's number. He picked up on the second ring.

"Zander Closet Company, this is Andy."

My heart rate quickened, and I shrugged out of my jacket. For some strange reason I tended to feel warmer than normal when Andy was around—or on the phone . . . or in my thoughts . . .

"Hi Andy. It's Tobi."

"Hey! How are you?"

"Good. Busy." I pinched myself in the arm as payback for the robotic-sounding answers and tried again. "I got your message. I think shooting the demo closets is a wonderful idea. I've already contacted Sam, and we can be at your office at eight o'clock sharp on Saturday. Will that work?"

"Absolutely. That's perfect."

My stomach tightened and I glanced at the clock on my desk. That green pepper beef was taking its sweet time. "We'll see you then. Thanks, Andy."

I was about to bid farewell when he spoke again, the topic changing along with the tone in his voice. He'd been enthusiastic when I'd identified myself at the beginning of the call, but now his voice had taken on a deepness that made my stomach flop around. (Where was the delivery guy—hunting down the cow?)

"Wait! Don't go yet. What were you dancing to at that traffic light?"

I grabbed the electric bill and used it as a fan. "Dancing?"

Andy laughed, a deep sound that echoed across the line. "Yeah. You *were* actually listening to music, weren't you?"

He had me. If I denied listening to music, he'd think I was nuttier than he already did. So I caved. "Dancing in the Dark," I whispered. How he heard me, I don't know, but he did.

"Know it well. Love Bruce."

I sat straight up in my chair. Okay, so Andy Zander was good looking, sweet, drove a nice car, was willing to overlook the negative attention my slogan was creating, *and* liked Bruce Springsteen? Torture . . . that was what this was, pure torture. Mary Fran must be using those voodoo dolls again. I nodded at the phone.

"Tobi, you still there?"

"Um, yeah. I-I'm sorry you had to witness that this morning."

"What? The dancing? I loved it. Started my day off with a smile."

I set my fan down and wiped my hands on my jeans. "Glad to help."

Andy laughed. "What kind of car was that?"

"Oh no! Carter's car!" I jumped to my feet, nearly strangling myself with the phone cord.

"Carter? Who's Carter?"

"My upstairs neighbor. He lent me his car, and I completely forgot to bring it back." My eyes flew to the clock and I stared at the soft green numerals that made up the time—7:05. Carter was due at the theater at seven-thirty. "I've got to go, Andy. I'm sorry."

I think he said he understood. That he'd see me on Saturday. But I'm not entirely sure. I kinda hung up without listening for his response. Just like I kinda knocked the Chinese food delivery guy over when I ran across the parking lot to Carter's powder-blue 1975 Ford Granada.

18

I'd hit the hay shortly after handing Carter his keys and eating my takeout dinner, exhausted after a zany day. It was like my mind was doing everything in its power to ignore the bits of information I'd gleamed but not yet processed. And I was good with that. Avoidance is a marvelous coping skill.

Even when I awoke at six, to Gertrude's incessant yapping, my thoughts refused to linger on the Hohlbrook mess. Instead, they jetted their way to Slogan Land, which is where I'd been ever since, with the lone exception of a brief working-from-home-today phone call to JoAnna. She didn't question why; I didn't offer an explanation.

I sat down at my draft table, munching my Puffs, and letting my gaze travel across the countless scribbles and balled-up pieces of paper that represented nearly eleven hours of brainstorming, mumbling, jubilation, frustration, and—finally—creative, usable ideas. The same sun that was rising when I started was now setting for an early autumn slumber.

A soft tap at my door yanked me from my special place and dropped me into reality. Or as close as 46 McPherson Road *was* to reality.

I carried my Puffs to the door, cheeking several that weren't quite ready to travel the esophagus-slide just yet. When I reached the door, I opened it to find Carter on our shared doorstep. A very *bald* Carter. As in no hair. None. Zip. Nada.

"Hey, Sunshine."

I was truly speechless. I had absolutely nothing to say to, or about, his baldness. So I just stared.

"What's wrong?" Carter scrunched up his face and studied me, much like I imagined vegetarians would scrutinize me and my carnivorous ways, if given the chance.

I wiped my mouth on the sleeve of my pajamas (so I opted for creativity over cleanliness that day—sue me) and stifled a belly laugh. "Well, Daddy Warbucks, how 'bout you tell me?"

Carter's hand flew to his head and felt around his scalp, his cheeks turning the same shade of crimson as the housecoat I spied lurking on the other side of the bushes. I, of course, laughed. And laughed. And laughed. And laughed. It had to be a full minute before I gained enough control over myself to hear Carter's response.

"Ah geez, I forgot to take it off before I left. I was just trying out some new theatrical glue to see how it held." He peeled back his fake skin to reveal the Annie-red he'd yet to change. "Better?"

"Much." I motioned him out of Ms. Rapple's eavesdropping zone and into my apartment, stepping back so he could pass.

"So what time do we head out?" he asked, looking around, his eyes coming to rest on the fruits of my labor.

"Head out? What are you talking about?" I shoveled the last spoonful of Cocoa Puffs into my mouth and followed him over to the draft table.

"The yuppie bar, remember? You're dragging me there on what I suspect is some sort of recon mission."

My mouth dropped open. "Oh my gosh, I completely forgot!"

Carter eyed my lavender-colored satin pajamas and nodded. "I can see that. You sick?"

I waved my spoon-holding hand in the air and quickly crunched the last mouthful of dinner (actually that'd be breakfast, lunch, *and* dinner in one bowl). "No, I'm fine. I've been working. Trying to come up with something that'll knock their socks off."

"And who might *they* be?" Carter asked as he stuck his fake scalp into his back pocket.

I held my breath as he lifted my most recent brain child off the desk. "New Town," I explained. "It's that master community out in St. Charles that's been in all the papers."

Carter's eyes nearly doubled in size as he wrapped his arms around my waist and turned me around in a circle. "Tobi, that's fantastic! You are soooo on your way, Sunshine."

It was probably wrong that I didn't correct him right away. I meant to. Really. But there was something about his enthusiasm that I wanted to savor for a brief, shining moment. So I did. When he finally put me down, I fessed up.

"I don't have the account . . . *yet*. But I'm going to."

Carter studied my face for a moment. "Well, okay. At least they're talking to you."

I kneaded the spoon handle between the thumb and middle finger of my right hand. "Actually, that's not really the case either."

"Meaning?"

"Meaning no one from New Town has come near me. Yet."

"So what are you doing then?"

I turned on my heels and headed toward the kitchen, looking over my shoulder as I walked. "I'm putting together a pitch they can't ignore."

A slow, cockeyed smile spread across Carter's face. "Oh, I get it. You're gonna do a little client-plucking? You go, girl, that's the way to play."

I rounded the corner into my kitchen and dropped the bowl into the sink. "It's not a tactic I'd normally consider. Seems kind of underhanded, you know? But when you consider who they're working with, it doesn't bother me so much. In fact, it kind of lit the fire."

Carter's laugh carried into the kitchen (not a tough thing to do when my entire apartment could just about fit into the Hohlbrooks' closet). "Let me guess. New Town's rep is John Beckler?"

"Uh-huh." I pulled a glass from the cabinet, popped open a can of Carter's can't-live-without-it cherry soda, and carried it back into the living room. "Unfortunately, by stealing from John, I steal from Mike. But Mike's okay. He gets it."

"Thanks, Sunshine." He took the can from my hand and took a long, slow gulp. "Is New Town a big moneymaker for Beckler and Stanley?"

I grinned. Carter was a smart cookie. "You bet. New Town and Hohlbrook Motors pretty much write the paychecks over there."

Carter took another gulp and chased it down with a wide smile. "Good for you. It's about time you give that slime a run for his money."

I rose up on my tiptoes and planted a kiss on Carter's cheek. The guy just understood me 100 percent.

He looked at the papers on my draft table, and I watched as his eyes skirted the curvy words and slogan-created images. "Wow, Tobi, these are good. Really, really good."

My heart soared. I actually felt it lift in my chest. Knowing Carter believed in me and my talent was both humbling and exhilarating at the same time.

"Thanks." I pointed at the ad mock-up I'd created—the sketches of the lake, the fishing dock, the bikes, the stage performers. "I went out there yesterday to check the place out, and it was amazing. It had the feel of a quaint vacation town."

Carter nodded, a smile playing across his lips as he read my pitch ideas. "These slogans are amazing: *Paradise without the car ride. Who says vacation has to end?* How do you do that?"

I stared at the slogans I'd written and the pictures I'd drawn and felt the familiar twinge of a brainstorm coming on. "Do what?" I murmured.

"Create images with words?"

I grabbed a pen and a pad of paper from the table and started jotting notes. "I don't know. I just see it. But you're not so bad at it yourself, Your Simile Highness."

He took a moment to preen at the title and then leaned over my paper for a closer look. "So what are you doing now?"

"A commercial idea just hit me, and I want to get it down before I forget." I outlined the concept in my own Tobi Tobias shorthand (translation: gibberish that is understandable by no one else but me).

"What's that on the car?" Carter swept his hand across my paper, his index finger stopping on the top half of the sketch coming together beneath my pen.

"Suitcases."

"But I thought you said New Town *was* the vacation."

"I did." I set the paper down on the table and turned to face Carter. "Focus for a minute. Picture a car with suitcases strapped to the top. A family of four inside. Car pulling out of the driveway."

"Okay. Keep going."

My heart started to race as the image played itself out in my thoughts, movie-style. "Picture the kids in the back seat, turned around, their arms resting on the shelf by the back windshield. Their heads down, looking forlorn."

"Yeah . . ."

"The wife is in the front seat, her forehead pressed against the window, a pathetic look on her face."

Carter laughed. "I want to see you draw a pathetic face."

I stuck my tongue out quickly and then kept talking. "All of a sudden the husband says, 'Think it's too late to cancel Hawaii?'"

Apparently Andy *and* Carter had both missed the memo about women and the all-important initial response to their hard work, because he stood there, his eyes closed, his mouth motionless. Why didn't he get it? It was brilliant. Or maybe not.

"Oh my God, Sunshine, that's awesome!"

"See, I'm thinking if it was so awesome you'd have reacted a little quicker."

He grasped my arm and shook it. "I was picturing it. And it's incredible. Tell me you didn't just dream that up this morning."

"I didn't. I came up with it just now, while you were looking at the mock-ups."

"Unbelievable. Wish I had your talent, Sunshine."

"Are you kidding me? You have amazing talents. Have you seen the way the cast looks in every single one of your shows? Have you seen how you've transformed *me* in the past?"

"You're easy. You've got the goods and then some."

The goods? Really? I've got the goods? God, I love this man. I smiled. "Thanks."

Carter's eyes traveled my unclean hair, my make-up free face, my pajama-clad body. "I still get to doll you up before we leave, right?"

The bar.

I sighed. Getting so wrapped up in Slogan Land had enabled me to momentarily forget the unforgettable. But no matter how hard I tried, there was one indisputable fact I simply couldn't ignore. All the cutesy slogans in the world wouldn't mean a thing if I didn't catch a killer and refocus the media's attention.

"Yeah, you do." I pulled a strand of my hair through my fingertips and curled my lip. "I'll take all the help I can get."

Carter squeezed my arm and then made his way over to the door. "You, my dear, are beautiful no matter what. Even now—like *that?*— you're as delightful as a warm summer breeze across pure, untouched, white sand."

I laughed. I couldn't help it.

But he didn't seem to take offense. He simply grinned back at me and pulled open the door. "Get yourself showered. Put on those chocolate-brown slacks with that goldish-brown crocheted top. Throw on those heels you got a few weeks ago. It'll be perfect. I know just the hairstyle for it."

I had every faith in the world that by the time Carter was done, plain-Jane me would be looking like one hot mama. Carter McDade was a miracle worker like no other. (Okay, except God, of course.)

I closed the door and headed for the bathroom, my mind already focused on the warm steam and the shoulder-massage shower setting that had earned its rightful spot on my list of loyal friends.

My fingers had just undone the first few buttons of my pajama top when I heard another tap at my door. I did a quick check to make sure I wasn't revealing anything (even flat-chested women need to be prudent, according to my mother) then retraced my steps to the front door.

"What'd you forget?" I asked as I pulled on the knob and peeked my head out. Sure enough, there was Carter, his back to me, his Annie-red hair covered, once again, by fake, wrinkled skin. "Something to spit shine that scalp with?"

Daddy Warbucks's twin brother turned around, his eyes crackling with unmistakable excitement. My mouth dropped open (pretty much to the ground) and I stood there, speechless. A strange reaction, no doubt, to a man I'd seen just five seconds earlier. Only this wasn't that man.

And no, it wasn't the real Daddy Warbucks. Or even the guy hired to play his part. It was—

"Grandpa Stu? Are you okay? Did somebody die? What are you doing here? How did you get here? Didn't you lose your license?" The questions poured from my mouth with no apparent end in sight. "How long are you staying? Does Mom know you're here?"

Grandpa Stu simply waited for my version of twenty questions to come to a halt. When I finally stopped rambling, he spoke. His voice was soft but strong, the kind of sound that made people sit up and listen. "Goodness me, child. Have I taught you nothing?"

I gave him one of my *uh oh this is a trap* looks.

He wagged a disapproving finger at me. "Asking the questions and waiting for the answers is never as much fun as deducing them on your own."

"Okay. So I'll deduce: You bypassed the no-driver's-license issue by hopping a train from Kansas City, right?"

He nodded.

"And you arrived sometime in the last hour or so—"

Another nod. Damn, I was good.

"You didn't call Mom and tell her because you didn't want to get stuck out in the burbs."

A mischievous smile accompanied the latest nod. I was on to something. The cocky sparkle in his proud eyes erased any doubt.

"It's been driving you nuts being out of things here. The thought of a real, live murder mystery was a bigger pull than the senior special at Denny's."

He tapped his foot in mock irritation at that comment. But I also noticed he didn't deny it. I was on a roll, no ifs, ands, or buts about it.

I set the suitcase down in the little hallway (fancy word for a space the size of Ms. Rapple's mouth—wait, bad example) and turned. "The only thing I can't figure out is how you got from the train station to here? Did you take a cab?"

Grandpa Stu simply looked at me in silence. He was playing hardball and trying to read his face wasn't an option. You see, unlike me, he knew a thing or two about poker faces.

"Oh, come on. Help a girl out."

"How about a hug for your grandpa, instead? Think I can score one of those?" He opened up his arms and I ran in, just like I had since I was old enough to stand. Being wrapped in those arms was, hands down, the best place to be. We held each other for a long moment, and then I stepped back to get a better look.

His hair was gone. We'd already established that. His eyebrows, thick and white, sat atop ocean-blue eyes that twinkled like the brightest stars in the night sky. The navy blue sweater he wore fell over his shoulders—his once broad, strong shoulders. My throat tightened and my eyes watered. Grandpa Stu was no longer the spry man I remembered. Sure, he was still in fine shape for eighty years old, but he wasn't exactly the *same*.

"Now let me take a look at you, Sugar Lump."

I obliged and moved a few steps back, executing a near-perfect curtsey as I waited for the once-over.

"You've always been a little waif of a thing, but have you lost weight?"

Should I fess up and tell him about my diet of Cocoa Puffs and chocolate bars? Did I tell him that four hours was a good night's sleep? That if I slept any longer than that, I dreamed of someone ripping my heart out of my chest and stomping on it over and over? Nah. He'd figure it out anyway.

"Maybe a pound or two. I've been real busy the past week with the new client and then the whole murder thing. It's been a little stressful around here."

He sat down on the loveseat and slipped off his tasseled loafers, satisfied for the moment with my explanation.

"So what'd I miss? You didn't figure out who the killer is yet, did you?"

"I wish. I've learned that Mitzi Hohlbrook is Preston's second wife. Someone as different from his first wife as you could imagine. Preston's maid seems to think there was something going on between Mitzi and my client's cousin, but the cousin denies it and I believe him. Regardless, the maid and even Preston's secretary are both convinced that Preston had finally realized his marriage was a mistake."

"Was there a prenup?"

Leave it to Grandpa to cut to the chase. "I don't know. I need to ask the housekeeper that tonight."

Grandpa shifted forward on the sofa, his quick smile deepening to reveal the kind of dimple that set hearts aflutter in his Sexy Seniors Single Group back home. "Tonight?"

Oh, good God. Open mouth, insert foot.

I tried to make the upcoming jaunt to The Car Crash sound as unappealing as possible. "Carter and I are just going to head over to a bar about twenty minutes away. The Hohlbrooks' housekeeper and the next door neighbors' housekeeper like to hang out there on Wednesday nights. I thought it would be a good place to get some information about the neighbors and pump Preston's maid a little bit more as well."

Without really thinking, my shoulders hiked up and my head sank into my neck, a classic duck-for-cover pose if there ever was one. Grandpa was silent. I peeked out through closed eyes to make sure he hadn't had a stroke or anything, but he was gone, the only remnant of his time on the couch an indent where his buttocks had been.

"Grandpa? Where'd you go?"

I turned just in time to see my grandfather pull a fringed cowboy shirt and a pair of black leather pants from his suitcase. "Great. I brought some of my dress-up clothes just in case. One can never be too prepared when there's a mystery to be solved."

Cocoa Puffs churned in my stomach at the image of my grandfather in black leather pants and a cowboy shirt. It sunk to my toes when he pulled out an Army fatigue hat.

"I'll fit right in. The leather gets me in with the biker dudes, the shirt with the rednecks, and the hat with the hunters and patriotic fellas."

Dudes? Rednecks? Patriotic fellas? Who was this masked man?

I was just about to offer a feeble protest, something about the dangers of loud music and the health risks of secondhand smoke to senior citizens, when he spoke again. "See if you can't rustle up something better than what you've got on now, okay Sugar Lump? Your grandma always said you catch flies with honey. Remember that."

"Um, Grandpa?"

"What is it, Tobi?" He pulled his navy blue sweater over his head and shimmied into the cowboy shirt. Once it was completely on, he shook his upper body to showcase the movement of his fringe. "Snazzy, ain't it?"

I had to look away. The whole thing was almost painful. "I don't need to worry about catching flies. I'm going to this bar to talk to two *women*."

My grandfather patted my back, slung his black leather pants over his shoulder, and shot me the wink I'd loved all my life. Only I preferred when it was accompanied by a new life lesson or a trip to the ice-cream parlor, not my grandfather's social life and choice in barroom attire. "They like honey too, Sugar Lump. Trust me."

19

I can only imagine what the neighbors thought when we walked down the sidewalk and piled into Carter's powder-blue Ford. Sure, the car was always a sight to behold, but I was fairly certain it wasn't the vehicle people were raising their window shades and steadying their rockers to see. It was the people getting into the car. As in, *us.*

Our only saving grace was the fact that it was dark and the streetlamp closest to the car wasn't working. That absence of light made it much tougher to be completely sure of what (and more importantly *who*) they were seeing.

Still, I expected the late Joan Rivers and her daughter to pop out from behind a bush and hammer us: *What were they thinking, America? Who dresses like that?*

My answer? I hadn't a clue. I mean, really, what *were* we thinking? And what happened to my trouser-wearing grandpa whose only fashion boo-boo used to be black knee-highs with brightly patterned shorts?

I looked over at Carter as he pulled away from the curb and headed down McPherson Road toward Euclid. He didn't look much different than normal. Well, his normal for this week, anyway. His hair was still Annie-red (with a sprinkle of glitter he threw in as we were walking out the door) and he wore his standard denim jacket and moccasins. But he'd agreed to take off the Can't We All Just Love One Another tie-dyed tee and replace it with a fairly innocuous button-down shirt. With any luck, I'd find an opportunity to flip the collar down.

I half-turned on the front bench seat and glanced back at Grandpa Stu. He was beaming from ear to ear and looking out the side window like an anxious puppy on the way to the park. The whole time Carter had been doing my hair and makeup, Grandpa's mouth had been running on warp speed. If I didn't know any better, I'd think he was simply starved for human contact. But I did know better. Grandpa met his fellow senior citizens for breakfast, lunch, and dinner every day. He went golfing and fishing with the men, dancing with the women. So I knew it wasn't simple conversation he was craving. He was salivating at the idea of living out one of the many mystery novels he plowed through in a given week.

"So what are we doing at the pet shop again?" Carter asked, as he turned onto Maryland heading towards Newstead.

"Mary Fran had to close up early to get Sam to one of his follow-ups with the orthodontist. So that means Rudder didn't get fed at his usual time. He's going to be ripping off his bandana and staging a coup if we don't stop by and give him a snack." I dug my hand into my backpack and felt around for my key ring. "It shouldn't take long. You can come in."

Carter nodded and pulled into a parallel parking spot about halfway down Newstead.

"How do you do that so well?" I asked as I gathered my assorted stuff and pushed open the passenger-side door.

"Do what?" Carter stepped out onto the sidewalk and held my grandfather's door open. "Park?"

"Parallel park. On the first try. Usually takes me a few tries if I try at all."

I fell into step beside Carter and my grandfather. There was a chill to the air, a hint of the winter that was to come. Grandpa Stu shivered and pulled his Harley-Davidson biker's jacket (no, I'm not kidding—wish I was) tighter across his body.

Carter laughed. "I took driver's ed."

"So did Tobi. She got a perfect score on her written exam but failed on the parking. The second and third time wasn't any better," Grandpa Stu said.

I stopped. "Wait a minute. Of course the third time was better. I got my license."

My grandfather cleared his throat. Not a normal got-a-frog-in-my-throat kind of clearing. Oh no, that'd be too easy. This was an oops-I-walked-into-that kind of clearing.

"Grrraaannndpaaa!"

Carter folded his arms across his chest and waited, his right eyebrow cocked to the heavens in glee. He was loving this.

"Okay, okay." Grandpa Stu raised his hands into the air, palms out. "Remember how I left you while you were waiting to take that third road test? Told you I'd be right back?"

"Yesssss?"

"I moved the cones."

Carter laughed out loud. I stood, rooted to the cement beneath my feet, my eyes shifting side to side hoping none of the street cops were listening as my grandfather confessed—in full voice—how he fixed a government-run test. The man had finally lost it.

"No, you didn't!" I never realized you could whisper a yell. But you can. Quite effectively, I might add.

"Yes, Sugar Lump, I did. About five feet on the back cone, about five feet on the front cone."

I thought back to that day, to the exact moment I swung the car into the parking spot, absolutely floored that I'd made it with such ease. Now I knew why. My grandpa Stu had fixed the test. Waving my hands around, I marched ahead of them to the pet shop. I was mortified. Shocked. And grateful. Because I knew in my heart, if he hadn't done that, I'd still be marching into that motor vehicle department every thirty days, trying to pull into a spot that was half the size of the car (okay so maybe not *half,* but no more than two-thirds, tops).

I ignored their whispered remarks and belly laughs and focused, instead, on unlocking each of the six locks Mary Fran had installed on the front door. Not to keep anyone from breaking in, but to keep Rudder from breaking out. We'd caught him studying the process of key insertion more times than any of us could count.

"B-bout, bout time."

Rudder Malone was worse than my mother when there were three of us teenagers at home and she was trying to usher us out the door for Sunday Mass. She'd said that very same thing. Even tapped her foot the way Rudder did, only I swear he did it better.

"Wow, he sure is demanding, isn't he?" Carter shut the door behind my grandfather and walked over to Rudder's cage. "Nice bandana you've got there, buddy. That shade of green is perfect with your eyes. Like an evergreen tree in a sea of pines."

I waited. Could feel Rudder's desire for a nasty retort. Fortunately, Mary Fran and Sam were fairly easygoing. Which, in turn, limited Rudder's repertoire of words. Sounds though, were a different matter entirely.

"R-r-r-z-z-z!"

Carter jumped back. "What the heck was that?"

"His response."

"To what I said? About his eyes?"

I snickered as I walked behind the counter and opened the refrigerator. "Could have been. Though I'm thinking it was directed at your 'demanding' comment." I pulled out a Tupperware container of pre-chopped strawberries and popped the lid open.

"B-bout, bout time."

"Geez, Rudder, I'm getting it." I plucked out four pieces and walked over to the cage. "You really need to learn some patience, pal."

"Pa-patience. Patience pal."

If only his beak was connected to his brain.

When I'd placated Rudder with his evening snack, I crossed the room to Baboo. "Hey there, Baboo. How you doing, big guy?"

Baboo looked at me with his yellowy eyes and said nothing. He looked better. Seemed less tense. But he was still heartbroken. You could sense it the moment he looked at you.

"P-pphhtt. P-pphhtt. P-pphhtt."

I pulled Mary Fran's stool over to the cage and sat down. "Hush, Rudder. Eat your food."

Carter and Grandpa Stu came over to Baboo's cage and peered inside.

"This the bird that belonged to the murder victim?" My grandfather asked as he stuck his finger between the wire slats.

"Bend it like this, Grandpa." I pushed my bent finger through the cage and waited while Baboo looked at it. "They like that better. Mary Fran says it's less threatening."

Grandpa Stu bent his finger in imitation and looked at the African grey. "Baboo. Baboo."

"P-pphhtt. P-pphhtt. P-pphhtt."

"Quit it, Rudder." I looked over my shoulder and looked daggers at the bandana-clad troublemaker.

"What's he saying?" Carter asked.

"Darned if I know."

As annoying as his attention-seeking tactics were, I was gleefully aware of one thing: Rudder hadn't snorted since I walked in. Maybe, just maybe, the fact that I'd been busy lately had given him time to forget my minor little idiosyncrasy. A gal can hope, can't she?

"You never answered me, Tobi. Was this the murder victim's bird you told me about?"

"Oh, sorry, Grandpa. Yes, Baboo was Preston Hohlbrook's bird." The words had no sooner left my mouth when Baboo jumped off his perch and faced the corner.

"Would you look at that?" Grandpa Stu said, pointing toward Baboo. "He heard his owner's name, and it's made him sad."

I suspected my grandfather was right. My heart ached for this creature who'd lost his beacon. "Mary Fran says that's why he has almost no feathers left. This particular species is very loyal and often expresses stress by pulling out their feathers."

Carter leaned against the counter, his gaze fixed on Rudder. "I bet that bird was traumatized."

"Rudder?" I laughed and then cringed at the faint snort that followed. Fortunately, it went unnoticed. "His biggest trauma is getting one less kiwi than he's used to."

"No, not Rudder. The other one. Baboo."

I set my foot on the rung of the stool. "You mean from losing Preston?"

Carter shook his head. "From Preston's *murder*."

"Huh?"

"Where was"—my grandfather lowered his voice to a whisper as he said the name—"Preston murdered?"

I shrugged my confusion. "They're thinking the bedroom. At the very least he was dragged through it on the way to the clos—"

Then I stopped. I'd finally learned the language. Without anyone moving the orange cones. "You're thinking Baboo witnessed the murder?"

Carter and Grandpa Stu nodded in tandem.

My heart nearly broke as I looked back at the bird who'd turned his back to all of us, unwilling or unable to share his grief. I stepped off the stool and motioned toward the door. "Let's leave him alone. He needs his space."

I grabbed my backpack off the counter and headed toward the door, Carter and Grandpa Stu in tow.

"It's too bad Baboo isn't talking," Carter muttered as I turned off the lights and opened the door to the outside world.

Too bad is right.

"S-snort. Snort. Snort. Snort."

I didn't look back as I pulled the door closed, locking each and every lock. Carter was right. Baboo could tell us so much. If he'd talk. But since that was proving more and more unlikely with each passing day, the only hope I had left was that he might teach Rudder the art of silence.

20

"Yowza at ten o'clock!"

I looked over my shoulder as I wound my way through the chest-to-chest crowd that lined the dance floor, certain (okay, praying) that I'd heard wrong. After all, the music was thumping as loudly in my ears and chest as it was inside the walls of The Car Crash. Surely that kind of deafening volume could distort a few words and wreak havoc on a sentence, right? Wrong.

While I'd been circling the room, scanning the tables and stools for Deserey, my grandfather was checking out the merchandise (and I don't mean the colorful T-shirts with the bar's logo ironed on the front). And as much as I hoped a *yowza* was a geriatric sleep-aid he took before bed each night, reality was hard to ignore. Grandpa Stu, in all his fringed-cowboy-shirt-tight-black-leather-pants-army-hat-wearing glory, was on the prowl.

I shot my best help-me face at Carter and flared my nostrils ever so slightly (*slightly* being the key word, since I'd promised Carter I would do my best not to ruin the look he'd slaved over). He nodded and whispered something to my grandfather, who rolled his eyes in response. Heaven forbid I put a damper on his mating ritual.

I continued on, threading my way between the throngs of women in skimpy tops (and even skimpier bottoms) and the kind of guys who found that attractive. Sidestepping a couple who brought new meaning to the phrase *joined at the hip*, I accidentally bumped into a man facing the opposite way.

"I'm sorry. Are you okay?" I touched his arm briefly, only to jerk away when he turned. Gary Zander. The hint of surprise that skirted his face was quickly chased away by a smile that set my radar pinging off the ceiling.

"Tobi Tobias! What a nice surprise," he shouted over the music. He wrapped his arms around my waist and pulled me in for a hug, his fingers finding their way through my crocheted top at record speed. "What are you doing here? You with someone?"

I resisted the urge to jerk my knee upward and opted instead to extricate myself as delicately as possible. He was, after all, my lone source of decent income these days.

"I'm here with a few people." I looked around wildly, hoping that Grandpa Stu had ignored Carter's whispered comment and found his way over to Miss Yowza anyway. An old man in leather pants and a sweeter-than-life redhead wouldn't exactly be seen as competition by a guy like Gary.

What I needed was a sidekick with a muscle-sculpted body and limited brain capacity. A problem, considering human cloning was illegal in this country and only one Gary Zander was available at the moment. And the original version was already standing there, hitting on me.

"Did you see the loser?" Gary asked, his breath warm and sticky against my ear.

I stood there, speechless, wondering how to answer such an obvious question without losing my one and only client. So I shrugged my confusion and waited for more information.

"Over there." Gary's right hand found a resting spot on the small of my back while his left hand pointed across the dance floor to a table inhabited by loud, obnoxious men who were drinking, smoking, and belching in true triathlon fashion.

I searched the men, tried to pick out a common face to the two of us, but came up empty.

"Who?" I finally asked.

"The ad idiot." He pointed in the same direction again, only this time I knew exactly who to look for. And I found him in mere seconds.

John Beckler sat just behind and to the left of the table I'd originally searched. His eyes were trained back on us, a scowl etched across his face. I watched him for a moment or two, determined not to look away. When I finally did, I spotted Mike next to him.

"His partner is so disgusting. See that ashtray in front of him?" Gary's hand slid up my back and stopped in the spot where the cami ended and the crocheted holes left access to bare skin. "He's been spitting his damn chew into it for the past half hour. If you look closely, you can actually see a mound of the crap from here. It's gross."

I refrained from lashing out at Gary in defense of Mike. Yes, my former boss had a nasty habit. He knew it. His wife knew it. Everyone knew it. But people dealt with stress in different ways. Chewing and spitting happened to be his way. Mine was Cocoa Puffs. (Okay, so Cocoa Puffs played a multifaceted role in my life.)

I looked back at John, a scowl still gracing his leathery face. No wonder Mike was chewing so much. John was *not* a fun person to be with when he was in one of his moods. But, as always, Mike was the consummate team player and business partner. And if going out with John from time to time kept their working relationship more even-keeled, he did it. Point for him. Me, I'd taken John Beckler for as long as I could, until the relentless putdowns, the competitive jockeying, and the account-stealing—oh, yes, more times that I can count—finally pushed me over the edge and into the role of small-business owner.

Sure, Gary Zander was a playboy. A slimy playboy. But he was what he was, and he made little attempt to be anything else. John Beckler, on the other hand, was a chameleon. One minute he'd be charming and hardworking, the next he'd be backstabbing and lazy. If they were the only two men left on earth, I'd pick Gary in a heartbeat.

"He passed by me the other night when I was, ah, waiting for someone. Except instead of spitting into ashtrays, he was emptying his chew onto a stone walkway, into a birdbath, and—you get my point. All while talking on his cell phone." Gary repositioned his hand on my back, his skin uncomfortably warm against mine. "Anyway, those two are lousy ad guys. Giving up on them and taking a chance on you was the best move Andy and I have made in a very long time."

I pulled my gaze off John and Mike and turned to face Gary. As annoying as the man was, he had a way of making me feel good. And when your ego was the size of a nickel, it was refreshing to get a confidence boost from time to time, regardless of the source.

In fact, the whole bar-scene thus far had been an ego boost. It was one of those places where men weren't the slightest bit shy about showing their appreciation for a pretty face. Their methods were varied like the ages and body types in the room, but they all had a few commonalities. Slow, lingering eye contact and opening lines so carefully crafted that one misspoken word resulted in an *oh crap* look from which only the truly strong (and psychotically persistent) ever recovered.

Like Gary.

"You wanna dance? I've got rhythm in places you wouldn't imagine." His eyes traveled slowly down my body and back again, a sparkle igniting his eyes.

"I don't have rhythm or want to dance, but I'm sure you can find someone who does." I poked my head upward in periscope fashion and looked around for Carter and Grandpa Stu and finally located them over by a pinball machine in the back left corner with Miss Yowza looking on in awe. Nothing like back-up when you needed it.

I swung my head in the direction of the bar, desperate to find something, anything I could use to get me out of standing next to a gyrating Gary with my former boss looking on. I knew I could— should—say hi to Mike, but I really wasn't in the mood for dealing with John Beckler.

And that's when I spotted Deserey. Though, truth be told, if I hadn't spent so much time talking to her on Monday, I'd never have recognized her. Her dark hair was no longer clasped behind her head in a tight bun. Instead, it cascaded down her shoulders in soft waves. Gone was the housekeeper uniform she starched as crisp as a board, in its place, a turquoise sheath that was sure to turn many a head. A sparkly turquoise bag was clutched in her hand. She was sitting at the corner of the L-shaped bar, her body turned toward the woman at her right, arms moving as she related something of great interest to her companion, a companion I was willing to bet big money was Larry and Linda Johnsons' housekeeper, Glenda.

"I've got to go, Gary. I see one of my friends." I took off through the crowd without so much as a glance over my shoulder, anxious to begin my detective work for the night (and to get out of dancing with Mr. Hands, formerly known as Mr. Roving Eyes).

I ran through a list of opening lines and decided a simple greeting was best. Deserey and I had clicked on Monday. There was no reason to think she'd forgotten that or the invitation she'd extended to meet her here.

"Deserey. Hi, how are you?" I pulled to a stop next to her bar stool and squeezed her shoulder gently. "It's good to see you out having a little fun."

Her face lit up in recognition and she slid off the stool. "Hi, Tobi! You look gorgeous. I love that top."

"Thanks. You look great too."

Deserey smiled, revealing ultrawhite teeth in the process. "Tobi, this is my friend, Glenda. She works for the Johnsons. I told you about her, remember?"

I didn't miss the quizzical look that shot across the other woman's face or the way her eyes narrowed when she met mine.

"Yes. Hi, Glenda. I'm Tobi Tobias. It's nice to meet you. Deserey speaks very highly of you."

The woman's features softened and she scooted over a stool, patting the one she'd just left. "Sit." I smiled my thanks and made myself comfortable as she continued on. "Tobias. Tobias. Why does that name sound so familiar?"

"Tobi is the woman who created the slogan for Zander Closet Company *and* the one who found Mr. Hohlbrook." Deserey lifted her half-empty glass and raised it to her lips, her eyes closing momentarily as she sipped the amber-colored liquid.

"Oh, okay, I remember now. All this media talk about your slogan predicting Mr. Hohlbrook's death must be really hard on you," Glenda said, her eyes pinning me.

I held my reply until I'd asked the bartender for some water and had helped myself to a pretzel from the bowl on the counter. "Yeah, it's been hard. Real hard. But it's nothing compared to the pain Deserey is carrying." Glenda nodded her assent and I looked at Deserey. "How are you holding up?"

She shrugged. "They're releasing his body tomorrow. We'll hold his memorial service on Friday." Her voice cracked as she pulled the red stir stick from her glass and tapped it absently on the bar. "And because of his company and all those employees, Mr. Hohlbrook's attorney is coming to the house in the morning to do an emergency reading of his will. All these people will be traipsing around the house with their hand out, hoping for something. It's going to be hard to get things ready for the post-service reception with so many people underfoot."

I studied Deserey as her hand moved the stick in a series of figure eights, her voice, her words, barely audible over the beat of the music. The woman was in pain. No fancy dress or new hairstyle could erase that fact.

Without thinking, I slid my hand across the bar and squeezed Deserey's. "Would you like a little company while that stuff is going on? I could help you ready the house for the reception."

Her face fell, her eyes watered. "Tobi, I'd love that. I can't ask you to help clean the house—I've got that down to a science—but I think the company would be nice."

"Consider it done." I thanked the bartender for my water and stole another pretzel from the bowl. "What time should I come?"

Deserey thought for a moment. "Um, how about nine thirtyish? The lawyer is coming at ten."

"Nine thirty it is." I squeezed her hand one last time and then looked back at Glenda. "How are the Johnsons taking all of this? It must be hard to lose their neighbor in such a horrific way."

Glenda snickered. "You'd think so, wouldn't you? But my employers are, hmmm, how can I say this tactfully? Let's just say Larry and Linda are a different breed. They want attention. They want praise. They want to be worshipped."

I listened politely, aware of one huge difference between the two women. Never in all our time together had I *ever* heard Deserey address her employers by anything other than their surname—even when it was painfully apparent that she considered Mr. Hohlbrook and his first wife to be her family. Yet, here was Glenda, all too willing to sully her employers to a complete stranger.

It was the difference between top-notch and mediocre.

"Those last few days leading up to the Showcase," she continued, "Linda had me recleaning sections of that house that I'd cleaned fifteen times in a row. All because she wanted it to be better than the Hohlbrooks' home. I wasn't surprised, of course. When it comes to anything related to the Hohlbrooks, Larry and Linda are determined to come out on top, no matter how they have to do it."

I shivered at her choice of words.

"You should have seen her after that segment on the news about your slogan. The television crew framed each shot with the Hohlbrooks' home in the background, and you couldn't see so much as a tree in our yard. Linda was furious. She badgered Larry for hours, carrying on like an absolute banshee. But it wasn't just her. He hated the way Mr. Hohlbrook was respected in this town. Drove him nuts. No matter how many charities he tried to get involved in to one-up Mr. Hohlbrook, no one ever seemed to notice."

"Did he have a temper?" I figured I was safe asking since the china-throwing incident had come to my attention from two different sources. (Though, in all fairness, the two sources had heard it from the same mouth—Glenda's.)

The woman guffawed. An honest-to-goodness guffaw. I wondered, briefly, if Rudder could imitate *that* noise.

"A temper? Think of a two-year-old who throws himself on the floor when he doesn't get the lollipop he wants: What's he do?"

When I realized she was waiting for an answer, I closed my eyes and tried to remember my last trip to the grocery store. A sheer nightmare if there ever was one.

"Kicks. Screams. Hits," I prattled off.

Glenda snapped her fingers together. "Voilà. I give you Larry Johnson."

I sat there quietly, trying to decide how much stock I put in Glenda's words. It didn't take a rocket scientist to see the woman liked gossip. And it didn't take a rocket scientist to see she didn't like her employers. So how much of what she said was true? How much was exaggerated for the good of the story? And could someone who smashed a set of expensive china during a temper tantrum kill someone out of jealousy?

The first few notes of "Y.M.C.A." carried across the room and I shivered unexpectedly. Call it intuition. Call it luck. Call it whatever you'd like. But when I heard that song, I knew immediately who'd be on the dance floor. I turned slowly on the stool and peered over the heads that separated me from a front-row seat.

Somehow, someway, Carter and Grandpa Stu had talked two unsuspecting (more likely, drunk) cohorts onto the lighted dance floor and were acting out the song that had both delighted and frightened generations of music lovers since its debut.

Although it was a tune that had seen its heyday long before I was born, "Y.M.C.A." was one of my grandfather's favorites. He liked to dance out the letters regardless of where we were when the song came on: restaurants, department stores, block parties, my sixteenth birthday party—oh yes, he did. While most kids' grandparents yelled, "Turn off that crap" when the Village People came on, my grandfather would invariably yell, "Turn it up." He said he liked the beat. I think it had more to do with some odd loyalty for the common, everyday slob, as evidenced by his evening's choice of attire—a nod, no doubt, to Jeff Olson's cowboy, Alex Briley's army man, and Eric Anzalone's biker dude.

I slid off my stool and grimaced. With any luck, neither Deserey nor Glenda (nor the entire bar, for that matter) would associate me with the crazy old man and the Annie-look-alike shaking their booty for the world to see.

"It was nice to meet you, Glenda." I shook her hand and then turned to Deserey. "I'll see you at nine thirty tomorrow, okay?"

Deserey nodded, her eyes on the dance floor behind me. I would have been mortified even further if not for the slow smile that crept across the woman's face. Her unbridled glee made me think of an expression my grandmother used to say. It was one she always used on me when I'd beg her to make Grandpa stop his nutty antics when my friends were around: *One woman's embarrassment is another one's joy, Tobi. And the joy is much more fun.*

As I made my way back through the crowd, I stole a sideways glance at the floor. Grandpa Stu had just made his *Y*, followed by Carter's *M*, and then the poor, unsuspecting drunks next to them made the *C* and the *A*. The applause was thunderous, the laughter contagious, as they continued the song to the bitter end. I stood near the door and waited, a smile tugging at my lips. As much as I wanted to pretend I didn't know them, I also knew I couldn't imagine my life without them.

It was a full fifteen minutes before Carter and Grandpa Stu made their way over to me. They were waylaid every five feet by their adoring fans, including Miss Yowza at my ten o'clock. As I stood and waited for them, I found myself having to step aside every so often to allow people in and out of the door. But that was okay. My vantage point gave me an opportunity to say good-bye again to Deserey and Glenda when they headed out to their cars, as well as a hiding place (behind the 300-pound bouncer) when Gary headed out to the parking lot a short time later.

"Hey there, Sunshine. How'd we look?"

I smiled at Carter and gave my grandfather a quick hug. "You guys were a hit. I'm surprised the manager didn't ask you back."

Grandpa Stu cleared his throat and puffed out his chest. "He did."

I fell in step between my two favorite guys in the world as we made our way out to the parking lot and Carter's Granada.

"So, what'd we miss? Did you get any good dirt?"

I looked over at my grandfather and grinned. "Well, if the house-keeper isn't being dramatic, the next-door neighbor hated Mr. Hohlbrook. Oh, and guess what? There's going to be an emergency reading of Preston's will in the morning and *I'm* going to be there."

We got into the car and settled back against the seats.

"Who was that young man who had his hands all over you? He someone I'm going to meet before I leave?" my grandfather asked from the backseat.

"Young man?"

"Aka Mr. Muscle Man," Carter said as he turned the key and backed out of the parking spot.

My stomach flip flopped. "You mean, Gary? Uh, no. He is not, nor will he ever be, my young man. He's simply a client who's a little—"

"Forward?" Carter asked.

"Handsy?" my grandfather interjected.

"Let's go with . . . interesting."

My grandfather snorted.

"Aha! So that's where you get it from," Carter said, smacking his left hand against the steering wheel as he shifted into drive with his right.

I ignored him. Much the way I ignore Rudder. But amid all the jokes, I realized something I'd neglected to find out. I'd wanted to ask Deserey about Blake, see if I could pinpoint a reason for the huge difference in our impressions of the Zander cousin.

Making a mental note to broach the topic in the morning, I reached behind my right shoulder and pulled the seat belt across my body. When it was clicked into place, I looked out the front windshield.

And that's when I saw them—Gary and Deserey. Together. And arguing.

I turned around in my seat as Carter drove by, my eyes glued to the pair.

Deserey's back was to me, but it didn't matter. Her anger was as red hot as Gary's. As he raked a hand through his hair in frustration, my eyes closed in on one thing . . .

Her purse. Her sparkly *glittery* purse.

21

Iflipped on my right blinker and slowed as I approached the Hohlbrooks' street the next morning, my thoughts bouncing between the argument I'd witnessed between Gary and Deserey in the parking lot of the bar and what, if anything, it all meant. The next few hours were destined to be interesting, and I needed to collect my thoughts and my game face.

For a brief moment during the night, I'd actually entertained the notion that Gary had been defending Blake against Deserey's wild accusations regarding an affair between the Zander cousin and Mitzi. But then I remembered the bad blood between Gary and Blake and discarded that theory. Yet nothing else made sense. At the moment, anyway.

When I got to the house, I'd simply ask Deserey about the incident outright. After all, it's not like I'd been eavesdropping or sneaking around trying to see what she was doing. The Village People and I had simply driven by and witnessed the argument. It would be more strange *not* to inquire, right?

"Right," I muttered to myself as I turned into the Hohlbrooks' driveway. A half dozen cars were parked along the right hand side of the circular drive, their occupants filing toward the front door with their heads bent low. If I had to guess, based on their attire and posture, I'd say that most of them were seated on the board of Hohlbrook Motors.

Preston's death brought more than just sorrow to those who knew and loved him. It also brought financial uncertainty to the hundreds of people who worked for him. There were the salesmen, the mechanics, the secretaries, the higher-ups—all folks who counted on their job as a source of income. And now, the owner of their company was dead, a victim of foul play.

I passed the line of cars and headed toward the parking area in back where I'd seen a Zander work truck just three days earlier. I wasn't there for the reading of the will, so it seemed inappropriate to enter the home as if I were.

The early morning sun felt good against my face as I stepped out of the car and headed down the stone walkway toward the Hohlbrooks' back door. Cardinals, finches, and blue jays flittered about while a small robin splashed happily in a nearby bath. If I didn't know any better, I'd think all was well in the world, that no one was hurting and no one was sad. But I *did* know better.

When I reached the back door, I peered inside. Deserey was mechanically scooping muffins out of tins and transferring them to a wide serving plate with a lace cloth. Her shoulders drooped as she worked, her hand stopping to wipe her brow a few times.

I knew there was very little I could do to ease her pain, but still, I hoped my presence would make the morning more bearable. At the very least, I could roll up my sleeves and help ready the house for tomorrow's reception.

I was just about to knock when Deserey suddenly looked up, our eyes meeting through the glass. The momentary surprise that flashed across her face was quickly replaced by a small smile as she waved me in. Considering the stress the woman was under, I'd take any iota of happiness she could muster. It was a start anyway. Baby steps . . .

"Hi, Deserey."

"Hi, Tobi." She gestured toward the archway that led to the front section of the house. "I've got to set these out for the guests; I'll be right back. Make yourself at home."

I peeled off my jacket and hung it on the brass rack beside the door. "Can I help carry anything?"

"That would be great—" Deserey cut herself short and shook her head. "No, I can't ask you to do that."

Grabbing the silver tea pot and tray of cups from the island, I met her tired eyes with a smile. "You didn't ask. I offered."

I shrugged off the gratitude that crossed her face and followed her through the archway and down the massive front foyer. A smattering of hushed voices came from the living room where people were obviously still in shock over the passing of Preston Hohlbrook. You could hear it in the pockets of conversation that emanated into the hall and in the tone of people's voices.

Deserey led the way into the living room and set her platter of muffins on the buffet table that she'd erected in the far corner. Her hands expertly removed the cups from my tray and set them out next to the tea pot. The muffins were placed nearby with a tiny rack of assorted spreads.

"Ms. Tobias? Is that you?"

I turned from the table and recognized Charlotte West immediately.

"Hello Ms. West. It's nice to see you again." I reached out and squeezed her hand. The stress of the past few days was evident in the many grooves and lines around the secretary's unsmiling eyes.

As I stood there and looked at her and Deserey, I couldn't help but recall something my grandfather once told me. He'd said it at a time when I was struggling with finding my place in high school: *You are known by the company you keep.*

And he'd been right, of course. I'd resisted the urge to change myself in favor of a higher rung on the popularity ladder. Instead, I'd chosen to enjoy my four-year high school career with the people who valued the things I did. When senior year came and it was time to cast votes for class superlatives, there had been one common theme in the way I'd been received by everyone. I wasn't voted most popular, or best chess player, or greatest athlete, or most likely to succeed in business. The superlative I'd received had been simple: most caring.

Deserey was a nice woman—loyal, true, hard working. Charlotte West demonstrated the same basic attributes. They both believed in Preston Hohlbrook and mourned his loss. Their decency and values had surely been shared by the CEO of Hohlbrook Motors.

"Are you here to help Deserey?" Charlotte West asked softly.

"I'm here to support her. She's struggling." I saw Charlotte nod in response, then watched the way she looked around the room and motion to a gentleman seated on the floral couch near the front window. The man stood and crossed the room toward us. His shoulders were broad, his posture strong and assured. His salt-and-pepper hair was cut short; his clothes were impeccable.

"Tobi Tobias, this is Tom Riker, vice president of Hohlbrook Motors." Charlotte stepped back so the man could extend his hand to me.

I grasped it and smiled. "It's nice to meet you, Mr. Riker."

He cocked his head to the side and studied me for a long moment, but oddly enough, I didn't find the silence to be awkward. "So *you're* Tobi Tobias." His mouth crept upward, his eyes sparkled. "I was expecting a—oh forget it. Just one more indication he's flipped his lid."

I was about to inquire about his odd statement when the tap-tap of stiletto heels made everyone turn and not a few eyes roll. Mitzi Hohlbrook.

Preston's widow stood in the archway, her hands clasped in front of her. This was a Mitzi I'd not seen before. A woman wearing a black suit that managed to hide her implants (how, I had no idea). Her long mane was pulled into a bun at the nape of her neck. I shuddered. There was something truly unnerving about a person who could transform their image so severely, so suddenly, and make it look effortless.

"Preston's attorney is settled in the library, and he is ready to begin the reading. He's asked that you all come in now." Mitzi tugged at her suit jacket and then nervously pushed a strand of hair off her face. Her discomfort in this life, with these people, was palpable and I couldn't help but feel as if, by changing her clothes and hair to fit the day's crowd, a little part of Mitzi had died along with Preston. Though, if I really thought about it, I knew it had died the day they got married.

I waited with Deserey as the mourners filed out of the living room and moved toward the library. Her shoulders drooped low.

"You okay, Deserey?" I asked quietly.

She busied herself by straightening the buffet table, her voice cracking when she finally answered. "All of this—the will, the memorial service tomorrow—it's just making it all real. It's not just a bad dream."

I draped my arm across the housekeeper's shoulders and pulled her close. Her pain was so real, so raw.

"You too, Deserey." Our heads both snapped up at the sound of Mitzi's voice—a voice that was no longer hesitant and humble as it had been when she addressed the room of Hohlbrook Motors' personnel just moments earlier. This tone was reserved for the help, and I found it nauseating.

"Excuse me, ma'am?" Deserey asked.

"The attorney wants you in there too." Mitzi turned and marched away, her chin pointed upward, her stiletto heels tapping firmly across the foyer.

Deserey's eyes were wide and confused as she looked at me. "Why on earth would they want me in there?"

I dropped my arm from her shoulder and took hold of her hand. "Because you were part of Preston's family. Now get in there. I'll be waiting when you come out."

She went. Nervously. I could see it in her tentative steps, the way she wiped her hands repeatedly on her straight black skirt, the way she'd stop every few feet and look back at me.

When she was finally out of sight, I finished straightening up the table and looked around the room, my gaze falling on the couch where Andy and I had sat less than a week earlier. I could still sense his hand draped behind me on the back of the couch, feel the warmth of his skin when he'd patted my shoulder.

I closed my eyes quickly and willed myself to think of something, anything, else. My thoughts had gone to Andy Zander too often lately. I needed to remember that even if my heart had fully recovered from Nick, Andy was my client. And he had a live-in female friend. Hanging my thoughts on an impossible relationship would be nothing short of stupid. And stupid, I wasn't.

Still, my mind replayed the events of that morning, including the way Mitzi had shed her sequined gown for the hot-pink cocktail dress. I smirked as I recalled her explanation for the change: *A few of my, sequins rip—popped off. I think I was just too much woman for those little threads.*

Too much woman? Or too much silicone?

I headed aimlessly out into the hall. It was weird to be on my own in a house like this with nothing to do except wander.

Without thinking, I found my way down the paneled hallway that had caught my breath just last weekend. The picturesque view of the bird sanctuary was peaceful and calming. I strolled over to one of the cushioned window seats, sat down, and pressed my head against the glass.

I'd so wanted to talk to Deserey, to ask her about the argument I'd witnessed in the parking lot. Instead, I was killing time in the hallway while chunks of her beloved employer's life were divvied up. Everyone waiting for their share of his fortune, while Deserey waited for someone to tell her that news of Preston's death had been a horrible mistake.

Only it wasn't. Not by a long shot. I grabbed the fringed throw pillow on the other end of the window seat and hugged it to my body. Life just wasn't fair sometimes. Especially when good people got caught in the crosshairs.

The morning sun streamed through the plate glass window, and I lifted my face to its warmth. Somehow, no matter how grim things seemed, the sun had a way of making me feel like anything was possible. Whether it was finding a client, paying bills, creating a slogan, or trying to find my way through a murder maze. I opened my eyes slowly and looked out at the birds as they flew from their feeder, to the tree, and back again. Happy, peaceful. The way everything should be.

Leaning back against the post, I pulled my legs up onto the cushion. I wasn't above basking in front of a window if that was the only place to get my recommended daily allowance of UV rays. The sun glistened across the strap of my ankle boot and reflected off a small shiny circle I hadn't noticed at first. I sat up, reached across the cushion, scooped the object up, and stared at the small, round silver sequin between my thumb and index finger.

And then it clicked. All of it.

Deserey and Gary arguing . . . The housekeeper's hatred of the Zander with the "hots" for Preston's wife . . . Mitzi's need to change clothes the morning of the shoot—the comment about her sequins being ripped off . . . The sparkly fleck that Gary had pushed out of his hair not more than ten minutes later . . . I'd seen that speck skip across the window seat, disappear under the same fringed pillow that I now held.

It wasn't Blake who was fooling around with Mitzi Hohlbrook, it was Gary!

I dropped my legs to the floor and jumped off the seat, my thoughts racing a mile a minute. It all fit, every last piece. Except one.

I'd been right next to Gary when Mr. Hohlbrook had called to complain about Blake. Why would he finger the wrong man?

Unless . . .

It wasn't *Mr.* Hohlbrook who called.

After all, it was *that* phone call that gave Gary the role of temporary closet installer, gaining him more frequent access to the Hohlbrook home and Mitzi. Not to mention the fact that it also resulted in a sidelining of his cousin and archenemy, Blake.

My stomach churned as I thought of the implications for Andy and his company, the inevitable hit to its reputation. Never mind the destruction that would be caused if Gary's misdeeds went beyond canoodling with the homeowner . . .

I shuddered.

Gary Zander was a playboy, plain and simple. But just because he couldn't keep his eyes and hands to himself, didn't mean he was capable of strangling someone and stuffing him in a closet, right?

God, I hoped not.

I wandered down the hallway and into the kitchen looking for what, I didn't know. A clue? An answer? Probably both. Just something, anything, that would point me in a direction other than Andy's brother.

A car door slammed out back and I jumped. My nerves were shot, my mind reeling with questions for which I had no definitive answers (at least not ones I liked). I glanced at the clock and prayed Deserey would finish up in the library and be able to deal with whoever was here. I simply wasn't in a place conducive for idle chitchat.

But the house remained quiet. The door to the library remained closed. Which meant one thing: I was on deck to answer the knock at the back door.

I walked across the hardwood floor and yanked open the door, my mouth falling open at the sight of the man who turned to face me.

Gary.

The shock I felt at seeing him was reflected in the eyes that peered back.

"Tobi. What are you doing here?" Gary shifted his weight from one leg to the other, his bottled tan doing little to mask the sudden whiteness in his face.

"Deserey asked me to come." I supposed that was a slight distortion of the truth, since I was the one who'd suggested it, but those were semantics I didn't feel the need to pick through for Gary. Instead, I focused my attention on the way he gulped when I said the housekeeper's name.

"You friends with Deserey or something?" Gary brought a clamped fist to his mouth and cleared his throat, once, twice, three times while he waited for my response.

I let him sweat for a few seconds. When I did respond, I kept my answer short. "Yes."

"Oh."

Scintillating conversation, sure. But it wasn't getting us anywhere. Nor was it answering the parade of questions marching through my head. So I took a gamble. A huge gamble.

"I saw you two last night."

"Who?" Gary asked.

"You and Deserey. In the parking lot. Arguing." I folded my arms across my chest and waited.

He raked his hand through his hair (no sequins this time) and dropped his shoulders. "Crap."

I waited.

He shifted. He coughed. He shifted again. Finally, he met my gaze head-on. "I did something stupid. Really stupid."

"Let me guess. Blake wasn't ogling Mitzi Hohlbrook, was he? You and Mitzi staged that call so you could install the system and have access to her." I saw his eyes widen, his mouth drop open, his cheeks redden ever so slightly. But I kept going. I mean, why not? If he was going to grab me and stuff me in the back of his truck for a quick trip to the river's bottom I might as well know everything before I sunk. Right? "Did you kill him?"

The genuine shock that splashed over his face caused a ripple of relief in me. My body sagged in response.

"What? Are you crazy? How could you think that?" Gary asked, his voice rising with each new word. "Why? Why would I kill him?"

I leaned against the doorjamb and sighed. "I'm sorry, Gary. I didn't know what to think. I just knew that everything pointed to you in terms of who was fooling around with Mitzi, and I guess the rest started stacking up."

Gary gestured me towards the three small steps that led to the stone walkway and sat down. I pulled the door shut and followed suit. He dropped his head into his hands and exhaled loudly.

"You're right. Mitzi and I were—*are*—attracted to each other. I know we went about it the wrong way, but having me install the closet gave us a chance to spend time together." He picked his head up and wiped a hand across his mouth. "Mitzi called me that day in your office. I pretended it was her husband. And as you know, it worked."

I wrapped my arms around my knees and linked my fingers. I had so many questions I wanted to ask, but didn't. This was Gary's turn to explain. And at the rate he was going, I figured he'd answer all my questions anyway. So I kept my mouth shut and listened.

"We thought we were being discreet, that her husband hadn't caught on. But he had."

And that's when I caved on the shut-mouth thing. The question flew out of my mouth before I even knew it was there. "Did he say something to you? Catch you two together?"

Gary shook his head. "Friday night, around nine o'clock, I picked Mitzi up. She told her husband she was going out with a friend. Only I think the tiger-print plunge-neck top and black mini skirt probably tipped him off."

"Why do you say that?" I asked.

"Because when Mitzi was leaving, he told her he *knew*. That it was time they both faced facts."

"Did he elaborate?" I prodded.

"No. But Mitzi was hysterical when she got in the car. Kept saying over and over that she was going to lose everything. I tried to calm her down, get her mind off it, but she was distracted all night long."

"Wait." I held up my index finger briefly and ran through the last few things Gary had said. "Did Mitzi *ask* him to elaborate?"

Again, he shook his head. "No. Apparently his phone rang and when he saw the number he rolled his eyes and said something about people not knowing when to give up. He answered it, agreed to meet with someone, then told her to go out and have fun. Told her they'd talk in the morning."

"He knew she was fooling around and told her to have *fun*?" I asked.

"I know. Weird, huh?"

Maybe. Unless he really didn't care anymore. I looked out at the still water in the bird bath and tried to process everything I'd heard. "When did you drop her back home?"

Gary's cheeks turned crimson, and he looked at the steps beneath his feet. "Look, I know I need to tell Andy about this, and I will—but not this minute, okay?"

I didn't answer.

Gary pushed off the steps, walked over to the birdbath, and peered at his reflection in the water. "I brought her back around six in the morning."

"Six in the morning? Sam and I were here at eight."

"I know. We wanted to make sure she had enough time to shower and dress. She used one of the guest bedrooms and planned to tell Preston she decided to sleep in there because she'd been too upset to get into his bed," Gary explained.

I looked away, focused instead on the bird feeder that hung from the ash tree to the right of the walkway. "And when Andy and I saw you coming out of the bathroom with your pants unbuckled?"

Gary tipped his head upward and stared at the blue sky for several long minutes before making eye contact with me for the first time all morning. "I hung out in the kitchen while she got showered and dressed, figuring I could explain my presence away with the whole photo shoot thing. Anyway, after you arrived, I guess she went off to freshen her makeup and that's when I saw her in the back hallway. One thing led to another and, well, I had a hard time keeping my hands to myself, and so we messed around a little."

"And you didn't see Preston? Or anyone else that morning?" I knew the questions were stupid even before I uttered them aloud, but I inquired anyway.

He shook his head. "No. Just Deserey. And she was livid."

"Can you blame her? You'd just returned from sleeping with her employer's wife." I knew my voice sounded snippy, but I really didn't care.

Gary crossed the distance between us in mere seconds, grabbed hold of my hands, and held them tightly. "I know I was a little forward with you a few times this week, but I was hurting. Mitzi hasn't wanted to talk, and it hurts like hell. But she'll come around. I know she will. It's too good for her not to." He closed his eyes briefly. "Tobi, we didn't plan for this to happen. We really didn't. Something just clicked between the two of us. I wish I could explain it, but I don't know how."

I inhaled slowly, deeply, searched for the courage to say what needed to be said. "Ask Blake. He understands all about unplanned clicking."

22

My head was pounding by the time I returned to my apartment at two thirty. The morning's drama had taken my emotions on the ride of their life, hurtling me through hills and dips that included everything from empathy and anger, to fear and confusion, and finally a startling detour into elation.

During the ride back to the Central West End, I'd briefly entertained the notion of stopping at the office to get a little work done. But when I thought about it, *really* thought about it, I knew I couldn't. I mean, what was the point? There were simply too many untied bows (read: stuff that made no sense) to ignore. And until I pulled those last loops tight, I'd be useless to everyone around me.

I turned the key and pushed the door open, anxious to be alone with my thoughts and a big bottle of Tylenol. Instead, a medley of BenGay, burned Pop Tarts, and heavy cologne greeted my olfactory sense with a sledgehammer to my aching head. Grandpa Stu.

I'd known he was still there. I'd pointed him in the direction of breakfast and kissed him good-bye on my way out the door that morning. But somehow, amid all the confusion of the past few hours, I'd completely forgotten the fact that my apartment was not mine alone. Not for the next few days anyway.

"Hiya, Sugar Lump. How'd it go?"

Suddenly all desire to be alone with my thoughts disappeared, in its place a reality I'd known all my life. There was no one better to have by my side during troubled times than my grandfather. He took one look at me (not a pretty sight, I'm sure) held out his arms, and waited for me to cross the room and plant my head against his chest. We stood that way for several long moments before I finally stepped back and sighed the biggest sigh of my life.

"Tell me about it." That's all he had to say. It's all he ever had to say to make the flood gates open and my troubles pour forth.

"I thought I had it figured out. I thought I'd narrowed Preston Hohlbrook's killer to one of two suspects, but I was wrong. I mean, I didn't want to believe he could do it, and I'm relieved to realize he didn't. But I just don't know what to make of things now."

Grandpa Stu simply nodded for me to continue, his eyes trained on every nuance of my face as I spoke.

"The whole idea that Andy's cousin had been making moves on Preston's wife didn't ring true once I met Blake. He's too decent. Too honest. Too in love with his wife. Yet Deserey had shown such anger when she spoke of the Zander employee and the way he'd been making moves on Mitzi that I guess I left open the possibility that my radar was off with Blake just as it so obviously was with Nick." I willed myself to slow down, to annunciate my words clearly so my grandfather could follow along despite my propensity to ramble when I was stressed. "Then, last night, I saw Deserey and Gary arguing in the parking lot of the bar. And things started to click in my mind even though it didn't truly hit me until I saw the sequin on the window seat cushion."

His eyebrow rose, but he remained silent.

"I started to wonder if maybe I'd been too quick to assume Deserey's anger was directed at *Blake* Zander. After all, there are two other Zander men. I knew it couldn't be Andy; she'd already said it wasn't and . . ."

My grandfather picked up where I left off. "And you sense that he's a truly good man."

I stared at Grandpa Stu. How he knew that, I hadn't a clue. I'd only brought Andy's name up once when we talked on the phone. Probably uttered it a second time (okay, maybe six or seven times) over the course of the past twenty-four hours since he showed up on my doorstep, suitcase in hand.

I ignored the knowing sparkle in my grandfather's eyes and continued. "So that left Gary. Especially when I factored in that Gary was the one who'd taken the call about Blake, made the command decision to remove him from the Hohlbrook job, and stepped in as the installer."

"There was no call, was there?" my grandfather asked, pleased with himself.

I shook my head. "There *was*, only it was staged. By Gary and Mitzi."

Grandpa Stu leaned back against the sofa and brought his right foot up to rest on his left knee. I recognized the pose. It was his infamous sleuthing pose. Or the early stages of it, anyway. "Then how can you be so sure he didn't do it? He seems a safe bet in my book."

"I asked him outright."

My grandfather's foot dropped to the ground with a thump. "You *asked* him? Tobi, what would have happened if he had and he decided to get rid of you too?"

I put my hand on his knee and squeezed, gently. "I'm here, aren't I?" I leaned to my right and planted a kiss on his temple. "Besides, Gary Zander's behavior may be questionable at times, but despite all his womanizing, I think he's an okay guy. I guess my gut knew that even if my brain didn't."

"Okay, so what about Mitzi? If this Preston fella was as wealthy as the papers say, maybe she killed him for the money."

I could see how his mind could make that leap. It was the same one mine made when I realized Gary wasn't responsible for Preston's murder. So I pointed out the same thing Gary had told me.

"She couldn't have. She was with Gary all night long. Even Deserey attested to that when I asked her after the reading of the will." I slid out of my jacket and tossed it onto the armchair. The apartment was stifling hot despite the crisp autumn temperatures.

My grandfather shrugged his apologies. "Sorry, Tobi. I was cold, so I turned up the heat."

I smiled an okay at him and forced myself to ignore the utility meter (aka cash sucker) spinning in my head. Sam and I would begin work on Zander's print brochure on Saturday, which meant another paycheck.

"So how'd the will go? Mitzi keep her lifestyle?" My grandfather resumed his sleuthing pose and waited for my reply.

"No! I mean, yeah, she got some money. Probably enough to keep her from ever having to work. But she didn't get the two biggest assets." I felt the same shock and disbelief at my retelling of the events as I did when Deserey shared the outcome around crying jags and stunned silence. "Hohlbrook Motors was essentially divided. Fifty percent of all profits will go to the Loving Hands and Helping Hearts charity his beloved first wife founded. The other half will be shared among the four employees who have been with Preston since the company's birth—including his secretary, Charlotte West."

"And the house?"

"Deserey got it." The words still seemed so strange, so unbelievable. But I was thrilled for the woman who had loved Preston and Alana Hohlbrook with every ounce of her being.

I recognized the look that flashed across my grandfather's face. It was the same expression I'd seen in Gary's when Deserey shared the news of her new home.

"No," I said in a preemptive strike. "Deserey had nothing to do with Preston Hohlbrook's murder. I'm positive of that. She didn't have so much as an inkling she would get that house. No one could fake that kind of surprise, not even an Oscar-winning actress."

Grandpa Stu stood and walked over to the front window, parting the curtain just enough to peek outside. What he was looking at or for, I had no clue. "How'd Mitzi take news of the house going to the maid?"

I half turned on the sofa so I could have a better view of my grandfather. "She wasn't thrilled. But I think she was able to overlook it somewhat thanks to the money *she* got. I overheard her whispering to Gary afterward that she'd been afraid she'd be cut out completely."

He straightened his shoulders and cleared his throat, all the while looking at whatever it was he was watching. "How do you think Deserey will handle a house like that?"

I pushed off the sofa and wandered over to the window, curious to see what had captured my grandfather's attention. All I could see was Ms. Rapple and Gertrude.

"I think she'll be fine. She has taken such pride in that home, in keeping it the way Mr. Hohlbrook liked. If anything, I think her biggest problem will be coming to accept it as *her* home rather than her employer's." I leaned against the wall and rolled my eyes at Gertrude's restroom selection. Not a big surprise considering I'd already replaced two mums in as many weeks.

"So who killed Preston Hohlbrook?"

I pulled my gaze off Ms. Rapple's ornery little pooch and fixed it on my grandfather. "I haven't a clue. Which means the media continues their degradation of my slogan and me."

"Then don't give up until you figure it out."

My grandfather had a way of cutting to the chase. His listening was second to none, his shoulder perfect for crying jags. But when push came to shove, he'd leave you with a comment or suggestion that would plague your thoughts until a solution was found. Like now.

I was just about to tell him I was trying, to run him through the paths I'd followed over the past five days, but my effort was cut short by a knock. I pushed off the wall and headed toward the door, my thoughts once again on the list of suspects that had dwindled to none.

I tugged the door open and grinned when I saw who it was.

"Hi Sam. Come in." I stepped back and let Mary Fran's son pass by, a large black backpack straddling his shoulders. "Think you've got enough homework in there?"

The tow-headed teenager snickered. "My teachers apparently don't. They keep giving us more and more and more."

My grandfather walked over, shook Sam's hand. "Hello, son. When are you going to quit growing? You must be eating your mom out of house and home."

Sam's face broke into a wide grin as he returned the firm shake and then used his extended arm to pull my grandfather in for a quick hug. "Grandpa Stu, when'd you get into town?"

"Yesterday, 'bout five or six."

"It's good to see you, sir." Sam lowered the backpack down his arms, set it on the floor behind the sofa and planted a quick kiss on my cheek in the process. "Mom said you stopped by the shop last night to feed Rudder. What'd you think of Baboo?"

I felt my body deflate at the thought of Preston's bird—at his obvious sadness, at the way he'd stopped speaking, at the fact that I had failed in finding the person responsible for his beloved owner's death.

I walked into the tiny kitchen area, grabbed a handful of cookies from the jar, and carried them out to Sam. He took one without hesitation. "He looked better than the day I brought him to your mom, but he still wouldn't talk. In fact, when he heard us mention Preston's name, he turned his back to us. It was really quite heartbreaking."

Sam quietly chewed. When he was done, his eyes strayed to the two remaining cookies in my hand. "It's true he's not talking to us. But we're pretty sure he's communicating with Rudder."

I handed Sam the last of the cookies. "Why do you say that?"

Shoving the pair into his mouth, Sam mumbled a thank you. "Because Rudder's learned a new sound over the past few days, and he didn't get it from mom or me. Or anyone else for that matter. Which leaves Baboo."

My grandfather left his post at the front window and grabbed his black-leather loafers from the unofficial shoe-drop spot beside the door. "Got any polish, Tobi?"

Polish? What would I polish? I shook my head and continued my conversation with Sam.

"At least that's some comfort, I guess. It's been tearing me up thinking this bird is suffering so horribly, and I haven't been able to do anything to help—" I lost my train of thought at the sight of my grandfather and a wad of paper towels. He was a man on a mission.

"Baboo will be okay, Tobi. Mom's fairly optimistic that he'll pull through this. And she thinks Rudder is the best medicine of all."

I couldn't help it, I laughed. "Interesting, considering Rudder gives *me* agita . . ."

"Martha sure looks pretty today," my grandfather said quietly.

"*Martha?*"

"Yes. Your next door neighbor, Martha Rapple. She was outside just now and she looked—"

"Since when are you on a first-name basis with Ms. Rapple?" I inquired, my stomach feeling the slightest bit queasy as I waited for his response.

"Since we had thirty minutes alone in the car yesterday." My grandfather held his fingers side by side and shoved his left hand into his shoe.

"Excuse me?" I stole a glance in Sam's direction to see if I was missing something, but he looked as perplexed as I felt. "You spent thirty minutes alone in a car with Ms. Rapple? Yesterday? How? When? And, even more importantly, *why?*"

Grandpa Stu turned his shoe-topped hand from side to side and carefully inspected his loafer. "When I called Carter to ask him to come get me at the train station, he was running out the door to that theater place he hangs out at all the time. I told him I wanted to surprise you, so he suggested I call Martha. She was more than happy to oblige."

I bet she was. In the two years I'd known her, Ms. Rapple was only pleasant when my grandfather was visiting. Even Mary Fran and Carter had picked up on it, giggling at the idea of fixing them up and sending them on a date. I'd said something about hell freezing over and discarded the notion right then and there. As a result, I'd never let my mind dwell on the remote possibility that the interest might one day be mutual.

I pulled my bottom lip inward with my top teeth and tried to think of something to say, something to do to stop the wreck before it happened. Unfortunately, the only ideas I came up with had me throwing myself across the door and grounding my grandfather for the rest of his life. Neither of which I imagined would go over very well.

"*Pphhtt.*"

I snapped my head up and stared at my grandfather as he hocked a giant, wet loogie onto his shoe. When he was pleased with its circumference, he began slowly working it into the leather with a paper towel. When it wouldn't spread any further, he did it again.

"*Pphhtt.*"

Sam clapped his hands and laughed. "That's it! That's it! He's spitting!"

I looked at Mary Fran's son. "What are you talking about?"

"That's what Rudder's doing! He's spitting! *That's* the sound that Baboo taught him!"

I heard the garbled sound escape my lips, felt the cool linoleum against my knees. But I couldn't stop the room from spinning. Sam's words, sweet and innocent, had knocked the air from my lungs, their terrifying reality hitting me with a sucker punch to the gut I would never forget.

23

Have you ever looked at a picture from a slightly different angle only to spot something in the background you'd never noticed before? Or listened to a song you'd heard a million times and finally realized what the fifth word in the third line was—and that it totally changed what you'd *thought* the song was about?

That's what my world felt like at that exact moment. The picture's seemingly inconsequential background was now the focal point. The strange rambling lyrics were now poetic. And I was a certifiable idiot for not putting two and two together until now.

I took several slow, deep breaths and opened my eyes, anxious to see if the walls had stopped spinning. But I couldn't see them, didn't know if they were spinning or moving or sticking their tongue out at me. All I could see were two worried faces pressed close to mine, each wearing the same clueless expression I'd been sporting since finding Preston Hohlbrook's body.

"You okay, Tobes?" Sam pressed the back of his hand to my forehead while my grandfather checked the pulse in my neck. "You look a little—"

"Sick," Grandpa Stu interjected. "You need a puke bucket?"

Good Lord, a puke bucket? I hadn't needed one of those in ten years, thanks to a disinterest in alcohol, a good immune system, and stellar eating habits. (Okay, so maybe *stellar* was a stretch, but how often do you hear of people getting food poisoning from Cocoa Puffs and chocolate bars?) It was a decade-long streak I wasn't about to break now.

"I'm okay. Really." I struggled to my feet and accepted the bottle of water from Sam's outstretched hand. The cold liquid felt good against my throat and slowly helped to wipe away any lingering fog. "I . . . I just . . ."

My grandfather's whitish-gray eyebrows dipped downward as he studied me from head to toe. I recognized the look as one I'd gotten many times over the past twenty-eight years. Usually when I'd been talking a mile a minute and he was trying to catch up.

"What's going on, Sugar Lump? What did I miss?"

I reached out and squeezed his hand. "It's what *I* missed, Grandpa. Not you. It was right there all along, and I just didn't see it. Now that I do, it makes perfect sense."

"Tell me about it." He turned his hand inside mine and led me over to the sofa, Ms. Rapple no longer the focal point of his thoughts or actions. It was a comforting place to be and one I didn't take for granted.

I sunk onto the cushion beside my grandfather and rested my head on his shoulder the way I had so many times before. Yet this time was different. I'd run a race completely on my own, and I'd figured out so much about myself in the process.

"I know who did it, Grandpa."

Those six little words felt incredible as they rolled off my tongue and out my mouth. It was what I'd been trying to figure out all week, what I'd focused virtually every waking thought on since realizing the answer was about more than just fitting the final piece in a tricky puzzle or finding a way to salvage the reputation of my company. It was about right and wrong. About finding justice in the wake of evil.

I felt his shoulder pull back just before he guided my focus onto him via a finger beneath my chin. "What are you saying?"

"I'm saying that I know who killed Preston Hohlbrook. Baboo's been trying to tell us since that very first morning. Only no one listened."

Sam walked around the end table and dropped onto the armchair. "You mean the noise he taught Rudder?"

I nodded. "Exactly. Think about it. He said one sentence over and over that first day. Do you remember what it was, Sam?"

Sam scrunched his face in concentration. "All I remember is something about his daddy."

"His daddy?" my grandfather asked.

"Yes. That's what he called Preston. He would say 'Baboo's Daddy' and then make that spitting sound. He did it two or three times before we ever went in the closet and found Mr. Hohlbrook's body. Remember?"

Finally Sam's eyes showed the confirmation I'd been waiting for. "Now that you say it, yeah, I remember. But what does that have to do with the killer? And how does that tell you who did it?"

I turned to my grandfather. "Do you remember what you and Carter said at the pet shop the other night? About Baboo being a witness to the crime? He was! That sound is his way of trying to tell us who did it. It's a sound he must have heard during the crime and/or the hiding of Preston's body."

"But who would spit like that during a crime?"

"Someone who is addicted to chewing tobacco. Someone who chews and spits it morning, noon, and night." I heard the rise in my voice, felt the quickened beat of my heart as I rushed to explain my thought process. "Someone who saw the writing on the wall for his company."

"Who?" Sam asked.

"Mike Stanley." There was something enormously validating, yet painfully sad, about saying his name aloud, voicing my suspicions for others to hear and digest. I recalled our lunch together and the way he'd reacted when I said Zander Closet Company was their agency's loss and my gain.

It was sure looking that way, wasn't it? The loss potential there was enormous.

I'd taken the comment as confirmation that he, too, saw Preston's murder as a blotch on my career. A blotch that was so big, so messy, that I'd never be a threat to Beckler and Stanley—or any other advertising agency in town.

Yet that's not what he'd meant at all. The success of my slogan was getting noticed by big clients. His and John's big clients. The loss potential to their company was enormous. A loss he had to nip in the bud.

My grandfather closed his eyes and said nothing for a full minute, his finger tapping his chin as he sat in silence. Sam's mouth gaped open while he looked around the room in an obvious attempt to place a name he'd heard many times before.

When Grandpa finally spoke, his words were slow and measured, as if he was unsure of how to proceed. "That's the fella you used to work with at that ad agency, isn't it? The one who took you under his wing and showed you the ropes? The one who encouraged you even when your other boss was being so lousy?"

Sam chimed in as his memory, too, clicked into place. "I thought you liked him."

I blinked at the sudden burning in my eyes. "Yeah. That's him. And I did like him. I respected him. Looked up to him. That's why this hurts so much.

"Look. I know how this sounds, I really do. But there are pretty substantial dots that led me to him. Baboo's noise just connected them all together." I looked from my grandfather, to Sam, and back again, and waited for any sign that they were following my train of thought.

When there was none, I continued. "I think it hit me this morning. Or, rather, my subconscious. But Sam, when you pinpointed Baboo's sound to a spit, my mind immediately went to Mike. And that's when everything started to make sense." I half-turned on my cushion so I could see both Sam and my grandfather at the same time. "The other night at the bar, Gary said he'd seen Mike while he was waiting for someone. That he was spitting his chew onto the stone walkway and into the birdbath."

"How does that make him the killer?" Sam asked as he slid off the arm chair and moved closer to the sofa.

"Gary always parked by the service entrance to the Hohlbrook house. It's the same place I parked this morning." I stopped to take a breath, then hurried on when I saw the blank look on my grandfather's face. "There's a stone walkway and a birdbath on the way to the Hohlbrook's back door."

I heard the conviction in my voice as I put my cards on the table and waited for my *atta girl*. But it didn't come. At least not in the fast-and-easy manner I'd expected.

"There are stone walkways and birdbaths in yards all over St. Louis," Sam said quietly.

"But don't you see? Gary was waiting out in the driveway for Mitzi on Friday night." I heard the exasperation in my words but couldn't stop it. This was easy. The puzzle was fitting perfectly. Why couldn't they see that?

"Did Gary say that's when he saw Mike?" My grandfather rubbed his hands over his eyes and mouth and then leaned his head against the back of the sofa. He looked tired, worn out.

"Well, no. But it fits." The words poured from my mouth as I tried to make them see what I was seeing, to realize I was right even though it was painful for me to admit. Mike Stanley killed Preston Hohlbrook. "Gary didn't want to tell me who he'd been waiting for, and now I know why. He didn't want to admit he had a thing with Mitzi. But sitting in his truck, waiting, he'd have had a clear view of the stone walkway and the birdbath."

"Okay. Let's say you're right. Why would this Stanley fella have been at the Hohlbrooks' house on a Friday night?" Grandpa Stu crossed his arms against his chest and waited for more details.

"Because my slogan for Zander was getting fantastic media coverage and Preston had noticed. He hated the campaign Beckler and Stanley had created for Hohlbrook Motors and wanted to talk to me. Losing Hohlbrook Motors would have been devastating for their agency.

"And, on top of that, Andy told me that he'd taken a call from Craig Miticker about me. They're old college buddies. I wasn't privy to the conversation between them, but whatever was said left Andy with the distinct impression that Craig Miticker was interested in working with me too."

"Who's Craig Miticker?" Sam asked from his spot on the floor.

"The brains behind New Town out in St. Charles." I grasped Grandpa Stu's knee and rushed to fill in the blank spots. "Losing Hohlbrook Motors would be pretty devastating to Beckler and Stanley all on its own. But losing New Town *on top* of that would have been absolutely crippling to their hold in the St. Louis area. A dozen little companies, heck *two* dozen little companies, can't compare to the kind of revenue one of the big accounts can bring in."

"Interesting . . ."

I stared at my grandfather. "It makes sense to you, doesn't it? Please, Grandpa, you've got to see this."

He scooted forward on the sofa and pulled me in for a quick hug. "Oh I see it, Sugar Lump, I see it. But we still need confirmation. You can't take this to the cops without a little more to go on."

"Confirmation of what?"

"That it was really Mike that Gary saw, and that it was really Friday night that he saw him." Sam pulled up on his knees and tossed me the phone.

"You're a smart young man, Sam," my grandfather said as he raised his hand to the teenager. Sam grinned and high-fived him back.

Normally, I'd have seized that statement as an opportunity to pout, to demand my well-deserved accolades. But today wasn't normal. Nothing about this scenario was normal or right.

"Call Gary." My grandfather pointed at the phone.

I jumped up, walked over to my backpack, and rifled through it until I came to Gary's business card. Consulting the mobile number on the bottom left corner, I punched in the numbers and waited (not so patiently).

"Gary, here."

"Gary, it's Tobi."

"Hey." His voice was lacking its usual playboy banter, its tone now wary. It's funny, but I'd turned a corner in my thinking of Andy's brother. Sure, I still disapproved of his playboy ways, how could I not? But as disappointing as that was, I'd seen something real, something genuine in his eyes when he spoke of Mitzi that morning. The apprehension in his voice over telling his brother what he'd done had also been real. And so was the reason: He didn't want to disappoint Andy.

"I need to ask you a very important question." I wanted to tell him it was okay, to reassure him I wouldn't tell Andy about his fling with Mitzi, but I had more pressing things to discuss with him. "Remember how you told me you waited outside for Mitzi on Friday night?"

"Yeah . . ."

"Did you see anyone while you were sitting out there? Anyone at all?" I held my breath as I waited for his reply, felt my grandfather's cheek against mine as he moved in to hear.

"Besides Mitzi?"

I bit my tongue from screaming yes at the top of my lungs. Instead, I gave my assent in a more subdued manner. "Yes, besides Mitzi."

"No. Why?"

I felt my stomach drop to my knees as my grandfather straightened up and moved away.

"Wait! That's not right."

I sucked in my breath at the change in Gary's response. Grandpa Stu's eyes widened, and he resumed his pose just in time to hear Gary continue.

"I saw Mike. Mike Stanley. But he was on his cell phone and looked like he was pretty engrossed, so I'm not sure he saw me."

Grandpa's fist rose into the air and I caught Sam's smile in return. We had him. We had the killer right where I suspected.

"Did you tell the cops that?" I asked quickly.

"No. Mitzi didn't want my name getting wrapped up in this. She was afraid our"—he stopped, sucked in a breath, and then let it out—"affair would bring the cops sniffing around at her door. And Lord knows I didn't want Andy to find out either."

My grandfather slid his hand over the mouthpiece of the phone. "Ask him what else he remembers."

I nodded. But as I was about to inquire, our conversation from that morning loomed large in my thoughts. *When he saw the number he rolled his eyes and said something about people not knowing when to give up.*

"Oh my God," I muttered aloud, as more pieces began to fall into place.

"What?" Gary asked.

"This morning, when you were telling me about Preston's reaction to Mitzi going out Friday night, you said he got a call. That when he saw the number, he rolled his eyes and commented on people not knowing when to give up."

"Yeah, that's right. Mitzi said he was tense when he hung up the phone."

"How long was Mike on the phone when he passed you by?" I asked, knowing what the answer would be.

"Not long. Maybe a minute or two. Certainly no more than that."

I looked at my grandfather as he pulled away from the phone for a moment, his eyes beaming with pride as he met my gaze straight on. His lips mouthed the words *good work.*

But I wasn't done. Not quite yet. "Gary, is Mitzi around by chance?"

There was a hesitation on the other end, and I rushed to allay his fears in favor of the final confirmation I needed. "Look, Gary. What you do with your personal life is your business. I'm not asking about Mitzi to check up on you. I'm asking because I think I figured out who killed her husband. Is she there, Gary?"

The slight background sounds evident during the call were muffled momentarily and then replaced by a now familiar voice.

"I'm here, Tobi."

"Mitzi, when you left the house Friday night, who did you pass?" The question was rather rhetorical since I knew the answer. But it was really just the initial step to get me where I wanted to be.

"Mike Stanley."

"Were you expecting him?" I asked quickly.

"I wasn't. But I think Preston was," Mitzi said, her voice quivering.

"Why do you say that? Did he tell you he was waiting for Mike?"

"No. But when I was walking out, he told me to leave the door open. That he needed to have a word with someone who was on their way in." It sounded as if Mitzi blew her nose before continuing. "Mike was the only person I saw."

I'm not sure if I thanked Mitzi for her time, or even if I said good-bye. The only thing I was aware of was the look on my grandfather's face when I pulled the phone from my ear.

"It's him, isn't it?"

I nodded, my voice suddenly missing in action. It was a hollow victory in a lot of ways. Sure, Preston Hohlbrook's killer would be brought to justice, and my agency could get out from under the media's high-powered spotlight. But in discovering the whodunit, I'd lost someone I'd looked up to, respected. And that's the kind of loss that was hard to set aside.

Grandpa Stu slid his arm around my shoulders and met the side of my head with his own. As always, he got it. Got me.

We stood that way for what seemed like an eternity. Until I broke the silence with a question I wanted to ask, yet knew was unanswerable. "What is it about men and my inability to find decent ones? I mean, I really believed Nick was the one I was going to spend the rest of my life with. I thought he was my soul mate—the person I was going to have and to hold from this day forward, forsaking all others, you know? But he wasn't. He was bedding another woman the whole time. And with Mike, I thought I'd found a mentor—someone who could show me the ropes of the advertising world with honor and integrity. Yet he had neither." I closed my eyes against the tears I refused to shed. Crying didn't fix things. Understanding did. "When am I going to get with the program and start *seeing*? Or, better yet, when am I going to finally cut my losses and stop trying?"

"Hopefully never." Grandpa Stu turned and faced me, his wrinkled, yet powerful hands holding my forearms. "Sugar Lump, they weren't men. Not that Nick fella who broke your heart, or this Mike Stanley person who broke your trust. Real men don't do that."

I looked up at my grandfather and peered into the eyes that had guided me through life with love and faith. Then I looked at Sam, at the gentle, loving young man who had more wisdom and sensitivity than guys three times his age.

Once again, Grandpa was right. All I needed to do was find a man of their caliber, somewhere between the ages of fifteen and seventy-five.

24

The ride out to Brentwood was quiet. Some of that, I suppose, was the simple fact it was seven forty-five on a Saturday morning. Some, because my passenger's face was buried in the front page of the *St. Louis Post-Dispatch* reading the print version of the past day and a half of my nutso life.

"Hey, it says in here that Mike Stanley confessed," Sam said.

Looking out my (okay, *Mary Fran's*) side mirror, I slid into the far left lane of Highway 40. We were making good time, but I didn't want to run the risk that a few pokey lights on Brentwood Boulevard would make us late for the closet shoot. "He did. Apparently, when the cops pulled him in for questioning, he caved. Said he never meant to kill Preston, but that their argument got out of hand. And then fear took over."

Sam reached into the bag between our seats, extracted a glazed Krispy Kreme donut, and shoved it in his mouth. "Annnd ou ere ight?"

"Come again?" I asked with mock seriousness as I stole a sideways glance at my friend's son, his mouth stuffed with glazed-covered carbs.

He shot his left index finger in the air for a moment, and I looked back at the road in time to see the half-mile warning for the exit I needed. With a quick glance into the rearview mirror, I maneuvered Mary Fran's Beamer across the two right lanes.

"What I asked was if you were right? You know, about the reason he killed Mr. Hohlbrook."

"Ohhhhh, is that what you said? Because I distinctly heard 'ou ere ight'."

It felt good to laugh out loud, to goof off without worrying about my company, or Zander's reputation, or who killed Preston Hohlbrook. It was done. Over with. Time to move on.

"C'mon, Tobes. Cut me some slack here. I'm hungry."

I flicked on my blinker and exited onto Brentwood Boulevard North. "You're *always* hungry, Sam."

"Now you sound like my mother." The teenager wiped his face with the napkin and tossed it into the empty sack.

"There are worse things than that." I stopped at the first of three lights that stood between us and the offices of Zander Closet Company. "Anyway, yeah, I was right. Mike didn't want to lose the Hohlbrook account. It was one of the agency's biggest cash cows. He saw it as the card that would make the entire house tumble. He knew that kind of loss would be devastating. Get this, he even tried to blackmail Preston into staying with Beckler and Stanley, but it backfired. Blackmail only works on people who have—"

"Skeletons in their closet?" Sam interjected, a face-splitting grin moving across his face in tandem with the mischievous sparkle that danced in his eyes.

"Yeah. Skeletons." It was hard to ignore all the ways my slogan fit into the goings-on of the past week. But it was a coincidence. And I knew that. Or, at least, I kept telling myself that. "After Mike killed him, he actually thought he still had a chance at keeping the Hohlbrook Motors account at Beckler and Stanley. Thought his chances were *better* in fact, because they could start fresh with a new CEO. Can you believe that? And that's not all. He claims he didn't set out to tie the murder to my slogan, but when he decided to shove the body in the closet he realized the potential it created and the clients it would help them keep."

"Go, Tobes."

"Huh?" I looked my confusion at the tow-head in the passenger seat.

He pointed out the front windshield. "It's green. You can go."

"Thanks."

"Tobes?"

"Uh-huh?"

"There's something I don't get," Sam said as he looked out the window at the cars and buildings.

"What's that?"

"Where was Mike's chew? The stuff he spit out? Why didn't the cops find it in Mr. Hohlbrook's room?"

I grinned. Sam was smart. Like his mom. "He didn't need chew to spit. Never did. It had become such a habit that, oftentimes, he simply did an air-spit. I suspect that's what Baboo heard."

"An air-spit?"

"Yeah. Same basic noise but only air comes out."

Sam nodded and then posed yet another question as he reached down to his camera bag and hoisted it onto his lap. "Is Mitzi going to face charges for not telling the police she saw Mike that night?"

"I don't think so. She was scared. Mike had left her a voice mail that same night, threatening to tell everyone he saw Gary waiting in the driveway for her." I pulled into a parking spot by the front door and shifted into park. "She knew Preston was suspicious but didn't want to give him concrete proof. She was afraid of being tossed out on her ear without so much as a penny."

"So why didn't she blab when she realized Preston was dead?"

"Because somehow, Mike had convinced her that the affair with Gary would nullify anything Preston had left her in his will." I grabbed my purse and reached for the door handle.

"She believed that?"

"Yeah. Believability was one of Mike's biggest assets. Trust me, I know."

"He sure must have been desperate, huh?"

Desperate didn't begin to cover it.

We climbed out of the car and walked side by side up the front steps.

"Rich people can be kind of screwy, huh?" Sam pulled open the door and motioned me in.

"Some, I suppose. But Preston Hohlbrook was a good man. And even Mitzi is okay. She was just out of her league. What's *really* screwy is someone who is so competitive and so desperate that they'd take another person's life to keep their edge."

I stepped into the elevator, with Sam in tow, and pushed number three. "Time to focus. We need great stuff today, okay?"

Sam flexed his right arm and puffed out his thin chest. "No problemo, Tobes. We'll light it on fire."

I leaned my head against the elevator wall and sighed. "No fire, please. Murder was enough." The chime for the third floor sounded, and the doors skirted open in front of us. I stepped out and eyed Zander's door at the end of the long hallway. In all the drama of the past day, I hadn't stopped to wonder if Andy would be mad. Until now. He'd specifically told me to stay out of the investigation and I'd pretty much (okay, out and out) ignored him. But he had to understand, right? I mean, his company's reputation wasn't the only one on the line. And besides, once I got to know Deserey and Baboo, Mitzi and Blake, and yeah, even Gary, I couldn't walk away. It just wasn't what I was about. I could only hope Andy would understand.

"Eight o'clock on the dot," I mumbled under my breath as Sam pushed open the door and strode into the waiting room. The office was silent except for the quiet hum of the fluorescent overhead light. "Andy? Are you here?"

"Yup. I'll be right there."

My skin tingled at the sound of his voice, and it didn't scare me any longer. It was as if finding Preston's killer had given me a courage—a belief in myself that I'd allowed Nick to squelch. And that was *my* fault.

I flipped open a magazine and stared, unseeingly, at the first page. My thoughts had wandered me back to one of my grandfather's fondest sayings: *Every experience in life makes you who you are, Tobi.*

And, once again, he was right. The breakup of my engagement with Nick had been devastating. It had made me judgmental, wary, and even a little cynical. But *I'd* allowed it to have that effect. Nick was one guy. Just like Mike Stanley was one guy. There were far more good people in my life than there were clunkers. I just needed to find a way to learn from all of them, because in learning I would grow stronger. Better.

I was just making a mental note to give my grandfather a big hug when Andy came around the corner. I immediately noticed the way his hair glistened from the overhead light, the way his hand touched Sam's shoulder as he passed by, the way his tall, lean form moved across the waiting room and stopped in front of me.

"I told you to stay out of it. To let the cops do their job." His emerald-green eyes searched my face, worry etched into the lines that framed them. "I felt sick to my stomach when Gary called and told me last night."

"You talked to Gary?" I asked in a soft voice.

"Yeah. He told me everything." His eyes bore into mine, and I looked away.

"He's okay, you know. Sometimes things just click between people." I heard the words as they flowed from my mouth, words I never thought I'd ever say, let alone believe. But I did. I'd learned a lot the past week. About greed. About deception. About appearances versus reality. And about love.

"Yeah. I know they do. Trust me." His words caught me by surprise. I pulled my gaze off the floor and put it back, squarely, on him. But it wasn't his eyes I saw. Or the way he set his mouth. In fact, I didn't see anything. I simply felt the strength and warmth of his arms as he pulled me into an embrace. "I'm glad you're okay, Tobi."

I knew my cheeks had to be red when he eventually let me go and stepped backward. I tried to think of something, anything, to say that would ease the electric charge in the room. But truth be told, I didn't want the charge to go anywhere. It felt too good.

"So, should we get started?"

We both turned and looked at Sam, the sheepish smile on his teenaged face virtually impossible to ignore.

I cleared my throat and walked around Andy. "Yeah, we probably should. We don't want to keep Andy all day. I'm sure he wants to get home."

Home to his roommate, the one who keeps him up all night . . .

The thought was no sooner making a lap through my thoughts when I felt ashamed. Just because I was ready to start living again didn't mean I had the right to begrudge someone their happiness. There'd be another Andy out there for me. Somewhere. Someday. I knew that now.

"I'm not in any rush. I figured I'd be fielding some phone calls after the article in this morning's paper so I brought my roommate here. She's back in my office. Although, what, exactly, she's doing in there is anyone's guess." He stopped, his eyes widening as he did. "Hey, you wanna meet her? She's real sociable."

Sociable?

Without waiting for an answer, Andy took hold of my hand and led me down the small hallway toward his closed office door. "She's real sweet. An amazing listener. Poor thing's gotten quite an earful lately."

I willed myself to be pleasant as he turned the knob and motioned me into his office. A flash of white and orange jumped down from the desk, ran over to me, and brushed lovingly against my legs. And, as I stood there speechless, I knew beyond a shadow of a doubt who it was.

I bent down and scooped her up, held her to my face as the tears began to flow. "Oh, Sadie. I've missed you so much."

"What? You know Sadie? How? Why?" Andy's hand rested on the small of my back as he led me over to his desk.

When I found my voice, it emerged from my mouth in a quiet, raspy sound. "Yeah, I know Sadie. And you're right, she's an amazing listener."

"Hold the phone. So *you're* the guy? The grungy one my mom's always telling Tobi about?"

I looked at Sam standing in the doorway, but I didn't really see him. My mind was already trying to piece everything together.

"Okay. I'm confused," Andy said. He leaned against the desk and pulled me alongside him. "How do you know Sadie? And"—he swung his gaze onto Sam—"who's your mom and why did she call me *grungy?*"

"Mary Fran Wazoli. She owns the To Know Them Is To Love Them pet shop," Sam answered as I rested my head on Andy's shoulder and tried to drink up everything that was happening.

Grungy was not a word I'd ever use to describe Andy or his choice in attire. I couldn't imagine a drop of paint on anything he wore.

"Mary Fran is your mom? Wow, she's a great lady. A little persistent, but great."

And then it hit me. His off-duty Saturdays. Blake teaching him to build . . .

"Remember the lopsided dollhouse? That's Andy's attempt at building one. He put himself on painting duty after that one."

"Persistent, how?" I asked, though I knew the answer before he uttered a word.

Andy's laugh rumbled deep in his chest as he continued to hold me with his right arm. "Every time I go in there, she keeps telling me about this woman she wants to fix me up with. I keep telling her I'm not a big blind-date kinda guy. But she keeps trying."

"She's relentless," Sam and I said in unison.

Andy nodded.

I set a squirming Sadie down on the ground and smiled as she ran to Sam. "She's been after me to meet a man that came into her shop not long ago and took home one of the cats. I told her no way. I've been on one of her blind dates before."

"They can really stink, huh?" Andy said, his hand still lingering across my waist. "It's kind of funny she's been after us for the same thing, don't you—"

I turned my head to the left and met his rounded eyes with a knowing smile. The reality bus had finally pulled into his station, too.

"Wait. Are *you* the one she's been trying to fix me up with?" he asked, his voice a curious mixture of surprise and excitement.

I felt my cheeks warm as I slowly nodded. "You've got Sadie. And that's the man she's been carrying on about."

"Wow."

We both stood there in silence, each alone with our thoughts and the odd way that things had come together.

"Well, should we let her?" he finally asked.

I looked back at Andy, at his questioning eyes and their undeniable sparkle. "Let her what?"

His left hand rose up from its perch on the edge of the desk to brush a stray piece of hair from my face, my skin tingling at his touch. "You know. Fix us up. On a blind date. With each other."

The earnestness with which he spoke brought a school-girl flutter to my stomach, and I knew without hesitation what my answer would be.

"Can I borrow your phone? I left my cell out in the waiting room."

He searched my face for a long moment then pushed off the desk. "Sure can. Press nine for an outside line. I'll get Sam going out by the displays and give you a little privacy."

"No. Stay." I picked up the phone, punched in the familiar number, and motioned for Andy to come listen. I held my breath at the feel of his face so close to mine as I waited through one, two, three rings.

Maybe she'd headed into the pet shop early.

"Hello?"

"Hi, Mary Fran, it's Tobi."

"Are you and Sam okay?"

I felt the phone move with my grin. "We're fine. Great, in fact. But I have a question."

"Okay, shoot."

"Remember that guy you wanted to fix me up with? The one who took Sadie?"

I swear I could hear the woman jog in place on the other side of the phone.

"Yes . . ."

"Let's do it. I think I'm ready."

Andy and I both jumped back from the phone as screeching filled our ears. Happy, excited screeching.

"Really? What's the catch?" Mary Fran finally asked when she'd gotten her enthusiasm in check.

I threw a gentle elbow at Andy as he laughed too close to the phone.

"No catch, Mary Fran. I'm just ready for a little fun. That's all."

"Well, it's about time. We'll talk about it when you guys get back here, okay? And don't think for one second I'm going to let you change your mind, got it?"

I laughed. "Got it. See you soon."

I handed the phone to Andy, his hand lingering longer than necessary on mine.

"This is going to be fun," he finally said.

I nodded. And then stopped. A thought had entered my mind that I couldn't ignore. It was a question that needed to be asked. I crossed my fingers behind my back and jumped right in.

"Andy?"

"Uh-huh?"

"You don't have a foot fetish, do you?"

Love Tobi?
Keep reading for a sneak peek at *30-Second Death*
Coming soon from Laura Bradford and Lyrical Underground

1

Hell had officially frozen over. And, oddly enough, there was no swell of background music, no thunderous blast like I'd always imagined. There was simply crunching. Loud, deliberate crunching.

In fact, it was the *cruncher* and the *crunchee* that had turned the fiery flames of the dreaded underworld into the clichéd icicles referenced at the end of virtually every nasty break-up.

In English? My best friend, Carter McDade, was standing less than five feet from my sofa eating a bowl of Cocoa Puffs.

That's right, the same guy who lectured me daily—sometimes hourly—on the gaps (okay, seismic gulleys) in my eating habits. The same guy who could draw a text-book food pyramid in mere seconds. The same guy who'd willingly and happily choose broccoli in a head-to-head with a Caramello bar.

Which is why his Puff-crunching pointed to one indisputable conclusion: Carter was stressed. Big time. A rarity in and of itself. In fact, my upstairs neighbor was the most positive human being I'd ever met. One of those happy-go-lucky, always-has-a-smile types. You know, the kind of person everyone needed in their life, but few were fortunate enough to have.

I was one of the fortunate. I was also dumbfounded. Utterly and completely dumbfounded by what to say and how to say it. So I took the not-so-subtle approach.

"What's wrong, Carter?"

"Uh-in."

Now I'll admit, I have a leg up when it comes to deciphering Puff-talk (it is, after all, my second language) but I was feeling pretty proud that I could decode it from even the most novice of crunchers.

"Nothing? Nothing?! Do you realize what you're eating right now?"

Carter looked at the bowl in his left hand and then the spoon moving toward his mouth with his right. "Uh-huh."

'They're *Cocoa Puffs,* Carter! Co-coa puffs. As in *chocolate*—or as you call it, sugar central. You know, void of roughage. In fact, if I do recall correctly, you refer to them as the downfall of mankind. The reason for society's ills."

I guess I thought if I berated the point it might sink in. But, then again, I was living proof that that tactic had failed. Just ask my mother. Besides, it was hard to hammer home drawbacks when I didn't believe a word of what I was saying. Why? Because I, Tobi Tobias, am a chocoholic. And proud of it, I might add.

So I did what any good chocoholic would do. I sauntered into the kitchen, grabbed my Bugs Bunny melamine bowl and matching spoon, filled it to the brim with the last of the crunchy brown puffs—don't worry, I've got four more boxes in the cabinet over the stove—and headed back out into the living room. I mean, let's face it: The expression *If you can't beat 'em, join 'em* was coined for a reason, right?

Not that my commiserating helped. In fact, when I returned, Carter showed no signs of having noticed my departure or subsequent return. His facial expression was still void of its trademark smile, and his eyes held a vacant look. Somehow, though, I managed to coax him onto the sofa.

"C'mon, Carter, spill it. It's Fiona again, isn't it?"

Call it a lucky guess, or simply all I had, but it was worth a shot. And judging by the look of complete mortification on his face as my words (and thus, his choice of food) registered in his subconscious, I'd hit the jackpot.

"Oh, good God, please tell me I'm not eating what I think I'm eating." Carter squeezed his eyes shut then opened them slowly, cautiously. A tortured gasp escaped his mouth along with a partially chewed Puff.

"It's okay, Carter, really. It's been a long time coming. I mean, you can't keep depriving yourself of the finer things in life, right?" I reached out and touched his shoulder, a teasing smile tugging my lips. "Thanks for letting me be a part of your spiritual awakening."

If looks could kill . . .

He rolled his eyes upward and then frantically wiped his tongue with the sleeve of his cable-knit sweater. "Ugh, how on earth can you eat this stuff?"

"Same way you just did, my friend. One yummy spoonful at a time." I winked and popped some Puffs into my mouth. I knew I was being ornery, but I couldn't help myself. Let's face it, I'd endured more pontificating about my eating habits from this man than I could possibly recall. So, this was, in a way, sweet justice. Comeuppance at its finest.

"My mind was compromised." Carter released a long, slow sigh and wiped his tongue one more time. "I swear, Sunshine, that woman will be the death of me yet. Mark my words."

I took the bowl from his shaking hand and set it on the end table to my right. It never ceased to amaze me how fast the sugar rush hit the chocolate virgins. Especially the stressed ones.

"What'd Ms. Princess do *this* time?"

"In the interest of time, it might be better if I tell you what she *didn't* do." Carter pushed off the couch and wandered over to the window.

"C'mon, Carter. What's the deal with Fiona?"

He let the curtain slip through his fingers and I scooted over on the sofa to make room as he dropped his wiry body down with a thud. "I told you we just started casting for *Rapunzel*, right?"

"Yup."

Carter stretched his feet out and propped them on my new-to-me coffee table. "I like this table by the way. Nice lines."

"Impressive topic shift, but it's not gonna fly." I bent my legs at the knee and pulled them under me, hugging a throw pillow to my chest. "So . . . Ra-pun-zel?"

He stuck his tongue out at me and rolled his eyes. "Okay. So, of course, Old Man Renoir wants the lead to go to his amazingly talented niece."

Did I sense a defrosting in Carter's opinion of his one-and-only nemesis? "Correct me if I'm wrong, but did you just call Fiona amazingly talented?" I asked for clarification purposes.

"Renoir's words, not mine. I'd choose something more, oh, I don't know—*fitting*. Like world-class troublemaker or irritant extraordinaire."

So much for defrosting.

"I take it you'd rather she didn't get the part?" I giggled as he touched his index finger to his nose and then continued on.

"This is *Rapunzel*, Sunshine. Fiona's hair barely touches her collar. And she won't even consider hair extensions." He stopped, inhaled sharply, and then threw his head back against the couch. "She wants to wear a wig."

Carter's unexpected tumble off the broccoli wagon was suddenly crystal clear. If anything, I was stunned it had stopped at Cocoa Puffs. This little development could have landed him at the checkout counter of Death by Chocolate on North Euclid.

"A wig? Does she not realize what you *do*?"

"Oh she realizes it. She just gets her jollies out of pushing my buttons. Has since the day her precious uncle Frank introduced us. Probably because my greeting lacked a bow and the obligatory peck on her hand."

It's true. Carter is hands-down the nicest, sweetest, most genuine guy I'd ever met. But he doesn't kiss up to anyone. Ever. He speaks with his heart 24-7 and doesn't give a hoot who you are or what you do for a living.

"Are you going to let her use a wig? I mean, isn't the whole hair thing why you're there in the first place?"

He pulled his legs off the table and sat ramrod straight. "Exactly! And I was salivating at the idea of doing this show. Think about it— the extensions, mixing up just the right shade of golden blonde. Oh my God, it was going to be so awesome."

It was hard not to notice the way his wistful tone morphed into anger as he continued, his voice growing deeper and more wooden with each subsequent word. "But now, I'm not sure I'll even have a job come Monday morning, thanks to Princess Fiona."

I'd never seen Carter quite like this before. Sure, he was theatrical, it was part of his shtick. But there's a difference between being theatrical and being a drama queen, and Carter was suddenly blurring the line.

"C'mon, Carter. Just because she doesn't want you to do her hair doesn't mean you're going to lose your job. You know that." I tugged at a loose thread on my throw pillow and waited for him to come to his senses.

"You might've been right, Sunshine, if I hadn't let her bait me into a fight. With her uncle standing less than ten feet behind me."

Uh-oh.

"You didn't know he was there?" I asked, though why I'm not quite sure. The answer was obvious, wasn't it? Carter had, after all, resorted to *chocolate*.

"Nope. Not a clue. But Fiona did. I'm positive of that." Carter pushed off the sofa and wandered around my living room, stopping from time to time to look at a few framed photographs he'd seen a million times over the past two years.

"But you just *disagreed* with her on the hair stuff, right?"

Carter snickered. "Disagreed? Oh no. Let's just say I kinda unleashed the past six months of Fiona-inspired frustration. And once I started, I couldn't stop."

I gulped. "How bad did it get?"

"Depends on what you call bad." Carter stopped at my draft table and picked up a sheet of long white paper with colorful block letters across the top and rough sketches in a series of hand-drawn boxes along the bottom.

"Try me." I tossed the throw pillow onto Carter's empty spot and stood. I'd spent the better part of the day working on my campaign ideas for Pizza Adventure but wasn't necessarily ready to share them with anyone yet. Even Carter, my biggest fan of all.

"Well, let's see—I told her how sick I was of her temper-tantrums during rehearsals, her constant screaming at the lighting guys, her Gestapo-like tactics when it comes to making sure no one even so much as *thinks* about eating something with peanuts anywhere in the building lest she break out in hives or whatever the hell happens to her, and, of course, her blatant hogging of the press anytime the theater gets coverage."

My mouth dropped open.

"Wait." He held up his hand, crossing-guard style. "Trust me, Sunshine. It gets better."

"There's more?" I asked.

Carter nodded. "I called her a spoiled brat with no chance in hell of ever making it as an actress."

Ouch. Okay, so maybe the notion of a new job wasn't so drama-queenish after all. *What to say . . . what to say . . .*

Carter continued with a sigh. "Let's face it—Fiona's not going anywhere. Not until she lands a real acting gig. And unless the little princess has a yet-to-be-discovered uncle living in Hollywood or happens to stumble across a role that doesn't require a whole lot of depth or ability, I'm toast at the theater house." Carter shuffled over to the four-by-four-foot square of linoleum that denoted my entry foyer and grabbed his navy blue parka from its perch on the door knob.

An acting gig... A role that doesn't require a whole lot of depth...

And then it hit me. Maybe I could get Fiona a job—the kind of job that would make Carter look like a hero and save his sanity at the same time. Sure, there'd be a few kinks to work out (like rescinding a semi-promise to someone) but if I could pull this off it might—

"I think it's time I face facts, Tobi," Carter said, his voice strained and tired as he slipped his arms into his coat and zipped it to his neck, his eyes meeting mine for the first time since he walked through my door an hour earlier. "A premature curtain call is about the only way I'll ever be rid of Fiona Renoir."

Photo credit: Carrie Schechter Studios

As a child, Laura Bradford fell in love with writing over a stack of blank paper, a box of crayons, and a freshly sharpened # 2 pencil. From that moment forward, she never wanted to do or be anything else. Today, Laura is the national bestselling author of several mystery series, including the Tobi Tobias Mystery Series, the Emergency Dessert Squad Mysteries, and the Amish Mysteries. She is a former Agatha Award nominee, and the recipient of an RT Reviewer's Choice Award in romance. A graduate of Xavier University in Cincinnati, Ohio, Laura enjoys making memories with her family, baking, and being an advocate for those living with Multiple Sclerosis.

Visit her at www.laurabradford.com or on Facebook.

CPSIA information can be obtained
at www.ICGtesting.com
Printed in the USA
LVOW12s1558030817
543713LV00002B/309/P

9 781516 102075